THE DREAM KEY

RACHAEL WATSON

—◆—

For everyone who has a dream and dares to make it come true

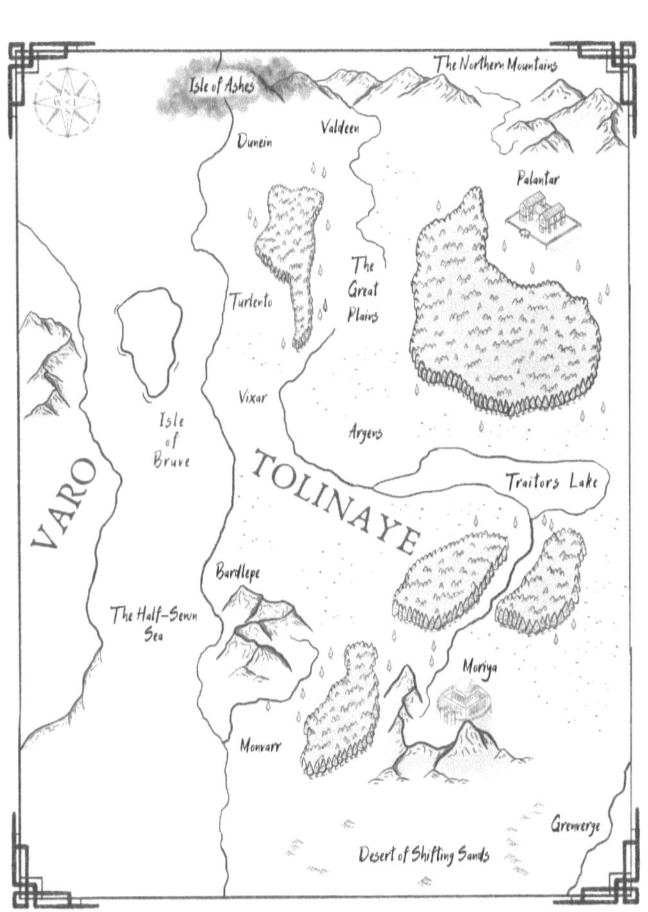

N
W E
S
Isle of Ashes
The Northern Mountains
Dunein
Valdeen
Palantar
The Great Plains
Turlento
Vixar
Argens
VARO
Isle of Bruve
TOLINAYE
Traitors Lake
Bardlepe
The Half-Sewn Sea
Moriya
Monvarr
Grenverge
Desert of Shifting Sands

1

— · —

KYLA

THE CITY OF PALANTAR

Kyla stood on the riverbank. Dawn light glinted on the surface of the water and birdsong came in fitful bursts from the trees. Across the water the northern mountains rose in the distance like grim and static sentinels, sworn to protect Tolinaye from the lands beyond.

At her feet a small boat, settled in the mud of the bank, waited to be pushed out into the water. It was narrow, hewn of rough wood and not at all as grand as Edmund would have wanted, but it was the best she could do at short notice.

Kyla winced at the thought of what Edmund might have said, and grief spread through her chest.

His body, small and shrouded in white muslin, lay in the bottom of the boat. The fabric was slick with some flammable oil, the scent of which made Kyla's nose wrinkle. Beneath it was kindling that would burn hot and fast, set in a shallow pool of yet more oil.

Kyla gripped the bow she held in her left hand and glanced down at the arrows in a bucket at her feet, each one dipped in tar that would burst into flame when touched to the fire burning nearby.

She was a good shot. Her arrow would find its target, burning Edmund's body, setting it alight so that his soul could mingle with the smoke and make the journey to the dead world. It was a ceremonial duty that Kyla determined to undertake with sombre deliberation, especially as none of Edmund's family had been able to make the journey north in time for the funeral, and she was one of the only true mourners present.

The sound of mumbled prayer from somewhere over her left shoulder distracted her, but she didn't turn. She had already seen the ill-matched mob of nobles and peasants that had gathered beneath the trees, a little distance from where she stood. She knew they were staring. She could feel their eyes like the stroking of unwelcome fingertips.

Moriyan soldiers were an unusual sight in Palantar, and her uniform, as red as fresh blood, drew the eye, but even so the crowd weren't there to look at her or her clothes. They were here to witness the send off of the ill-fated Moriyan soldier who had come to Palantar to do little more than die. Whether they were lamenting or celebrating Edmund's demise, or drawn to the river by curiosity alone, Kyla wasn't sure.

Beside her, Max sighed. The sound of his breath filled her with gratitude. He was alive, thank the God-Sage, but only just. It should rightly have been his body lying in the boat. Not Edmund's.

She wanted to reach out and grab Max's hand, squeeze it tight, make sure that he was really there. But she did none of those things. Not now, not here, where everyone could see.

Max scratched the back of his neck; a gesture that spoke his awareness, and awkwardness, at being observed. He tilted his head towards the crowd gathered behind them. "Do you think they know what killed him?"

"Would you be here if you knew the dead man had been killed by a death eel that had burrowed into his heart?"

Max grimaced and Kyla was immediately sorry she had been so explicit. After he had fallen in the water at Traitors' Lake, Max had been infested with the same eels that had killed Edmund. It had been grotesque, horrifying, and Max would surely have been killed by them too, had he not been saved by the most powerful healing Kyla had ever witnessed.

Max nodded towards the young woman who had healed him. "Do they know she saved me?"

Kyla shrugged. People loved to gossip, but what information they actually had Kyla wasn't sure. It was safe to say they knew something about the young woman, for they kept stealing glances in her direction.

Valora Tide. That was her name. Tide, like the ocean, ceaselessly beating the shore. She certainly had the power of the ocean in her, and more besides.

The power of the God-Sage.

Valora didn't look powerful. She had a twist in her back so severe that she could not fully raise her head. Standing next to her brother, Marlowe, a little way back from the river on a hillock that looked down on the crowd, she appeared more hunched than ever. Strands of unwashed dark hair hung down either side of hollowed cheeks, and her dress was plain and grey. Everything about her, aside from her curved spine, was utterly unremarkable.

Guards stood either side of the siblings, marshalling them like they were captives liable to attempt an escape. Perhaps Lord Aralorn, their grandfather, anticipated that they might try for freedom. Although why they would, Kyla had no idea. Valora was to become an acolyte, a handmaiden to the God-Sage himself. It was an honour, one of the greatest in all of Tolinaye. Valora would represent her province in the capital city, Moriya. It made no sense that she would try to escape that privilege.

Valora was staring at the boat bearing Edmund's body. Edmund, who would never have agreed to bring a crippled acolyte back to Moriya, where disease and deformity were all but forbidden. *The God-Sage deserves a pure city.*

Kyla shook herself. What did it matter that Edmund would have refused to accept Valora? He was dead. The decision was hers alone, and she was determined to bring Valora back. The girl was a channel for the healing power of the God-Sage. Kyla was sure of it. *Healing belongs to the God-Sage.* What other explanation could there be?

Yes, it was a risk to return to Moriya with a crippled girl, but it was one worth taking. Only once an acolyte had been found could Kyla be initiated into the Sacred Core.

It was the one desire that Kyla had held to with faith for years. Ever since her older brother had disappeared, forfeiting his role in the Sacred Core, Kyla was determined that she would take on that mantle.

A prickling sensation ran over her skin, distracting her from her thoughts. Someone was watching her. She shifted her gaze and Marlowe's eyes hit hers like a fist to the gut. His features showed no softness, his jaw set like stone; his expression was a mixture of hatred and fascination, as if he wanted to look away from her and yet was unable to.

Despite the loathing she read in his face, Kyla could not deny that he was handsome. Certainly not in a pretty way like Edmund had been, with his golden hair and red lips. No. Marlowe was a different sort of man entirely; his hair was almost black and dark stubble grew across his chin. His skin was deeply tanned and there was a fire, a violence to him that Edmund could never have truly known. He looked older than Valora, but it was hard to guess his age. Eighteen, at least.

Kyla tore her gaze away from Marlowe's, but as she did so she felt the strangest sensation of having left part of herself with him, as if he was holding some piece of her and would not let go.

She dug her boots into the mud of the river bank, reprimanding herself for letting her thoughts float away again. She owed it to Edmund to stay focused, to give him the send off that every nobleman deserved.

Nearby, a Palantarian priest by the name of Verbun began to murmur, leading the crowd in prayer. He stood at the side of the river, his long golden robes trailing in mud, whispering and offering Edmund's soul to the God-Sage. He waved his arms in the air, using his fingertips to draw the blazing ball of fire that represented the God-Sage.

A grunt. It was Arthur Chundle, the executioner, indicating that it was time to push the boat out. Max, who stood beside Arthur, pulled his sleeves right down over his wrists. That way, Kyla knew, he would not expose his skin. Skin that bore those strange shimmering scars, the remaining evidence of the wounds the death eels had inflicted.

Together, Max and Arthur bent down and shoved the rough wood. The hull of the boat splashed into the water and bobbed on the surface. Arthur pushed it again and it moved off into the current.

No one spoke as the boat bearing Edmund's body floated further downstream. The fire on the bank scented the air with woodsmoke, and the silence was broken only by its crackling.

When the boat had travelled far enough, Kyla pulled an arrow from the bucket and touched the head of it to the flames. It burst alight. She hoisted the bow, nocked the flaming arrow and let it loose. It arced over the river, a ball of orange fire, the God-Sage in miniature, seeming to flicker and flash in slow motion, before landing in Edmund's chest, right where his heart would have been.

It was but a few moments before the oil in the boat, the crisp kindling, the oil soaked shroud that clung to Edmund's form, took flame, and soon the boat became a bonfire, sending thick black smoke spiralling to the sky.

To the God-Sage.

Kyla bowed her head, but just as she did so Max grabbed her arm. His voice was sharp with shock when he spoke. "Something's wrong."

Her whole body became alert at his words.

"It's in the air," he said. "I can feel it."

Dark clouds had gathered in the sky. Had they been there a moment before? Kyla didn't think so. The air was heavy, laden with the threat of rain. The breeze blew stronger and leaves rustled in the trees overhead.

Arthur looked at the clouds and then out towards the boat, where flames rose up and smoke peeled into the sky.

"Storm's coming. We better hope no rain falls, or his soul won't make it to the dead world," he said.

Kyla's cloak whipped around her legs and she felt a change in her body, as if the wind had whistled right through her skin and chilled the bones beneath. This was more than a storm. She reached for another arrow.

"There." Max pointed to the water around Edmund's boat. It was rippling with a flickering darkness. Kyla's heart shivered with recognition.

"Death eels," whispered Max.

The boat began to rock from side to side. Kyla didn't waste a moment. She lit her arrow and sent the flames arcing over the river, crashing into the water around the boat. The arrow, still burning, thrashed like a dying star, impaled in some indistinguishable eel.

Max drew his sword and pointed it towards the river. "Where did they come from?"

Kyla loosed another arrow, and another, hitting yet more eels, but it made no difference. If the water became any more rocky, the boat would capsize and Edmund's body would fall in.

Some members of the crowd crept forwards, squinting out across the river to get a better look at the disturbance in the water. The pool of eels was spreading, fast. Whispers of alarm began, soon turning to shouts as the surface of the river became a swirling mass of eel flesh. Mothers rushed their children away from the water, whilst daring youths, trying to get a better look at the eels, stepped closer, their toes only a short distance from the river.

"Get back, get back! Keep away from the water!" Duncan, the physician, was hustling through the crowd, his voice raised and urgent.

Some people turned to look at him, but the youths still stood on the edge of the bank, toeing the water. One of them, a young peasant from the look of his rough clothes, had stooped to the water's edge and was peering in. A splash. He blinked and backed up, water on his face. He wiped it away and leant forward again, trying to see what had caused the splash. An eel leapt up, thrashing its thick muscular tail in his face. He yelled and batted it away with one hand.

"Ow." He clapped a hand to his nose. "It bit me, it bit me. That thing bit me."

A woman approached and urged him to drop his hand, trying to look at the wound. Even from where Kyla stood she could see the spreading blackness on the tip of the young man's nose.

Duncan had seen it too. He shouted even louder, his voice rough with anger. "It's the contamination. I knew it, I knew it." He swung round, searching for somewhere to focus his rage. Someone to blame. His gaze landed on Lord Aralorn, his next words shooting forth like an assault. "The body is contaminated with pestilence from Traitors' Lake! I warned you—"

"Silence." Lord Aralorn's voice boomed across the crowd, cutting Duncan short. The physician seemed to shrink and began to shift backwards through the crowd.

Kyla watched as the woman who had come to the aid of the young man with the bitten nose began to lead him away, between the trees, back in the direction of the slums.

A sudden movement drew Kyla's attention. The priest had raised his arms and begun calling to the God-Sage, asking for forgiveness. Beside him some of the crowd had fallen to their knees and begun to pray too.

"May the God-Sage be bountiful and merciful."

"The God-Sage deserves a pure city."

A flash, almost like lightning, exploded. Pure darkness followed. A child began to cry. Screams filled the air.

A chill breeze skimmed Kyla's skin and she felt a tightening in her chest. She fumbled for another arrow, but the fire at her side had gone out. She could see nothing. She glanced towards the river, hoping to see the flames of Edmund's boat, but saw no light there either. The boat must have taken on too much water, dousing the flames.

Again a flash of light. The entire surface of the river was a wriggling mass of eels. They were thrashing against the mud, crawling their way onto the bank. There were more eels here than Kyla had seen at Traitors' Lake.

People scurried back into the trees; even the daring youths dragged one another away from the river.

Kyla looked up in time to see eels squirming up the sides of Edmund's boat, pulling it beneath the water.

A third flash bit the sky in half, and in the burst of brightness Kyla saw him. A man, on the other side of the river, dressed all in black. Even from here, Kyla could see the tattoos that covered his cheeks.

Wings.

Max gasped. "A Nilari priest."

Kyla felt ice run from the top of her head to her toes. She had never seen a Nilari priest, but there was no mistaking this one. He wore a leather doublet, and a dark cloak embroidered with silver wings that glinted in the flashes of light.

The sky began to glow dimly, the sun's bright rays trapped beneath dark clouds. In the gloom the priest raised his arms high in the air, and from the mountains behind him a swarm of Nilari birds swooped down across the river. Kyla had never seen so many. Hundreds of them, forming a winged and terrible army.

The birds hit the water like stones, and for a moment she thought they wouldn't rise, but each one thieved an eel from the river, clasped it in golden talons and flew towards the crowd.

"Get away, get away!" A man was urging others away from the river, but there was no escape. The birds were flying towards them. People screamed, covering their heads with their hands as the eels rained down upon them.

A woman squealed as an eel landed on her head and tangled itself in her curls. She shook her head frantically until another woman came from behind, gripped the eel in one hand and tossed it in the mud.

Kyla threw down her bow and took a knife from her boot, lunging this way and that, piercing the bodies of the eels that had fallen amidst the crowd. Max too followed her lead, swiping his sword at the creatures.

"Move! Get back!" Kyla yelled, pushing people out of the way. "Don't touch them!"

More birds were coming from the hills across the river, swooping to the water to collect their writhing treasure and gliding swiftly towards the bank, before dropping the eels on the scattering crowd.

"There are too many! We have to run!"

Max was right. But Kyla wasn't going anywhere without the acolyte. Where was Valora? Kyla scanned the crowd, her heart thrumming. She could see the guards, stabbing eels with their swords, so preoccupied with the slaughter that they had forgotten about the girl entirely. What if Valora and her brother made their escape in the chaos?

Kyla pushed through the swarming crowd, forcing her way towards the hillock where the siblings had been standing. Panic surged like waves through her body, bringing flashes of catastrophe to mind. What if Valora was lost, or worse, dead?

She elbowed a woman aside, barely caring that she skidded and slipped in the mud. Kyla's path was clear and she caught sight of Valora, only a few paces away. Relief surged through her and she dashed towards the girl, intending to wrench her from the spot and haul her to safety. But she drew herself up. Something was wrong. Unlike everyone else, Valora had barely moved, and neither she nor her brother were looking at the birds or the eels, but at something else, something cradled in the palm of Valora's hand.

Kyla took another step forward, slower now and full of trepidation. Whatever it was Valora held in her hand, it was glowing with a pale blue light.

Marlowe was mouthing something Kyla couldn't hear. He was trying to close Valora's fingers to conceal whatever was glowing there, but the light spilled out between their hands.

Valora's attention snapped from the light in her hand to Kyla, as if some instinct had told her she was being watched.

A flash, bigger than before, lit the entire sky, shooting up from Valora's hands. Then it was all around her, as if Valora herself were the light, but only for a moment before it expanded further, coming towards Kyla like a forcefield. She shielded her eyes, turning away, ducking down, but the brightness was everywhere.

It shot upwards, outwards, cascading all around like the light of fallen stars, crashing down on the eel-ridden river.

Kyla expected the light to hurt, to pummel her body as it rushed towards her. But she felt nothing, and then it was gone.

She blinked and straightened. The clouds rolled back as though they had never been there. The sun peeked out, higher now in the sky. The chill on the breeze vanished.

Not a single Nilari bird flew in the sky, but here and there a bright blue feather drifted down, calm and slow compared to what had come before. The eels too were gone, leaving no trace other than their serpentine tracks in the mud. The water was still once more, but the boat bearing Edmund's body was nowhere to be seen.

What had happened? What power had been in Valora's hand?

Around her, everyone else looked just as confused, searching for the dark creatures that had been squirming their way from the water and dropping from the sky. The screaming faded, shock silenced the crowd. A few children were crying, but otherwise people were shooting frightened glances overhead and talking in hushed tones.

Kyla turned to look towards the opposite bank. The Nilari priest was gone. She felt a cool shiver run down her spine: who was he and why had he been there? And where, more importantly, had he gone?

Max was at her side. "They've vanished, Kyla. The eels."

"I see that." Kyla could barely keep the sharp edge from her voice.

"What do you think it was? Magic?"

Kyla ignored his question, but allowed herself a tiny shake of the head. There were only a few seconds left before the confused crowd would turn its attention on Valora. If she was quick, Kyla could question her before everyone started looking.

If it was some sort of magic, and it certainly looked to have been, then Kyla needed to know. She couldn't very well take an acolyte back to Moriya who was performing the sort of magic that was against the law. A healing was one thing, but causing thousands of eels to vanish in front of a crowd was something else entirely.

Leaving Max behind, Kyla closed the distance between her and Valora. She took hold of the girl's wrist and yanked her hand. "What was it? What are you holding?"

Valora's hand was clasped tight. She shook her head. "Nothing. It was nothing."

"Show me."

"Get your hands off her!" Marlowe pushed between them, trying to wrench them apart.

Kyla turned a fierce glare on him. "You get *your* hands off the acolyte. She's the property of the God-Sage now. Something just happened here, and I need to know what it was."

Marlowe became very still. "She told you it was nothing."

There was a raw violence in his eyes. Kyla felt herself squeezed into a place she didn't want to be. If she pressed too hard, she might get an answer she wasn't sure she wanted. If Valora's magic was anything other than the God-Sage working through her, there would be repercussions. Max, for one, would be condemned to death for having been healed by an illegal healer.

Someone would have to declare a verdict on what had occurred. No one could be allowed to leave the river, still wondering what they had witnessed.

"She's lying." Kyla kept her voice low, speaking only to Marlowe. "Everyone saw it." She gestured to the crowd around them, who were wandering about, blinking, pointing to the river, a mixture of relief and confusion clear on their faces. "Illegal magic—"

Marlowe stepped closer still. He let out a low growl. Kyla could feel his breath against her skin. "A Nilari priest sent an attack over the northern mountains, and you're worried about whether or not Valora acted in accordance with the God-Sage?" Kyla's hesitation was momentary, but before she could speak Marlowe whistled an exhalation through almost-closed lips. "You need an acolyte. For your healing circle. Isn't that right?"

Kyla shivered with the truth of his words. She needed an acolyte so she could join the Sacred Core, and she needed Max to be allowed to live.

"Valora saved your friend," Marlowe nodded in Max's direction, "and she saved all these people. You ought to be thanking her, not interrogating her."

Kyla inhaled sharply, outrage burning in her chest. How dare he? She was about to tell him to keep his opinions to himself when a voice crowed loudly from behind her.

"Praise be to the God-Sage!"

Kyla turned. Lord Aralorn was pushing his way through the crowd, moving with the vigour of a much younger man. His wrinkled face was deeply creased, but his eyes were full of purpose. His green velvet cloak flapped behind him, revealing a linen tunic of paler green beneath, the chest embroidered with the spiral of Palantar. He looked regal, and the peasants parted to let him through. He stopped just before Valora and raised his arms, spinning on the spot until all eyes were turned to him.

"All praise the God-Sage! He has once again shown his power through my granddaughter. What blessed glory you have all witnessed!" People began to mutter, and in the burst of chatter that followed his proclamation, Lord Aralorn stepped closer to Kyla and lowered his voice. "Don't you think, Miss Tarthwen?"

Kyla felt the eyes of both these men, the young and the old, Marlowe and Lord Aralorn, pressuring her to agree. Was it divine? Was it the God-Sage working through Valora in some unknown way? Or was it, as Max seemed to think, magic?

And if it was magic, and was declared as such, how many people would die for it? Kyla laid one hand on the sword at her hip, curled her fingers around the hilt and prayed she wouldn't have to use it.

Without waiting for her response Lord Aralorn raised his arms again, gesturing to every man and woman on the riverbank.

"We were attacked. That was a Nilari attack, from beyond the northern mountains. Those birds, those eels, that man! You all saw him, did you not?"

Every fibre of Kyla's body was alert. She scanned the crowd, trying to assess the effect of Lord Aralorn's words. A few voices were raised above the hum of discontent. People began shouting out in agreement. Yes, everyone had seen him.

Lord Aralorn continued, "A Nilari priest from beyond the northern boundary has used his magic against us! That is all but a declaration of war! Without the divine power our acolyte has demonstrated today, we might all be dead. Killed by those same eels that killed that soldier." Lord Aralorn swept an arm out towards the river, where there was still no sign of Edmund or the boat.

Kyla felt her skin thrum and tingle as she wondered how to respond. How could she give a verdict on what had occurred when she did not understand it? She needed time. There was no way to know for certain what had taken place. She opened her mouth to speak, but before she could say anything she heard a gasp from behind.

The priest, Verbun, came towards them, elbowing people aside. "That man is no priest. He may think of himself as such, he may even believe the Nilari are his gods, but they are not. I beg you not to use that word in conjunction with him."

There was a patter of agreement from the crowd, but Lord Aralorn looked taken aback at being corrected before so many people, and he was about to open his mouth when another voice cut through.

"Does it matter what God he worships? He's as much a priest as you are."

It was Marlowe, thinly veiled rage evident in his dark eyes. Valora was leaning towards him, imploring him to be quiet, her lips pursed, but the *shhh* that emanated from them was too timid to silence him. He shrugged her off.

Verbun drew himself up, the hem of his gold robes lifting slightly from where they trailed in the mud. "What do you mean, boy?"

"I mean that he holds to his delusion in the same way that you hold to your faith. There is no Nilari King, no race of winged creatures. There never was. Just as—"

Before he could finish Valora yanked on his arm and shouted his name, like he was a dog she was calling to heel. "Marlowe!"

Kyla held her breath. Had Marlowe been about to deny the God-Sage in front of all these people? Didn't he want Valora to become an acolyte? How did he dare do such a thing? In Moriya merely thinking it was enough to get you killed, let alone speaking it aloud.

Max's thoughts seemed to have run the same course as her own, for his eyes were wide and flitted from the priest to Marlowe and back again.

The attention of the crowd hung like a whip waiting to be cracked.

Verbun, nostrils flared, lips curling in disgust, stared at Marlowe. "Faith and delusion are quite different. That he holds to it with fervour does not make him a priest."

Lord Aralorn, anxious to shut down the discussion, fixed his gaze on Marlowe and barked, "Your opinions are not welcome here, Tide." Then he turned to the priest and lowered his voice, but the whisper was a front. It was clear he meant them all to hear it. "Pay him no heed, Verbun. The boy is not important."

Verbun inhaled deeply through his nose and, with one last vicious glance at Marlowe, turned his disgust across the river. "Those men are rebels, traitors of the worst kind. And that man... that man is the worst of the worst. His name is Yarmon Sacfron, one of the most fearsome leaders of the Nilari rebels."

Whispers began. Kyla had never heard the name Yarmon Sacfron before, but it was clear it meant something to the Palantarians.

Max drew near to her and whispered, "I thought all the Nilari priests..." He tripped over the word and quickly corrected himself. "...rebels had been killed?"

Kyla said nothing, but the idea that the Sages back in Moriya had concealed the truth from the people, from her, had already taken root in her mind. Just as she was wondering if there were frequent Nilari raids from the other side of the northern mountains, Verbun spoke again.

"Yarmon Sacfron hasn't been seen this side of the mountains for over thirty years. The last of the rebels to cross to our side was the man who—"

Lord Aralorn was suddenly at Verbun's side, his wrinkled face carved with deep, angry grooves. He pulled the priest closer to him and began talking, so quietly that Kyla could not hear, but it was evident from his stance and manner that he was giving the priest instructions. Verbun listened, tried to speak, only to be quickly shut down again by Lord Aralorn.

A moment later Verbun, having lost whatever argument the two men had been having, turned to Valora and bowed low, his arm curling before him with a wild flourish. "Praise be to the God-Sage."

There was a moment of confusion as the gathered people looked at one another, then again at Verbun for confirmation. He knelt at Valora's feet, and after the slightest hesitation, people nearby began to do the same, the movement rippling outwards until everyone on the bank was low to the ground.

"*The God-Sage deserves a pure city*," he said.

Max got to his knees too, and tugged on Kyla's arm. "Get down."

But Kyla didn't kneel. She watched as Valora removed a pouch that hung on a thong around her neck and slipped it into her pocket. She brushed her hands down over her dress, wincing as she did so, as if the motion caused her pain.

No one else was watching. The crowd were too busy kneeling in the mud, bowing their heads, pressing their palms to the earth. Then they raised mud-covered hands to the sky. "*May the God-Sage be bountiful and merciful.*"

Verbun pushed himself up from the mud to kiss the tips of Valora's fingers, still murmuring his thanks to the God-Sage. Valora was staring at him as if she couldn't believe what was happening, and Marlowe... He was staring at Kyla, a slight smile curling on his lips. He raised an eyebrow and mouthed the words *The God-Sage deserves a pure city.*

Kyla heard the prayers of the crowd, a mounting murmur that shook the earth beneath her feet. For the first time, it didn't feel reassuring.

It felt like the beginning of an earthquake.

2

— · —

MARLOWE

THE CITY OF PALANTAR

"They're looking. Everyone's staring at me," Valora whispered.

Marlowe felt his sister's hand reaching for his, her fingers grazing against the cuff of his shirt. He clasped her hand, intending to pull her closer, but she let out a small squeal and pulled away.

"What's wrong?"

Her eyes darted downwards, where her arm hung at her side. "My hand." She turned the palm towards him so he could see it. There, right in the middle, was a mark in the shape of the piece of metal they had discovered inside their mother's jewellery box. Round, like a wheel, but with crooked spokes. "It burnt me."

Marlowe wanted to grab her hand and inspect it. How could a piece of metal make a mark like that? Thoughts sped through his mind, ricocheting off one another. What was this small circle of metal? What power did it hold and why had their mother kept it? But the thought that rang louder than all others was that he ought to have trusted his first instinct when they had found it: he ought to have got rid of it.

"Why did you take it out of the pouch?"

"It was getting warm. As soon as the eels appeared. I could feel it through the leather, against my chest. I thought it was going to burn me."

"Where is it now?"

Valora glanced towards her pocket.

"Give it to me."

She shook her head. "It's mine—"

"It's not safe." His words were barely more than a whisper, but the low volume did nothing to conceal the hard edge to his voice. There were people on all sides, and if anyone should overhear them now, quibbling over the strange magical item, their lives would be short and their end painful. His palms were damp and sticky and he wiped them roughly on his trousers. "Give it to me, now. If they find that on you, do you think they'll still make you an acolyte? Do you think you can still pretend this is the work of the God-Sage? Do you think they'll let you live?"

Marlowe was sorry to be cruel, but she needed to know that this was serious. Understanding spread across her face, her cheeks paled and her chin quivered. She reached into her pocket with her good hand and, so that no one else could see, Marlowe moved to her other side, allowing her to slip the piece of metal from her pocket into his.

Then he took her good hand and pulled her closer. Whatever had just happened, he was in it with her. He would never desert her.

"Will they kill me?" she asked.

Marlowe kept his eyes on the guard in front of them, who was leading them through the crowd. His grandfather and Verbun had made a great show of their thanks for whatever it was Valora had done, or rather, and Marlowe allowed himself a little snort here, the God-Sage had done. It was, his grandfather had said, the greatest cause for celebration that the city of Palantar had ever known. The divine was amongst them, showing his power through Valora, and now they were to return to Aralorn Hall to dine in her honour.

Valora shook his hand, and hissed sharply to get his attention. "Marlowe, will they kill—"

"Shhh. Don't say anything."

He didn't know what they would do. When the guards had brought them to the riverbank, they had been rough, hauling Valora from the cart and pushing her to the top of the hillock. The fact that she was to be the next acolyte, a handmaid to the God-Sage himself, made no difference to how they treated her. She was still *that cripple*, the daughter of traitors, a child who should never have been allowed to live.

But now, after the explosion of light that had caused the eels to vanish, would people look at her any differently?

Marlowe wasn't sure. Rather than admiration on the faces of the crowd, he saw confusion. Yes, they had bowed when Verbun had bowed, they had been willing to follow his lead, but unless Marlowe was mistaken, Verbun's show of reverence had been forced. What other explanation could there be for the heated discussion that had occurred only moments before between his grandfather and Verbun?

Marlowe could almost read the questions in the priest's eyes, and in the eyes of the crowd too. *How could Valora wield the power of the God-Sage? How could a girl like her, with such a twist in her back, be an acolyte?*

After all, *the God-Sage deserves a pure city*, and Moriya of all places had little tolerance for physical disfigurement or illness. Valora was far more likely to be wielding illegal magic than she was to be the vessel of the God-Sage.

"I don't like it," Valora said. "I don't like how they stare."

"We'll be inside soon."

Marlowe could see his grandfather, Lord Aralorn, up ahead, marching towards his carriage. He was flapping his hands, gnarled knuckles flailing as he chirruped constantly, regaling Kyla Tarthwen with chatter that Marlowe couldn't hear.

Kyla Tarthwen.

His grandfather might have found Kyla impressive, but Marlowe was determined not to. So what if her ancient ancestor, Morden Tarthwen, had sliced the wings off the Nilari King, thereby single-handedly ending the Sage Rebellion and saving the land of Tolinaye? It was a legend, that was all. Marlowe was sure of it. What did it have to do with her?

Nothing, except that she had a lot to prove.

If Kyla toed the line, if she was willing to accept what his grandfather had forced on her: that it was the God-Sage and not some other incomprehensible magic that had saved them all at the river, then Valora was safe. But Marlowe wasn't at all sure that Kyla would accept it, and the thought made him nervous. He loathed being dependent on the whim of someone like Kyla Tarthwen.

When she had come to Palantar and declared that Valora was to be the next acolyte, Marlowe had sworn he would kill her, just as he meant to kill her father, Lander Tarthwen. It was he who had lit the pyre that had burnt Marlowe's parents.

Marlowe gritted his teeth. He had never killed anyone, and his threats to kill Kyla and her father had been words fuelled by anger. But was it more than that? Could he really end someone's life?

Aralorn Hall was gloomy, both outside and in. The stone facade was jagged and dull, and the windows set within it were small, little more than arrow slits, as if the place expected to be ransacked and raided at any moment.

The entrance hall was thick with dust, and light fought its way through the air. It was a space of stagnation. Why had he been so proud to have been in line to inherit this place?

Valora kept close to his side as they followed the guards towards the throne room, which also served as the feasting hall. The noise of celebration drifted to Marlowe's ears; music, a lute being played, the lilting melody of a young boy's song. He could make out the chatter of revelry, as if the throne room was full of hundreds of people who hadn't seen one another in far too long and had a lot to say. Had his grandfather invited every nobleman and his wife?

The guards led the way down the corridors as if Marlowe and Valora were strangers who had never set foot inside the place, despite the fact that Marlowe had practically grown up in this hall. He had spent his days here in the company of his grandfather, learning how to be a Lord and lead a city. He had enjoyed the luxury of it, though it was hard to admit it now, given how tainted the memories were by the fact that his grandfather had sanctioned his parents' execution and all but banished him from Aralorn Hall. The old man had ripped the love and luxury from his life all at once, as the hunter rips the guts from a pig.

One of the guards leant forward to open the door and the movement tore Marlowe from the bitterness of his thoughts. Another guard prodded Valora until she moved through the doorway.

Marlowe felt the pressure of a fingertip dig into his shoulder and he too toppled forward into the throne room. Light fell from two large windows behind the throne, before which was set a long table, covered in garlands of red flowers, interwoven with trails of ivy. Amidst the greenery were several vast decanters of wine, and the mingling of the rich oak-scented liquid with the earthy scent of leaves made the room smell like it did at the annual Morden Day celebrations. Even the joyful faces of the men and women in the room, Palantar's nobility, lent the space a celebratory atmosphere.

No one, aside from the Moriyan soldiers, looked like they had just come from a funeral where their lives had been threatened. The guests had swallowed his grandfather's story, that the God-Sage had performed a miracle at Valora's hand, as if it was the most delicious wine, and they were heady with relief.

Kyla and Max, however, wore expressions as sombre as their uniforms were red. They kept a little apart from the rest of the gathering, beyond the table, standing with their hands clasped behind their backs.

Marlowe saw his cousin, Nisia, dressed in a pale green dress with cream trimming, meandering amidst the crowd, treating both priests and young eligible suitors with the same easy charm. She flitted a hand towards the chest of one, touching her finger to his tunic, and tipped her head back, letting out a burst of gilded laughter. Marlowe couldn't help but envy Nisia's lack of concern, her freedom from anxiety. After today, her life would continue as it always had.

His would not.

Nisia stopped to speak with Verbun. Marlowe recognised the elderly priest who had attended Edmund's funeral from the days when his parents had dragged him to weekly services at the temple. Had Verbun noticed that Marlowe's worship had ceased after his parents were executed? Given the filthy look the priest had given him earlier, it was safe to say he had.

The buzz of chatter began to die down as people noticed their arrival, although Marlowe knew well enough that the silence was not for him, but for Valora.

Lord Aralorn stood up, his chair scraping against the stone floor. He held a goblet in one hand. Wine slopped over the edge and splashed onto the tabletop, but he didn't seem to notice.

"Lords and Ladies of Palantar, the God-Sage has seen fit to save us all on this day, using my granddaughter as his vessel. I am blessed indeed." Lord Aralorn took a slurp of wine, placed down the goblet, and then raised his hands over his head and began to applaud.

Others joined the clapping and the sound rose to a thunderous beat, but somehow it felt melancholy, with an edge of ridicule. Verbun, particularly, looked disapproving. He slammed his great hands together slowly, striking a rhythm that counted down to some unseen end.

Marlowe felt the heat of the gaze of the crowd and wanted to look away.

"We still look like prisoners." Valora rolled her eyes sideways, to indicate the guards who had resumed their places beside them. "It's because Grandfather thinks you want to escape."

Marlowe didn't respond. He wished that he had tried to escape. At least then Valora wouldn't have been exposed the way she had been at the river. And of course they looked like prisoners; they were treading the thinnest of paths: children of traitors, one of whom had wielded power beyond all comprehension. Their very lives depended on the interpretation of what had happened at the river.

Marlowe stared at his grandfather from beneath lowered brows. The hatred and resentment he tried to convey fell flat; the old man was too elated, too jovial, to notice. He believed he was the grandfather of the next acolyte, a young woman blessed by the God-Sage, and he was enjoying himself. How much of it was genuine, and how much of it was designed to convince Kyla Tarthwen of those beliefs, Marlowe wasn't sure.

"Sit, sit. Everyone, take your seats." Lord Aralorn waved everyone into their chairs, and the men and women who had been hovering around the table sat down. The young boy ceased his lute playing and perched on a chair against the wall. When everyone was seated Marlowe was struck by the fact that there were fewer people in the hall than he had at first thought.

Only he and Valora, the guards either side of them and his grandfather himself remained standing. Kyla had taken a seat on the far side of the table, next to where Lord Aralorn stood.

Nisia flailed a hand towards Valora and Marlowe. "Will you let them sit with us, Grandfather?"

"No. Not yet." Lord Aralorn pressed his palms flat on the tabletop and turned his attention to Kyla. "Before all these fine ladies and gentlemen, I need your assurance, Miss Tarthwen, that Valora will be accepted as acolyte when you return to Moriya."

Kyla, her eyes wary, sat back and gripped the arm of her chair with one hand. She looked as uncertain as Marlowe felt, and her lack of conviction speared fear into his chest. He needed her to agree. It was the only way to protect Valora.

"Trade has suffered in Palantar since..." Lord Aralorn shook his head, affecting some false remorse. "...since the execution of my daughter and her husband. They were traitors—" Marlowe could not hold back the hiss that escaped his lips. To hear his parents dismissed as such still pained him. Lord Aralorn shot him a silencing look. "—but my granddaughter is not. She is innocent. We have all paid harshly for my daughter's crimes, but I wish this to be a new beginning for Palantar. It is crucial that our trade routes will be repaired. Will you, Kyla Tarthwen, guarantee that Moriya will resume trade with us? And that the other provinces too will be permitted to trade with us once more?"

Kyla pushed her chair back and stood up. She looked at her hands for a brief moment before raising her eyes, glancing around the room and starting to speak. "Are we not to discuss what happened by the river?"

Lord Aralorn's eyes narrowed. "Yarmon Sacfron, leader of the Nilari rebels, showed himself. He attacked us. We will send a report to Moriya, to alert them to the possibility that he is raising forces in the north."

"I don't mean that. I am talking about whatever force dispelled him, his eels, his birds. Are we not to talk of that?"

Lord Aralorn stiffened, and his lips shrank back from his teeth. "It was the work of the God-Sage."

Marlowe gripped Valora's hand tighter. Her life, his life, hung by a thread. Kyla said nothing, but she stared unblinkingly at Lord Aralorn. The people seated near her had pushed their chairs away and were looking warily at her. The tension was thick.

Max, seated at Kyla's side, looked nervous. His fingers, which had been running up and down the stem of his goblet, froze.

Lord Aralorn's voice splintered the silence. "What other explanation is there?"

Kyla lowered her eyes to the table, and then slid her gaze to Max. He looked back at her, and something passed between them then, something so visceral that Marlowe felt he could almost see it. Of course! If Valora's power was deemed illegal magic, then Max would have been contaminated when she healed him. To condemn Valora was to condemn Max too.

"Will you—" Lord Aralorn would not wait for Kyla to speak. "—guarantee that Moriya will resume trade with us?"

Kyla inhaled and sighed so deeply that Marlowe could see her chest rise and fall from the other side of the room. She shook her head. "It is not my place to make such guarantees. The Sages will make that declaration, once Valora is initiated as an acolyte back in Moirya."

Lord Aralorn rubbed an aged hand over his upper lip several times before he spoke. The motion was smooth, the stubble that had been there only days before long gone. Marlowe felt nauseous at the thought of his grandfather preening himself for a funeral, excited at the prospect of sacrificing his granddaughter for trading rights.

"What if Moriya will not accept her? What if they refuse to take a cripple as an acolyte? What if someone—" Lord Aralorn fixed Kyla with a stony glare, before which anyone else might have cowered, but she stood firm. "—tried to say that what happened today was not the work of the God-Sage? What then? It is a risk, is it not? The Sages may not accept her. You—" He lingered on the word. "—might not accept her."

Kyla was still for a moment, then her chest heaved and she exhaled loudly again. "It is. But—"

"They are branded, are they not? The acolytes?"

Marlowe felt a jolt through his hand, where Valora's small, clammy fingers held his own. "What is he talking about?" she whispered.

Marlowe felt his chest tighten. He didn't know, but he didn't like the sound of it.

Kyla nodded. "They are branded. It's a ritual performed in the temple at Moriya."

"After which their role is indisputable. They are acolytes, and they are marked as such. They belong to the God-Sage. Is that not correct?"

"That's right." Kyla was beginning to look uneasy, as if she anticipated that she was about to lose control of the situation. "But it is an intricate and highly skilled endeavour. The acolytes are branded with molten gold."

Lord Aralorn brought his goblet down on the table with a thump and looked towards Verbun, the priest, who gave a nod to acknowledge some prior agreement or discussion. The priest stood up and clapped his hands.

A door on the far side of the room opened and three junior priests entered. One held a long iron pole, the upper end of which formed an outline of the God-Sage's image: a circle with ten flares bursting from the perimeter. It was red hot, glowing, as though it had been lifted from a fire just outside the room. The two other priests carried a pot made of thick metal, thick enough to bear the heat of molten gold. It hung from a wooden pole that they each balanced on one shoulder.

Marlowe could feel the searing heat of it from where he stood. He could smell the metallic tang of hot iron; the promise of scorched flesh.

The priests were making their way towards Valora. They were going to brand her, right now! He wouldn't let them. His heart began to hammer and rage flushed through his entire body. He charged forward.

"Don't touch her!"

"Guards. Arrest him." Lord Aralorn flicked his fingers towards Marlowe and the guards were quick to move, but Marlowe was faster. He had the iron pole in his hands, wrestling it from the priest. He could see the shock on the man's face, his eyes wide and cheeks pale: no one ever attacked a priest.

Chairs scraped against stone. People were standing up, gasping, muttering.

Nisia was on her feet. "Grandfather, please."

Her pleading did no good. Marlowe felt the hands of the guards on him, yanking him backwards. Another guard appeared and pulled the iron pole from Marlowe's grasp, handing it back to the young priest, who clutched it and stepped back, looking as if he would have preferred to be anywhere other than where he found himself right now.

"Get your hands off me!" Marlowe snarled and thrashed. Despite knowing that everyone was watching, that he must look like a wild animal, he neither cared nor was able to stop himself. If they were going to arrest him, he would do his utmost to resist. Another guard yanked Marlowe's arms behind his back, so hard and tight that he found himself unable to move.

He tried to find his grandfather amidst the seething mob of indistinguishable faces before him. The rows of rotten finery. His vision blurred. He blinked and finally found the old man.

"You can't do this!"

Lord Aralorn glared at him. "Who are you to tell me—"

"Wait, stop." It was Kyla. She was moving around the table, running her hands over the backs of chairs, dodging past gawking nobles. But she was too far away, the table too long. Marlowe was sure there was nothing she could do. Kyla too seemed to realise the hopelessness of the situation. She held up her hands. "The journey... She can't travel... You can't. Please, stop..."

The young priest paused, looking between Verbun and Lord Aralorn for confirmation. They didn't have long. The glow of the iron was dimming. He held the branding over the iron pot, ready to dunk it into the gold.

"What say you, Verbun?" asked Lord Aralorn.

"It must be done fast, if it is to be done at all."

"Then get on with it."

More guards had appeared, and two of them forced Valora to her knees. Another pulled down the front of her dress. The fabric ripped, revealing the upper part of her chest. Valora whimpered, biting her lip to withhold what Marlowe could only assume was a scream. Her features scrunched in the centre of her face, holding back tears. She tried to turn her head away.

Marlowe tore against the guards who held him, wrenching his shoulders forward, but he couldn't free himself. Words exploded from his mouth, hot and full of anger, leaving his throat raw. "You would do this to your own granddaughter? Isn't it enough that you executed our parents? You must inflict this pain too?"

Lord Aralorn's features were hard, his eyes like bone that would not yield to any emotion. "If we are fortunate, she may atone for all our sins."

He nodded at the priest, who pulled the branding iron from the pot, dripping with gold, and plunged it against Valora's chest.

She screamed.

Marlowe roared.

He lunged, his arms still pinned behind him. Rage propelled him forward. There was a loosening and Marlowe slipped from the guard's grasp. He was free, but the guard was grappling at him again almost instantly. Marlowe shouldered him off and the man fell to the ground. He was only a few paces from the priest, from Valora.

There was nothing for it but to charge at them, roaring and cursing. Marlowe surged forward, lost in the violence of his rage, more force than man.

Another guard appeared and yanked Marlowe off course, and all at once Marlowe realised it was hopeless. Two guards held him now. He could do nothing.

"No! No!" He yelled, shaking his head with each word. "Don't touch her! Leave her alone! Get off my sister!"

Blood rushed in his ears, a deafening *whoosh-whoosh* that sought to sweep him away. He felt dizzy, his legs weak. He lost all sense of himself, drowning in the agony of his own screams, yet hearing the noise as if it came from someone else.

It felt like an age that the iron pressed against Valora's chest, but it couldn't have been more than a few seconds. The room filled with the pungent smell of burning flesh. When the priest removed the brand there was a soft squelch as it pulled off the burnt skin. Valora collapsed, falling forward, held up only by the guards who kept her in place.

Nisia was sitting at the table, her face covered with her hands. Kyla and Max stood on the other side of the table, looking at one another with expressions of muted shock. Most of the gathered noblemen and women were still seated, barely moving. Some of the women clasped one another's hands, a frail protection against the barbarity of what they had witnessed.

Lord Aralorn sat at the head of the table, observing them all with a quiet dispassion.

"You heartless monster! You Nilari beast!" People were gasping, hands fluttering to cover open mouths, but Marlowe didn't care. Let them be scandalised. "How could you?" Without waiting for an answer, he spat at his grandfather's feet. The guards tugged harder at Marlowe's arms in response.

One of them growled, "Shut up."

Lord Aralorn glanced at the lump of phlegm on the stone floor, so recently hocked from the back of Marlowe's throat, but he did not look up, and Marlowe knew the response was not going to be a good one.

"Take him away. To the cells."

3

·

KYLA

THE CITY OF PALANTAR

The smell of singed flesh filled the air. Kyla tried not to breathe, if only for a moment.

"Great God-Sage, Kyla." Max spoke under his breath, but his tone betrayed all his horror.

Unable to think of anything else to say, Kyla bowed her head and fell back on the catechism. "*The God-Sage deserves a pure city.*"

She had known the acolytes were branded, but the mark was always concealed beneath their delicate white dresses. The ceremony during which they were marked took place in secret, which Kyla had always assumed was because it was an intimate dedication of the acolyte's body to the God-Sage himself.

But what she had witnessed here changed that. Now, she knew it was kept secret because it was brutal.

When Valora's skin had burnt, Kyla had wanted to scream herself, but Marlowe, who had screamed louder even than his sister, had made enough noise for everyone. Kyla watched him wrestle with his captors as they dragged him from the room, his dark hair sweeping back and forth across a face distorted by torment. She could feel his pain, his rage, as though it reached out and touched her soul. She put a hand to her heart to still the ache that had begun, and each breath she took was shallow and not enough, as if she was being crushed by some external weight.

The door clanged shut behind Marlowe and the guards, leaving a strange void, as if the only real person in the room had disappeared. Kyla felt a numbness flood her body, sealing her own emotions somewhere deep inside, and she could not help but be grateful for it.

A few moments of awkward, horrified silence followed, broken only when Lord Aralorn began instructing the servants to fill everyone's glasses with wine.

He caught Kyla's eye and waved towards Valora. "See, there's your acolyte. Branded, as required. Any doubt that her gifts are not the work of the God-Sage may be thoroughly assuaged. Does this satisfy you, Miss Tarthwen?"

Kyla felt the attention of the room fall on her as she balanced between treachery and piety. If it were so easy to claim all magic as the work of the God-Sage, why not brand every illegal healer, every secret witch and warlock that hid in the northern mountains? Why not, indeed, brand every Nilari rebel with the mark of the God-Sage?

Because, and here Kyla took a deep breath, a mark was not sufficient to change the soul of a person. Burning someone's skin did not make them a believer.

"Kyla," Max hissed. "Say something."

It was the sound of his voice that decided her.

"Yes," she said. "I believe Valora is a vessel of the God-Sage, and I shall return to Moriya with her as such. You have my word."

Lord Aralorn nodded sharply. "Good. Then you need not worry about her. My physician will bind her wounds and tend her injuries. I shall dispatch a letter to Moriya in the morning to inform the King and the Sages."

Valora was kneeling on the floor, whimpering. Duncan, the physician, came towards her. He was wearing the same green robes he had been wearing when Kyla had first seen him, before Max had been healed. In all the uproar, Kyla had not noticed his arrival. Perhaps he too had been informed earlier of what was to take place, and had been waiting outside the hall until his services were required.

He knelt beside Valora and opened a leather bag, which had been slung over his shoulder. He took out and uncorked several bottles, setting them on the floor beside him.

Kyla watched as Duncan tried to dab ointment onto Valora's burn. Valora in turn kept whimpering, clenching her eyes shut and moving away from him with stuttered jerks. The stench of burnt skin was worse now, and even from the other side of the table Kyla could see the wound, black, raw, red and still smoking.

"No need to look so concerned," Lord Aralorn said. "It is but a shallow wound, and will leave a pleasing scar. Duncan is more than capable of treating her. She will be taken for rest before your departure. And then you may take her away. She is yours now. I shall await word that trade may be resumed as normal."

The wound didn't look shallow, but Kyla didn't want to disagree. "Where will Valora sleep?"

"Oh, the cells, with her brother," Lord Aralorn said. "She'll be quite safe there. It's really the best place for her."

Kyla was about to object when she realised Lord Aralorn was no longer looking at her. He was staring over her shoulder to where four servants were crossing the room towards the table, carrying a silver platter so large that they had to rest it on their shoulders. It held a roasted pig with a crumpled, softened apple in its mouth.

"Oh look, look, our food arrives." He sat down, flapped out a linen napkin, and tucked it into the neck of his robes. "Take a seat, settle yourself, or you shan't be able to eat. My cook is one of the best in all Tolinaye, I am certain of it, and your appetite will be quite spoilt if we carry on this discussion."

But Kyla did not do as he had asked, and instead placed one hand on the tabletop and stood over him, leaning into his space. He pulled back and turned to look at her, one bushy eyebrow shooting upwards to hide beneath his tangled white hair.

"Miss Tarthwen, you have your own plate. Do not come so close to mine."

"Have Valora stay in my room. I insist. She's as important to me, to the God-Sage, as she is to you."

"Oh all right, all right. She is yours now, I suppose. Do what you will with her, but please sit down to eat." He waved at one of the servants. "Tell the physician where to take the girl. Quick."

As the servant scurried towards Duncan, Lord Aralorn rubbed his hands together and smacked his lips. "Quite delicious. Do you smell it? The pig?"

Max, on her other side, whispered, "I can't eat."

Kyla nodded. There was something disconcertingly similar about the smell of scorched flesh and roasted hog. "I know," she said. "But do try. Our journey tomorrow will be a long one."

With one final glance at Valora, Kyla resumed her seat next to Lord Aralorn. He seemed an unpredictable sort of man and she didn't want any more unexpected surprises. She passed him her goblet so that he might fill it with the scented wine, although she had no intention of drinking any of it. Instead she helped herself to one of the rolls of bread that had arrived at the table and crunched into it, but she could barely taste it.

Nisia, who sat not far away, leant across the table and grabbed a large decanter of pale liquid, shaking it at Kyla. "Take this with you, afterwards. Have Valora drink some. Have her drink a lot. She won't be able to sleep without it."

Kyla took the bottle, lifted the stopper and smelt the contents. She immediately turned her head away. Whatever it was, it was strong, and if anything would take away the pain of the branding, it was this.

"Thank you," she said.

Kyla made her way to her bedchamber. Her head was aching worse than ever and she needed to lie down. In one hand she clutched the decanter Nisia had given her, the other she drew along the wall in an attempt to leech the stone's stability through her fingertips.

Footsteps came running behind her and she turned, her hand springing from the wall to the hilt of her sword. She squinted at the figure darting towards her, visible only in bursts as it dashed between the light of the flames that flickered from sconces on the walls.

"Kyla, wait. We need to talk."

Max. *Thank the God-Sage*. She slid her hand from her sword. "Now?"

He nodded, pulling her into an alcove just off the corridor. Their bodies were so close Kyla could feel the nervous energy coming off him in waves. "Are you still going to take her?"

Irritation crawled up her throat. "Yes."

"You want to march into Moriya like a hero and make her an acolyte?"

"It's not about being a hero. We don't have any choice."

"But—"

"Don't do this to me. We're committed. She's been branded—"

"I know. But *the God-Sage deserves a pure city*, Kyla. You've told me a thousand times. Valora would never be accepted in Moriya."

"She wears the mark of the God-Sage. There is nothing more pure than that."

Max crossed his arms over his chest and pressed his lips together tightly.

"What? I can see you want to say something else."

"What if it *was* magic? What if it wasn't the God-Sage at all?" Kyla raised her hand in warning, but Max did not stop. He kept on in a rugged whisper. "No, listen to me. What happened to me during that healing was... something else. I was... dying. I can accept that the God-Sage may have been involved; we can pass it off that way, because healing is what the God-Sage does. It's what we know. It's what everyone knows. But today, at the river, those eels, that bright light... There's something going on here that's beyond the power of the God-Sage."

Kyla breath lodged in her throat. She coughed. "Nothing is beyond the power of the God-Sage."

Max fixed her with a hard stare. "It felt like magic."

Kyla felt a sudden frustration burst within. Why was he pushing her to agree with him, when agreement meant condemning him to death?

The words flew from her mouth. "There is no magic at work here. There is only the God-Sage."

Max's cheeks were red beneath his freckles, and she knew he was holding back. She didn't want to fight with him, not now when they were in a foreign city, far from home.

"I promise you, Max, the God-Sage saved you, I know it. I've told you before and I'll tell you again." She pressed a hand to her heart. "I feel it, right here."

For the first time, it felt like a lie. She stepped back, moving towards her room. She couldn't talk to him now, not like this. Anyone could come, anyone could hear them. Even discussing the possibility of magic out loud was a risk.

"Kyla, wait." His hand clenched about her forearm. "I feel it, beneath my skin. Something's not right. Ever since that day at Traitors' Lake, I've felt a sort of..." He paused, searching for the right word, and even before he spoke it Kyla knew what it would be. "...magic within me—"

"Magic?" She exhaled, a sharp, dismissive sound, and tugged her arm free of his grip. "It was death eels. That was what was inside you, nothing but those disgusting creatures, eating away at you." Even as she finished speaking she wished she hadn't been so harsh, but she'd been desperate for him to stop sharing his every thought with her.

He looked at her with eyes that trembled with hurt, and she tried to close the distance she had created between them by reaching out and putting her hand on his arm. She softened her voice and said, "Sorry. It's all been too much. I need to sleep, and so do you. We've a long journey tomorrow."

The room that had been allocated to Kyla the night before the funeral was far from luxurious, but it had yielded a far better sleep than any she had on the journey to Palantar. Her muscles still ached from the nights spent on the banks of the river, in the forest and in the back of Arthur's cart, but the pulsing at her temples right now felt worse than any of that. She longed to push back the green velvet cover that draped across the bed and slide between the sheets again.

But when she opened the door, someone was already in the bed. Valora. She was wearing the same grey dress she had been wearing at the branding. It flapped open at the neck where it had been ripped, and Kyla could see the bandages beneath.

Valora was shaking, her eyes closed, her hands tightly clasped together, the fingers of one hand pressing so hard into the back of the other that the tips were red and the nails blanched.

Kyla hesitated. She took one careful step forward, closer to the bed, but her approach was interrupted.

"Where's my brother?"

Valora hadn't opened her eyes and Kyla stood still, wondering if Valora knew, or even cared, to whom she was speaking.

"The cells, your grandfather said."

Valora was quiet for a moment and then a harsh sob rumbled in the back of her throat. If the girl was going to cry, Kyla wouldn't blame her, but she didn't want to encourage it.

Kyla walked over to a small table near the window, where there was a jug of water and some glasses. She placed the decanter that Nisia had given her down next to them and removed the cork. The smell of alcohol met her nostrils instantly. Powerful stuff. She lifted a glass, filled it with the clear liquid and brought it to Valora. "Here, drink some."

Valora blinked her eyes open. Tears quivered on her lower lashes. Her gaze settled on the glass Kyla held. She shook her head, and when she spoke her voice was taut with resentment.

"You didn't tell me they would do this." One hand wavered over her chest and she bit her lip. "You said it was an honour to be made an acolyte. You said—"

Kyla felt a strange weakness whip down her legs and she wanted to sit down, but instead she forced her voice to sound calm and held the glass out to Valora again. "Drink."

Valora eyed it suspiciously, leant closer, sniffed and turned her head away. "No. I'll wake with a splitting head."

Kyla gave a half-smile, trying to ignore the pounding in her own head. "The lesser of two evils, I fear."

Valora's eyes narrowed, considering the choices. A slight relaxation of her shoulders let Kyla know she had chosen to drink. She winced and groaned, each movement an agony as she struggled to prop herself up in the bed.

It was then that Kyla noticed that the fingers of one of Valora's hands were still clamped around something. It looked to be the little leather pouch that Kyla had seen her remove from around her neck, back when they had been by the river. She was holding it as though it offered her some sort of comfort. Did whatever was inside it have to do with what had happened at the river?

Kyla resisted the urge to reach out and force it from her hand, but she made a mental note to look later, when Valora fell asleep. Instead she proffered the glass once more. "It will ease the pain."

Valora nodded, but made no move to take the glass. Her other hand, the empty one, lay gingerly on the cover, and Kyla noticed that it wasn't moving naturally. The fingers were rigid, clawed.

"Is there something wrong with your hand?"

Valora shook her head, but slipped her hand beneath the covers. If she was determined to keep one hand hidden, then she would have to let go of the little leather pouch she held in the other to hold the glass of liquor.

But she made no move to reach for the glass with either hand. Kyla didn't want to upset her even more, so she lifted the glass to Valora's lips herself and let the girl sip at it. Her face scrunched up. "Yuck."

Kyla raised an eyebrow, still holding the glass close to Valora's face, and waited. After a moment Valora leant forward, allowing Kyla to tip the glass and its contents towards her mouth. She swallowed until the glass was empty.

The expression of pain that had been written on Valora's features softened. She lay back and closed her eyes. A drunken sleep was beginning to edge in.

Valora looked small against the bed, but even so Kyla wasn't sure it was wide enough for them both to share.

Not that it mattered; Kyla was doubtful that she would be able to sleep anyway after all that had happened that day. There was a chair by the window, and she sat there instead.

They were both silent for a few moments, and then Valora, her voice slow, spoke. "I won't go to Moriya without my brother."

"You'll have to, if your grandfather doesn't release him."

"Release him?" Valora let out a soft grunt. "He won't do that."

From what she had seen of Lord Aralorn, Kyla had no doubt that Valora's assessment was correct. "We have to leave in the morning. The sooner we get back to Moriya, the sooner you can join the other acolytes and the healing circle can be restored. You know it needs ten acolytes to function."

Valora, her eyes still closed, nodded. "I had heard that. And without the healing power of the circle—"

"The city is vulnerable to attack and disease," Kyla said. "The circle is our strength, our divine gift. Just like yours is for you."

"Mmm. You think it is divine? My healing gift?"

Kyla took a deep breath. She wasn't sure what she believed now, but she had to choose, and she had to come down hard. There was no room for uncertainty. "I do. People think illegal healers use magic, but they don't. They sell hope at a high price, but never healing. They're charlatans, all of them. They exploit the sick and the dying. All true healing, such as yours, is divine."

Kyla was pleased at how confident she sounded, and Valora was quiet as she absorbed the information. "And what about the eels? The way they disappeared..."

Kyla looked out of the window. It was dark outside. Heavy velvet curtains hung to one side and she stood up and pulled them closed, sending puffs of stale-smelling dust into the air. She spoke without turning back to look at Valora.

"You are marked for the God-Sage." It wasn't a direct answer, but it was all she felt able to give.

Silence followed, but Kyla sensed that Valora had not finished. Her body tensed as she waited for the girl to speak.

"My brother doesn't want me to go to Moriya, and he doesn't want me to be an acolyte."

Kyla turned to face her. "It's just as well he's locked up then."

Valora's lips twitched, like she had been about to say something and then changed her mind. She took a breath, and when she finally spoke her voice was brittle. "Marlowe says he won't do anything for a Moriyan soldier. Especially not you."

"Me?" Suspicion laced her words. "*Particularly* me?"

Valora nodded. "Yes. He hates you."

Kyla felt a strange pang somewhere in her chest, although the information wasn't entirely unexpected. "Oh?"

Valora's eyes were open now, her cheeks pale, her hair a shock of darkness on the white pillow.

"It was Lander Tarthwen who lit the pyre that burnt our mother and father." Valora's chin dimpled as she held back tears. She clenched her jaw and rigidity spread up her face.

Her eyes were stony when she raised them to meet Kyla's. "Your father killed our parents."

The words crept like frost over Kyla's neck, chilling her core. Her first instinct was to apologise, as if to say sorry might undo the fact that her father had been responsible for their execution. Kyla had known that Marlowe and Valora's parents had been executed as traitors, and she had known that her father had come to Palantar at the time, but she hadn't known it was his hand that had lit the flames that killed them. She wanted to say that she was sure her father wouldn't have done it if they hadn't been guilty, but looking at Valora's face, grief scrawled across it, she couldn't do it and she was sure it wouldn't have helped.

It explained why Marlowe had looked at her with such loathing when they had first met. It wasn't simply the expression of someone who didn't like Moriyans, or soldiers, or who didn't believe in the God-Sage. It was personal.

"What about you?" Kyla hoped the girl didn't hold the same level of vitriol towards her as Malowe did. She was, after all, not her father, but she didn't hold out much hope that she would be excused as such. Kyla could feel anger rolling off Valora as she lay in bed, singeing the air between them with its heat.

"I love my brother." Valora gritted her teeth. "He's all the family I have left."

It wasn't the question Kyla had meant to ask, and just as she was about to rephrase and ask again, Valora looked at her with eyes that were hard, but something behind the frosty glaze seemed to be melting. "I want to hate you. You represent the regime that killed my parents. The blood of the man who burnt them to death runs in your veins. Oh, I've *tried* to hate you—" Valora rolled her eyes towards the ceiling and her voice took on a slower, lilting quality. "—but somehow I can't quite manage it. Not after the healing..."

Kyla felt a heat rise to her cheeks at the mention of Max's healing. Her experience of it had been strangely intimate, and she could tell by the way Valora averted her eyes that she had found it so too.

Kyla remembered how Valora's hands clasped about her own, and the rushing sense that she and Valora were connected in some otherworldly way. But once it was over the feeling of connection had gone, leaving only a whisper of awkwardness, as Kyla imagined it might feel if she had kissed someone she didn't like and had to face them the next day. It felt shameful.

"It felt like I knew you," Valora continued. "It felt like—"

"Stop, now. You're weak and tired. You need to rest and heal as much as possible before the morning. I'll be here—" Kyla gestured to the chair at the window. "—if you need me."

There was a beat of silence. A breath, and then, "What did it feel like, for you? What did you feel—" Valora tried to sit up and fell back to the pillows.

"Don't strain yourself. Here, take a bit more." Kyla was glad to be able to stop the conversation; she had reflected on the healing no more than was absolutely necessary. It begged too many questions. If she started to examine it, everything might unravel. She refilled the glass with the potent alcohol and let Valora drink it. "It will take effect soon. You won't feel anything."

Kyla walked back towards the window and put the empty glass on the table. She picked up the decanter, inhaled the fumes that were rising from its neck. Would it do any harm to have a drink herself, to take the edge off a hard day? It might mute the ache in her head. She put the bottle down and fixed the stopper in the neck. Probably best not to.

She sat down, watching as Valora drifted into a drugged sleep.

Kyla could see the moon move across the sky, its pale light striping the floor through a gap between the curtains. Her body ached, but she couldn't sleep. Every so often Valora shifted in the sheets, groaning.

Perhaps she could take a look at whatever was in Valora's pouch now. If she was careful, the girl would not wake. She stood up and crept towards the bed.

There was a knock on the door and Kyla felt a shock of guilt run through her body. She stood straight and swung towards the door.

Max poked his head into the room and nodded at the bed. "How is she?"

"Asleep. But not comfortable."

Max nodded. "And you?"

"I can't sleep."

"Me neither. I can't stop thinking about what happened."

Kyla beckoned Max towards her, so they could talk without disturbing Valora. It wasn't entirely private, but as long as she was asleep it was better than having a discussion in the corridor outside.

Max let the door close softly behind him. "Can we travel?" he whispered.

"We have to. Tomorrow. We need to get back to Moriya as quickly as possible."

Max nodded. "Did you hear the people down at the river today? Whispering and wondering about Edmund. About what killed him. There's talk of something coming. Maybe plague, maybe something else."

"Like what?"

Max shrugged. "It's always the return of the Nilari, isn't it? That's the biggest fear. And after that Nilari rebel appeared out of nowhere... everyone's terrified."

"My brother doesn't believe the Nilari really existed." Both Max and Kyla turned towards the bed. Valora had her eyes open, but they were strangely unfocused, and her words were a little slurred. "He knows the *birds* exist, because we see them flying over the city every day. It's the people he means. You know, the winged men with teeth like talons. He thinks they're a legend to terrify the masses. To keep them under control."

"Does he?" Kyla asked.

Valora closed her eyes and nodded. "The Isle of Ashes too. He thinks it's nonsense. A great cloud over the northern mountains where the souls of the slaughtered Nilari rest? He says it's so unlikely to be true that he would burn every item of clothing he owned if it were."

Max gave a guffaw. "Every item? He'd regret that come winter."

Kyla glared at him and Max smacked a palm over his mouth, but his chuckling, muffled now, continued behind his hand.

"When you get to Moriya you'll see the wings of the Nilari King hanging over the healing circle," Kyla said. "They've been there for five hundred years, since Morden Tarthwen—"

"Marlowe thinks—"

"Marlowe isn't here," Kyla snapped. "What do *you* think?"

Valora was quiet.

Max, recovered from his fit of giggles, tutted and shook his head. "Leave her alone, Kyla. She's in pain."

"She's not. She's drunk."

Valora lay back, shook her head ever so slightly, and let it relax into the pillow. Kyla stood over the bed and waited a few moments until Valora's breathing became deep and regular, or at least as deep and regular as it was going to be. There was a breathless crackle in her chest that sounded with each inhalation. A few moments later a snore rattled in the back of her throat. She had fallen asleep. Thank the God-Sage.

Kyla tilted her head to one side and observed her. She was small, the green velvet coverlet hooked up across her knees and chest, which poked up at strange angles. She was fascinating, the shape of her, the contortion. Before Kyla had set eyes on Valora she had never seen someone with a body like hers.

Max came to stand beside her. Kyla heard air rasp in his throat as he prepared to speak, when something fell from the bed with a dull clunk and a clink.

The small leather pouch lay on the floor. Valora's uncurled fingers hung from the side of the bed, the leather thong still tangled between her index finger and thumb.

Max knelt to pick it up. He was about to slide it back into Valora's hand when Kyla snatched it from him.

"Hey—"

"Shhh." Kyla tipped the contents of the pouch into her palm. There were two gold rings, small, sized for women's fingers. She stared at them. There was nothing unusual about them whatsoever.

"What is it? What are you looking for?"

"I thought... I thought there was something in here. Something that caused that last blast of light, down at the river."

"Let me see." Max held his palm open, and Kyla, sure now that the rings were entirely unremarkable, dropped them into his hand. He pinched them between thumb and forefinger, held them up before one eye and then peered through them as if they were some kind of eyepiece.

Then his face took on a strange, confused expression and he held the rings away.

"What?" Kyla asked.

"It's like... Kyla... I think I can hear something."

Kyla cocked her head, listening. There was no sound other than their own breathing and Valora's gentle snoring.

"Not in the room. From the rings." His eyes were wide. "It's like the voices of the dead from the lake. Whoever owned these rings must be..." He gasped.

"Dead," finished Kyla.

Max nodded, closing his eyes. His eyelids flickered slightly, allowing a glimpse of white between them.

Then his eyes snapped open again. "They're her mother's."

"What else? Did you hear anything else?"

He shook his head. "No. I can't make anything out properly. I can only... sense what they are trying to tell me. It's as if... I don't know. It's as if hearing these voices is like learning to ride a horse. You can't do it straight away. You have to train. To practise. It's there though, I swear it."

"And there's nothing else?"

Max shook his head. "No. Whatever caused that blast of light, it wasn't these. They're completely normal rings. Her mother must have left them to her."

Kyla felt guilt gnawing at her again. Of course Valora kept her mother's jewellery close to her heart. It was probably all she had left. If Kyla had owned any of her own mother's jewellery, she was sure she would have kept it close too.

She was about to agree with Max's comment when the cuff of his shirt sleeve fell down as he held the rings up. It was only a slight slip, but enough to reveal his wrist and, around it, what looked like black tattoos, only they weren't still. They were moving.

Kyla grabbed his wrist. "What's that?"

Max looked down at where she held him. His eyebrows shot up and the colour drained from his cheeks, leaving his freckles pale and vulnerable. He dropped the rings from trembling fingers.

They clanked on the floor and Valora, disturbed by the noise, rustled the sheets and sighed. Kyla scrambled for the rings, clutching them in one hand before they rolled away.

Kyla and Max crouched, motionless, at the side of the bed, as if their stillness would prevent Valora waking up.

When it was clear she was still sleeping, Max, gingerly with the thumb and forefinger of one hand, eased up his sleeves.

Both his forearms were swirling with black marks, constantly shifting and blocking out the freckles, then exposing them again, like dark clouds crossing the moon's face. Were they on the skin or beneath it? It was hard to tell.

"Oh God-Sage..."

Max's horror, his wide eyes, his shock, was palpable. He shuffled backwards, trying to escape his own arms.

Kyla stared, all the possibilities racing through her mind at once. Was this what he had meant when he had tried to tell her before, and she had so thoughtlessly shut him down? Was something still inside him? Some poison from the lake, somehow sealed under his skin after the healing? Or did something infect him at the funeral?

"Did they touch you today? The eels, at the river?" Kyla whispered.

Max's lips quivered as he spoke. "I don't think so..."

He scratched at his arms as though he meant to unearth whatever was moving there, peel it off his skin, but it had no effect and only left red welts down his arms.

Kyla held his upper arms, willing him to calm. "Does it hurt?"

Max shook his head, and when Kyla saw that his initial fear had dissipated, she released him. He stroked one hand over the other forearm more gently now and then switched to the other side.

"Can you feel it?" she asked.

Max's eyebrows drew together, furrowing his forehead. "Not really. It's smooth."

"But... on the inside. Can you feel it there?"

Max shook his head. "It's not like the eels. It's like... the spirit of them, but without the bodies. It doesn't feel as if there's anything physically inside me anymore. It's like... the shadow of them."

Kyla reached out one finger and stroked it down his arm. He said nothing, letting her touch him. His skin felt soft, only disrupted by the fair hairs on his arms despite the black marks that squirmed beneath his freckles. Had Kyla had her eyes closed, she wouldn't have known anything was amiss.

"When did it start?" she asked.

Max shook his head. "I don't know. I didn't notice them before." He pressed his palm to his forehead as if he was trying to eke out some kind of clue, some more specific answer to her question. "There were silver scars before, you remember – they were there right after the healing. Nothing like this though. Nothing that moved." He looked up at her. "Do you think it's..."

Kyla knew he was about to say 'magic' and she didn't want to hear it. She pulled his sleeves all the way down, so they covered every trace of the black marks.

"It's... something. Keep it hidden until we can work out what it is. When we get back to Moriya, we can ask Gregor." Kyla felt her body relax even at the mention of Gregor's name. He was her priest mentor and had trained her in preparation to join the Sacred Core. "Gregor will know something, and if he doesn't he can go to the Great Library and find out if anything has been written about such things before." She paused, seeing that Max didn't look at all comforted by her words. "You will tell me, won't you? If it begins to hurt?"

Max slid his eyes to the left and then, after a brief pause, nodded. It was enough for Kyla to suspect that if the marks did start to cause him pain, he wouldn't be rushing to tell her.

"What about the voices?" she asked.

"The voices of the dead?"

Kyla nodded. "It's important, Max. Is that what you were trying to tell me, before? I wasn't listening then, I'm sorry. But I'm listening now. Something changed when you got to Traitors' Lake—"

"I touched the water. That's what happened. And then I could hear them, all those voices, babbling up from the lake. All those people who had been laid to rest in those waters..."

"Can you hear them now?"

Max's eyes glazed over as he directed his focus to his hearing. Then his eyes, once more alert, fixed on Kyla. "It's different now. There's a hum. Like hundreds of voices, all whispering at once. I can feel them, inside my body, rather than hear them with my ears. But there's nothing I can make out. No particular voice. I was listening during the funeral. I thought perhaps Edmund..."

Max closed his eyes. His lips were pressed tightly together and Kyla realised with a shock that he was struggling to hold it together. She rested her hand on his arm and felt him relax at her touch, but she sensed he needed more than she felt capable of giving.

"The voices are clearer when you're holding something? Something that connects you to the dead? Like these rings?"

Max opened his eyes, but in them Kyla saw only confusion and fear. There was no point pushing him any more, not now. She dropped her arm and nodded her head towards the door.

"Get some sleep, Max. We're leaving in the morning."

Max nodded and she watched as he crossed the room, but when he got to the door he paused and turned round. "People touched the water today."

Kyla felt her breathing grow shallow. After he had touched the waters of Traitors' Lake, Max had nearly died. It had been infested with eels, just like the river water at the funeral, which had splashed on more than one person in the crowd. The eels too had touched people. Max was watching her, waiting for a response. She gave a brief nod, to acknowledge that she heard him, that she understood his meaning, and then she said, "Go to bed, Max."

When he had gone, Kyla opened her hand and stared at the rings. Useless. They told her nothing about what had happened at the river. She lifted the leather pouch, intending to place the rings back inside, but as she lifted it she got a whiff of burning, like ash or smoke. She sniffed at it, inhaling the scent of burnt leather. She teased the neck open as far as it would go and looked inside. There was something there... something black. A scorch mark. She couldn't see it properly so she turned the pouch inside out. There, right on the leather, was a fresh burn mark. Kyla ran her fingertip over the design. It was circular, with spokes that met in the middle.

It looked like a tiny cart wheel, but the spokes weren't straight. They rippled on their way to meet in the centre.

Something about it looked familiar, but Kyla couldn't recall what; the memory was elusive, like the thread of a spider's web caught in a breeze.

Valora groaned and turned over in her sleep. Worried that the girl would wake, Kyla flipped the pouch the right way in, dropped the rings inside and shoved the whole thing back into Valora's curled, sleeping fingers, tucking her hand beneath the velvet cover.

4

MARLOWE

THE CITY OF PALANTAR

Marlowe had never been in the cells beneath Aralorn Hall, although he had heard all sorts of rumours about them, the most prevalent being that traitors were tortured down here with all manner of horrifying tools before they were finally burnt on the pyre. Had his parents been held here before they had died? Marlowe shuddered at the thought of it.

Now though, there didn't seem to be anyone else here. There was no noise, no human sound other than his own footsteps and those of the guards who had brought him down here. He was alone.

They reached a cell at the end of a dark passageway. One guard opened the gate, the other pushed Marlowe inside. It was dank, the floor slippery with some kind of lichen that grew on the rock.

The gate clanged shut and the guard clicked a heavy key into the lock.

"Don't let the rats eat you while you sleep." He grinned before turning and wandering back along the passageway.

Marlowe gripped the rusty bars, rough to the touch, and began to pull on them. The gate barely moved, but the oversized lock rattled. He began to shout, knowing it was pointless before he began, but he had to do something.

"Let me out! How dare you? They're taking my sister! Let me out, let me out!"

He had been sure after what had happened at the river that getting Kyla to agree to take Valora to Moriya would be the only way to save her life. But he hadn't known what his grandfather had planned. He hadn't known he meant to scar her with the mark of the God-Sage. He wanted to rage and kill them all, every last one of those over-indulged nobles who had done nothing but sit and stare. Even Nisia.

He called out again. "Unlock this gate... I swear I'll kill you all when I get out..." He shook the bars as violently as he could.

No response. Not even a sound. The guards must have retreated somewhere further off. The only light was the flickering of the torches fixed to the walls further down the passage: a golden glow that throbbed on the dark stone walls, shining on the patches of dampness. A rat scurried down the passage, and water plinked into green-hued puddles.

There was a small bench in the cell and Marlowe sat down, dropping his head into his hands. It was hopeless. Valora was branded. He could still smell her burning skin, as though the stench was lodged in his nostrils. It had taken months to forget the smell of his parents' burning bodies, to stop recalling it even when the breeze was as fresh as dawn; he was sure it would take just as long to forget this.

He sat that way for what could have been hours, listening to the muffled far-off chatter of the guards further down the passage. What time of day was it? There was no sunlight, no way of telling what length the shadows it cast might be. No way of knowing how far the sun had roamed across the sky.

What was Valora doing now? What was his grandfather doing? The soldiers? The nobles of Palantar? Were they still feasting in the hall? Drinking? Celebrating? Was it evening already?

He felt a little tired. Perhaps he could lie down somewhere. He dropped his hands to his thighs and touched on something in his pocket.

The little crooked wheel. He pulled it out and held it up, looked through it, flipped it round. The metal was strange; it gleamed in the flickers of torchlight like some sinister spectre, but it did not shine as regular metal might. What use was it? He cupped it in his hands, rubbed it, blew on it, licked it. He even tried speaking to it, gently coaxing it to help him get out of the cells.

He held his breath, waiting for something. For heat, for light. Nothing happened. Whatever it did for Valora, it certainly didn't seem to do anything for him. It lay like a dead weight in the centre of his palm.

He felt a fool for having hoped something miraculous might happen. He wasn't Valora. He had no powers, no talent for magic of any sort. Of course it did nothing when he was the one holding it.

Disappointed, yet also partly relieved – what would he have done if something had happened? – he slid the crooked wheel back into his pocket, but as it slipped in it clunked against something else.

The knife! Now this was more useful. It was Kyla's. The very same knife she had used to stab the eels that had exploded out of Max's body; the very knife that she and Valora had been holding when they had driven it through Max's chest. A knife wound that had healed, not killed.

Kyla had dropped it after the healing, when the blast had thrown her against the wall. After the shock of events that followed, she must have forgotten about it. He had found it tucked beneath a chair in the entrance hall of Duncan's house. Valora had fashioned a small leather sheath for it, and it had been in his pocket ever since.

He pulled it out now and let it sit in the palm of his hand. It was dense, yet it felt light. It was perfectly weighted. The hilt was twisted, two long arms spiralling together until they joined as clasped hands at the top.

He removed the sheath and pricked the tip of his finger with the exposed blade. It was sharp. What could he do with it though? It was all very well to have a knife, but no good if there was no one around he could threaten with it.

There was a clink as a rat ran along the bottom of the gate. The lock banged against the bars. Of course! The lock! Was the blade slim enough to fit inside?

Marlowe had picked more locks than he cared to remember, even when he had lived up at Aralorn Hall. His grandfather had a habit of keeping all the good wine locked away, in case the servants felt inclined to help themselves. The locks had never stopped Marlowe taking a bottle or two and sharing it with a serving maid.

He crept towards the gate, sliding his arms through the bars to the other side. It was awkward to clasp the lock like this, but the keyhole was hanging on the other side, facing outwards. He fumbled. The knife slid, dropped, splashed into a puddle that rippled bright with reflected light.

The sound echoed and light flickered further down the dark passageway. Marlowe held still, barely breathing. Someone was on the move.

The footsteps came closer.

The knife was outside his cell, lying in the passageway. He reached through the bars, struggling to grab it. It had fallen just out of reach. He pushed forward, the bars of the cell right up against his chest, digging into his armpit. Fingers scrabbling in the dank water. He grabbed it. The knife. He had it. He slid his arm back through the bars and into the cell, and sat back on the bench.

The guard appeared, holding a tray bearing one solitary roll of bread. Marlowe examined the man's face for a sign of suspicion, but found none.

The guard set down the tray outside the cell door. "From your grandfather. He said you didn't have time to eat at the feast."

Marlowe's first impulse was to grab the bread and try to stuff it down the man's throat, but bread was ultimately a rather useless weapon. The knife was better, but he didn't want to kill the guard through the bars of the cell, especially if he couldn't then open the gate.

He was hungry, too. If he wanted to get out of here, he would have to eat something. No point protesting the quality of the food and starving in the meantime, when no one would care if he lived or died down here.

"Thanks," he said.

The guard flinched, surprised perhaps at being thanked, and moved off again, disappearing into the shadows.

When Marlowe was sure the guard had gone, he crept forward and began to pick the lock. The little knife slotted into the keyhole perfectly. Marlowe barely moved, feeling the intricacy of the inner workings of the lock with the tip of the blade. He had to get just the right angle, just the right traction.

He eased his wrist, turning gently, perfect pressure.

Click.

The lock opened and Marlowe let the pieces of it fall into his hand, cupping them softly. He didn't open the gate at first, but reached through and grabbed the bread, pulling it through into the cell. He bit into it. It was as hard as rock. So much for gaining strength. He flung it at the wall. Crumbs sparked off from the brittle crust. He listened for the sound of footsteps but none came.

He pushed the gate, slowly, to avoid the creaking of rusty hinges. A moment later he stood outside the cell.

Now there were only the guards to deal with.

He held the knife, gripping the hilt, knowing that if he was to kill someone quickly with a small blade like this he would have to aim carefully at close range, forcing it between ribs to reach a vital organ, or creep up behind them and slice their neck open.

For all the fights Marlowe had been in down the back alleys behind the Three-Legged Mare, he had never actually killed a man, nor did he want to. But, if it was him or the other man, well... there was no choice, really. He was never going to opt for his own death over someone else's.

He crept along the passageway, pressing his back against the damp rocky wall.

"Where do you think you're going?"

Marlowe turned. One of the guards was standing behind him, glaring into the gloom.

Before Marlowe could do anything he felt the man's huge hands slam down on his shoulders, wrenching him towards him.

He held the knife tight. This wasn't what he wanted, but he had no choice. He allowed himself to be pulled into the great heft of the guard and, when he was close enough, thrust the knife deep into the man's side and twisted the blade.

The man released him and Marlowe pulled back. The guard fell to his knees, clutching the wound. Blood was already seeping between his fingers. Strange gurgling noises came from somewhere deep inside the man's throat.

Marlowe backed away, unable to take his eyes from the dying man. Blood was coming from his lips now, dribbling down his chin.

The man slammed into the ground, drooling blood and saliva onto the floor.

It was hard to watch and Marlowe wanted to run, but to run now was to die. He would be trapped in the cells, and when he was found he would be executed. He had to stay. He had to make sure the man was dead. He had to take the keys that were attached to the man's belt.

The man ceased his bloody spluttering. Marlowe approached the body, toed it with his boot. No response. But he had to be sure. He had to know for certain. He heaved the man onto his back, knelt down and rammed the knife through the man's windpipe. No response. He was dead.

Marlowe felt a shudder of repulsion course through his body. He had killed a guard. There was no returning from this.

He had to flee.

He began fumbling for the keys. Blood covered his white shirt. He would have to find another when he got out. This one was ruined; a flag that waved his guilt.

He took the keys, gripping them to stifle their clinking, and ran, heading back the way the guards had led him in.

His heart was smashing against his ribcage.

He leapt up the steps, nearly at the exit. Outside, it was dark. Perhaps midnight, maybe later.

Suddenly there was a shout from deeper down in the cells. "Murder, murder!"

He could hear other guards calling, shouting. He fumbled with the keys. Dropped them, picked them up. Tried one, then another, and finally found one that worked.

He pushed the gate open and stumbled out into the night air. But he couldn't stop. They were coming, running behind him.

He had to hide.

He scurried along a narrow street, keeping to the shadows. He waited, watching as a guard came up to street level, still shouting.

They would begin to ring the bell soon, to alert the city that a prisoner had escaped.

He didn't wait to watch. He ran to the stables, where he knew his grandfather kept his horses.

The bell began to ring, clanging through the cloudless night sky.

Marlowe hurried into the stables, skidding on the straw covered floor.

There was his horse, Marble, the one the guards had stolen from his parents' farmhouse when he and Valora had been forced to the slums. They had at least kept him beautifully, and even in this darkness Marlowe could see the sleek shine on his dark coat. The horse whinnied in recognition and Marlowe held a finger to his lips. Silence. The horse snorted in response, tapping its hooves on the floor as Marlowe unhooked the gate.

He swung it open, stepped inside, pulled a saddle pad and saddle from the wall, then a bridle too and fixed the tack with trembling fingers. A hunting horn attached to a strap hung from a hook on the back of the stable door. Marlowe unhooked it and looped it over his shoulder, just in case.

They burst from the stable at a gallop, moving like one beast, rounding the narrow dirt streets faster than they ought to have done.

If they could make it to the forest to the west of the city the trees would conceal them.

Marlowe squeezed his legs around Marble's girth, and the horse sped towards the western gate. It was open, thank the God-Sage!

Marlowe allowed himself a wry, dismissive chuckle. To think that his first impulse, despite everything that had happened, was to thank the God-Sage! But it was harder to shed the skin of faith that he had worn since childhood than he had expected it to be, and an open gate in this situation seemed like a miracle.

He set his eyes on the horizon, beyond the city, out towards the forest below. Out there, somewhere, was where he would find Valora.

5

—·—

KYLA

THE CITY OF PALANTAR

The bedroom door swung open, and Kyla's eyes snapped open at once. She was half-reclined in the chair by the window. Her body felt stiff but she bolted upright and stared towards the figure in the doorway. She couldn't make out who it was. There was the slightest hint of dawn light filtering between the curtains, but not enough to see by.

"Who's there?"

The door closed with a soft thud and someone paced into the room. There was the swish of fabric, the sound of a dress. A woman then, or a priest.

"It's me. Nisia."

Kyla watched as Nisia came towards her. She was fully dressed and bejewelled, large pearls dangling from her ears and around her neck. Either she hadn't yet been to bed, or she had awoken and dressed again in the early hours.

"What do you want?" Kyla asked.

"You have to leave. If you want to get back to Moriya, you have to leave now."

Kyla could hear the urgency in Nisia's voice, and felt her own heart start to beat in time with Nisia's panic. She sprang up from her seat, lifted her sword and began to fix her belt. She had taken it off only so she might feel more comfortable in her attempt to sleep in the chair. "Why?"

Nisia came to the window and pulled the curtain open, allowing more watery light to fall into the room. "The eels. Some people were... bitten." Nisia shrugged. "Something like that. There's rumour of a plague, a disease. Duncan, our physician, is advising we shut down the city. He said he's seen it, seen how fast it spreads. Whatever it was that happened yesterday, at the river... Some people are infected with it. Some of the peasants who came to the funeral."

Nisia was talking at such speed, her eyes darting around the room, that Kyla had difficulty keeping up with her.

"They've quarantined the slums and Grandfather wants to burn the infected houses, but the council are trying to convince him not to give the order. People are already unnerved by what happened at the river; if they find out there's a disease working its way through the slums, the city will collapse into chaos. But if it's as contagious as Duncan seems to think it is, then it's only a matter of time before people find out. His advice is to keep the city gates shut when morning comes. He wants to contain the sickness to save the rest of Tolinaye.

"But Grandfather would never agree. He won't sacrifice his city for the wellness of the rest of the Kingdom. Not when you're about to restore his trading rights. But if you don't leave right now, you won't be able to go. Grandfather will keep Valora here, and use her to heal the sick. There will be too many of them. She won't be able to do it. It will kill her. And if this is some Nilari plague, then you need to get Valora back to the healing circle, so at least..."

Kyla knew what Nisia meant. If there was a Nilari-sent plague coming, then they needed a functioning healing circle back in Moriya. "At least we have some form of defence," she finished.

Nisia was already moving to the bed, draping a fresh, grey dress over the end of the velvet coverlet before shaking Valora awake and telling her to get up.

Valora snuffled under the blanket, burrowing deeper beneath it.

"Get up. You must," Nisia urged.

A cross between a groan and a yawn came from beneath the sheets and then Valora's head appeared, dark hair, unkempt and wayward, cascading around her face. "Why? What's happening?" Her voice was thick with sleep, and Nisia ignored her questions entirely, helping her pull the torn dress over her head and slide into the new one.

As she assisted Valora, Nisia continued to talk over her shoulder to Kyla. "I've arranged horses and supplies. They're waiting for you in the courtyard below."

"Won't the gates be shut? They won't open until daybreak."

"I know the guards at the western gates. I've already told them to keep them open to allow you to pass through."

"And Max?"

"He's waiting for you."

Kyla, Max and Valora left Palantar through the western gates. Their departure had been hurried and disorienting, but thankfully the streets had been quiet. Word of the infection in the slums couldn't yet have reached the more salubrious areas of the city.

Behind them wispy clouds drifted like smoke across an orange sky. Ahead of them lay the thick darkness of the forest.

For all their initial urgency, progress was slow and they had already stopped several times to rest. The horses, sourced for them by Nisia, were little more than farm nags, their dusty brown coats too long and slightly mangy.

Kyla's horse struggled more than the others, given it had to bear the weight of two people. Valora sat ahead of her, slumped against her chest. Kyla supported her as best she was able whilst simultaneously holding the reins.

The girl's skin was pale and her cheekbones cast dark shadows, as if she had not eaten properly for months. Her eyes were barely open, the effects of the alcohol from the night before still apparent. Her head lolled against Kyla's upper arm, and her breath was warm through the sleeve of Kyla's tunic. When she spoke the words were damp.

"Marlowe. Where's Marlowe?" The words were little more than a mumble, but still they tugged at some inner pain Kyla was determined to ignore. Thank the God-Sage that Valora had not been more alert when they had dragged her from her bed, for Kyla wasn't sure how long she could have endured the girl's plaintive cries for her brother.

"He's still in the cells," Kyla muttered, but Valora gave no indication she had registered the answer and continued to talk confusedly.

Alongside them, Max patted the neck of the pony he sat on, and glanced over at the other, which he led by the lead rope. It lolloped along behind; a third steed for Valora, so that when she was recovered, she could ride alone. "Nisia overpaid for these horses," he said.

"Nisia didn't pay for them," Kyla snapped back, glad to be able to divert her thoughts from Marlowe. "I did." She touched two fingertips to the coin purse, where it hung from her belt, feeling the heft of it. It was still bulging, even after all the outlay.

"Is that... is that Edmund's?" Max's eyes grew wide. "Isn't that stealing?"

"No point sending all that gold to the dead world. The dead don't need gold. Besides, I had to use some of it to pay for the funeral. The boat, the muslin, the oil. I paid the priests for purifying Edmund's body—"

Max gave a small, cynical laugh. "That body was about as far from purified as the burnt-isle itself."

"They did what they could." Kyla cringed as she remembered how she had forced two gold tucks on the priests, despite their protests that they worked for the

God-Sage and not for any nobleman, and therefore did not require payment. One of them had been so irked that he had taken a tuck and shoved it into Edmund's mouth to pay for his passage to the dead world. Edmund's jaw, stiff after life had left, had given a disconcerting crack.

None of it, neither the gold nor the purification, had prevented the eels infesting the river. Had Edmund's soul made it to the dead world? Kyla shivered at the thought. Only the souls of traitors and criminals, forbidden a proper funeral, were said not to make it.

Max urged his horse on, but the beast made no attempt to walk any faster. Max cursed under his breath. "Whatever you paid, you wasted your coin."

"Nisia had to make do with what she could get. I don't think she reported our departure to Lord Aralorn."

"Maybe she should have. He might have given us better horses."

"He might not have let us leave at all." Kyla chewed on the inside of her cheek. What was happening back in Palantar? She had seen how the death eels destroyed a human body, and if they were carrying some sort of disease she had no doubt it would be a fatal one. How quickly would it spread?

The image of Marlowe, being dragged down to the cells, flashed through her mind. Would the infection reach him there? She pushed the thought away, trying not to question why, of all the people she had met and all the faces she had seen in Palantar, it was his that caused her most concern.

She drove her horse forward, heading towards the forest. To head south, back towards Traitors' Lake, might have been the fastest route, but Max had refused to go that way and Kyla wasn't going to push him. Nearly dying once after falling into those poisoned waters was more than enough. Besides, if the eels were capable of spreading disease, then the lake should be avoided at all costs, even if it made the journey twice as long.

At least this time she had weapons. A sword in a sheath that hung from her belt and a knife nestled in her boot. The only thing she lacked, the thing she missed, was a bow and a quiver full of arrows. But taking her shot from the saddle of a horse had never been her strength.

Just as the heat of the day was reaching its peak, they reached the forest. Dappled light forged its way through the canopy above, sending ripples of gold across the forest floor. The horses' hooves crunched through dead leaves as they weaved through the trees. The mingled scent of something sweet and something rotten, like crisp apple flesh and the decaying bodies of hidden animal carcasses, hung thick in the air.

"We need to rest," Max said.

Kyla didn't want to stop, but she couldn't force the horses on. They needed to eat, and Valora too would need a break. She was more alert now, which meant the numbing effects of the alcohol would be wearing off and pain would be setting in.

Valora's bandages were concealed beneath the new dress that Nisia had brought that morning. The girl looked well enough for someone who likely always looked somewhat sickly, but Kyla was sure the wound would be weeping.

They dismounted, fed and watered the horses, and unpacked some food for themselves. Nisia had asked the servants to prepare the bags, so unwrapping the muslin packages became almost like a game.

"What's this one?" Max bounced a circular parcel in one hand and then passed it to the others to feel.

Valora took it in one hand and prodded at it with the fingers of her other hand, which was still not moving naturally. "Pie. I can feel the crust." She sniffed it. "Cold meat pie. It's been a long time since I had meat pie. Can I?" She held it out, and looked to Kyla and Max, begging permission to unwrap it.

Kyla, her mouth full of bread, nodded and said, "Go ahead."

Valora removed the cloth and stared at it, her brows drawing together. "My mother used to..."

Her words dried up and she stared at the pie, as if it was so much more than a lump of buttered crust with meat inside.

Max leant towards her and spoke gently. "Shall I take it?"

Valora shook her head, but continued to gaze at the pie.

Max shot a concerned look at Kyla and shrugged his shoulders, asking the silent question, *What should we do?*

"My mother..." Valora began.

Kyla winced at the mention of the woman her father had executed. Valora might have claimed that she didn't hate Kyla, *couldn't hate her*, but that didn't mean that she wouldn't change her mind. Yes, the wonder of what they had shared during the healing was... immense, but afterwards they had been able to sit back and stare at one another as two entirely separate people. Whatever connected them was gone, but they still *existed* as individuals. Neither of them had died.

Kyla knew loss, and she knew what it was like to ache for someone who wouldn't come back. She knew too that whatever Valora thought they had shared during the healing, whatever bond they had forged, it could never be as life-changing as having to watch the execution of one's parents.

How must Valora feel, to find herself escorted from the city she had called home by the daughter of the man who, only a few months before, had lit the flames that had burnt her parents? It was unimaginable. No wonder Valora struggled between hating her and... whatever else it was she might feel for her. Kyla shuddered. She snatched the pie out of Valora's hand and cracked it in half.

She held a piece out to Valora, shaking it in her face. "Don't just stare at it. Eat it."

"Kyla!" Max's reprimand came almost instantly.

Valora's bottom lip wobbled. Kyla lowered the pie, shame coursing through her. She had been more cruel than she had meant to be.

"Sorry. I didn't mean—"

"It's not... it's..."

Valora gasped, her mouth freezing, half open, as if the pain was too much to express.

"It's the wound." Max moved closer and Valora gripped onto him with one hand. "Can you heal yourself?"

Valora shook her head and spoke through gritted teeth. "No. Never myself. My gift is not meant for me."

"It's the same in Moriya. Acolytes cannot be healed." Kyla muttered the words, more for her own benefit than anything else. Any evidence she could unearth that Valora fitted in with the other acolytes was something to be grasped and treasured. Something that might prove that choosing Valora had been the right thing to do.

Kyla opened one of the bags. It was stuffed with medication Duncan had given them. She pulled out a bottle. It was cold, and the ointment inside was thick and white.

"Will you let me put this on? It will hurt, but it will help."

Valora whimpered. Kyla couldn't see her face, huddled down as she was, but her hair, dark and knotted, hanging over her face, shifted. A nod.

Kyla loosened the neck of Valora's dress and removed the bandages. Beneath them was the image of the God-Sage, raw, flaming, and seeping some sort of pus. Realising it was going to be too painful, Kyla sifted through the bag until she found a leather flask, into which she had poured the remaining liquid from the decanter that Nisia had given her the night before. She held it out to Valora.

"Take a swig. A big one," she said.

After Valora had swallowed the alcohol Kyla waited a few moments before she rubbed the thick white ointment onto Valora's skin and replaced the bandages with fresh ones from the bag.

Valora sighed. The alcohol was taking effect. She twined her fingers into the leather cord that hung about her neck, from which dangled the small pouch she had clutched so desperately the night before.

Kyla began packing the bottles, forcing the cork tightly back into the neck of the one containing the white ointment. Max took a stroll to relieve himself further off in the forest, and Kyla found herself alone with Valora. She noticed that the girl still held one of her hands curled up, as if to move it caused her pain.

"Do you want some ointment?" Kyla held up the bottle and Valora raised a confused eyebrow. Kyla nodded at her curled up fingers. "For your hand."

Valora jerked her hand away and then, meeting Kyla's concerned gaze, she said, "I'll do it myself."

Suspicion rippled down Kyla's spine, but she kept her tone calm and handed Valora the bottle, knowing she wouldn't be able to open it one-handed. "Here you go."

Valora took the bottle with her good hand, clamped it between her knees and tried to prise the cork out. It was stiff because Kyla had forced it into place to prevent spillages in the bag, yet Valora didn't give up. She brought the bottle to her mouth, intending to use her teeth to clamp down on the cork.

Kyla reached out. "Let me. It'll be easier."

The light in Valora's eyes dulled as she handed Kyla the bottle and let the fingers of her damaged hand unfurl. There, in the centre of Valora's palm was a raw mark, a burn, the exact same shape as the burn on the inside of the leather pouch that had held the rings.

Kyla stifled the gasp that escaped her lips. Valora watched her, dark eyes suddenly alert, but Kyla asked no questions until she had finished applying the ointment.

She put the cork back in the bottle. "How did that happen?"

Valora shrugged. "Hot. It was hot—"

"What was?"

Valora hung her head, shaking it. Small bursts of noise escaped her lips, but Kyla couldn't tell if they were sobs or the beginnings of words. She didn't have the patience to wait.

"You know what I think? I think you had something in that pouch—" Kyla gestured to the leather thong that hung round Valora's neck. "—and that it burnt your hand that day at the river. At the funeral. I think it blasted the light and caused the eels to vanish." Kyla pressed her lips together and shook her head. "Your grandfather might think that it was all the God-Sage, but I'm not so sure. I think—"

Valora spoke quickly. "What do you think? What will you do?"

Tension crackled between them and Kyla sat back, scanning the girl's frightened face before choosing her words carefully. "It's out of my hands. You're marked for the God-Sage. Word will have been sent to Moriya already, that the acolyte is coming. They'll be expecting you." Kyla packed the ointment away, dusted off her hands and stood up, trying to affect a nonchalance she didn't feel. "My duty is to bring you back."

Valora eyed her cautiously. "What if it were up to you?"

Kyla stood up and stepped back, unsure what answer to give, but it wouldn't do any harm to keep Valora on edge. "I don't think you want to know." Valora shrivelled, and Kyla tried to lighten her tone when she said, "Where is it now, this thing that burnt you?"

Valora's fingers tightened about the pouch and Kyla felt a desperate fire run through her. *She had it on her*. It was in the pouch. Kyla tried to grab it but Valora swayed back, out of reach.

"I don't have it. I swear I don't. I don't know where it is."

"Show me." Kyla's voice was firm, leaving no room for refusal as she gestured to the pouch. Valora unlooped it from her neck with a tinkling of metal and, cautiously, held it out to Kyla. "Please don't take them from me. They were my mother's. The rings. They're all that's in there now. There's nothing else."

Kyla emptied the pouch, and the same rings she had seen back in Palantar fell into her palm. She shoved them back in and gave the pouch back to Valora, but remained standing over her, one hand on her hip.

"Do you know what it is?" Kyla asked. "This burnt circle—"

Valora shook her head. "It looks like a wheel. We—"

"We?"

Valora flinched, fear glistening in eyes so dark they were almost black. She held out her hand so Kyla could see the mark. "Yes. We. Marlowe and I. We think it looks like a wheel. A crooked wheel."

Kyla nodded. "That's exactly what it looks like."

Valora's eyes narrowed, but uncertainty softened her lips. "Does it... does it mean anything to you?"

Kyla shook her head. It had seemed familiar when she had first seen it, but no memory had come to her, and now, days later, that flicker of recognition didn't seem worth mentioning.

A crunching sound nearby made Kyla turn. Max had reappeared from the undergrowth, walking slowly at first, but then a worried expression fixed on his face and he hurried towards them. "What's going on?"

Kyla grabbed Valora's hand and directed her palm so Max could see it. The skin and the burn itself glistened with the ointment, but the pattern was visible beneath.

"What is it?" Max asked.

"Maybe you were right," Kyla said. "Maybe it was magic at the funeral." She thrust Valora's hand away and it fell into the girl's lap. She fixed her with a hard stare, unable to restrain the tremor in her voice. "Was it? Was it magic? Because if it was, there's more than just your life at stake."

"I don't know. I don't know—"

"Kyla, stop." Max was kneeling beside Valora, looking at her palm, his fingers hovering over the burn. "Does it look familiar to you? I think I've seen it before."

Valora had gone utterly still, holding her breath. "Where? Do you know—"

Max shook his head. "I can't remember. But I'm sure I've seen it before. How did you get a burn like that?"

"My mother. My mother gave me a jewellery box. She put her rings inside it, and told me to keep it safe. I didn't know there was anything else in there. I swear—"

"What else *was* inside it?" Kyla snapped.

In the face of all their questions, Valora began to retract, folding in upon herself. Tears shone in her eyes. If they weren-'t careful they would lose her completely; she would refuse to speak.

"Please, tell us." Kyla tried to speak gently as Max had done, but her voice had a stern edge she could not curb.

"There was a piece of metal, in the shape of this—" Valora held up her hand to show the mark. "—hidden in the bottom of the box. I kept it because it was my mother's. I didn't know it did anything before that day at the river. Before that Nilari... Yarmon..."

"The rebel. Yarmon Sacfron. What about him?"

Again she'd spoken too fast, too harshly. Valora shrank back. "I didn't know it did anything before he appeared. I swear I didn't."

"And when he did?" Kyla said slowly.

"It started to get hot and I could smell the leather burning." She gestured to the little pouch. "So I took it out and it burnt my hand. And then..."

Her words faded away, but Kyla didn't need to hear her speak them. Then the light had blasted, vivid and blue, like lightning in a storm, and everything had vanished.

Max turned to Kyla. "Great God-Sage—"

Kyla ignored him. She was watching Valora, tears streaming down the girl's cheeks, and rather than the anger she had expected to feel, she found something softer moving through her. "Where is it now?"

"I don't know. I don't have it anymore. I wanted to keep it, but I was frightened, after what happened at the river. The rings are all I have left. Please, let me keep them."

Kyla waited until she could feel the truth of Valora's words. Then she nodded. "My mother is dead too. I understand why you wanted to keep it. I would have done the same."

Max edged closer to Kyla and muttered, "It's different though, isn't it? Your mother wasn't executed as a traitor."

Kyla glanced at Max to let him know she had heard him, but she said nothing, aware that Valora was looking, urgently, between the two of them.

"Keep the rings." Kyla meant it to be her final statement on the matter, but she found Valora looking at her with eager eyes, and some impulse to satisfy the girl bubbled up in Kyla and words began to flow. "My mother died when I was born. I didn't know her. It's not the same, you know..." Kyla let her words drift off. How could she relate her own loss to Valora's? "It's not the same as what you and Marlowe experienced."

"Kyla—" hissed Max.

Kyla shot him a silencing look. She laid a hand on Valora's shoulder, felt it trembling and waited for it to lessen. Then she stood up and pulled Max with her, out of earshot.

"Why are you pushing me? Do you want me to condemn her? If I do, if I announce that Valora has used illegal magic, you will die. Do you understand that?" Max blinked, as if Kyla's words were a gale that blew in his face, but she didn't stop. "We don't know for sure what happened, and neither does she. Whatever made that mark on her hand, she doesn't have it anymore—"

"You believe her?"

"I do. We have to keep going. If we fail to deliver a branded acolyte to Moriya, I can only imagine what might await us—"

"You won't get your role in the Sacred Core, that's for sure." Max's eyes, pale and blue, were suddenly cold, and there was a harshness to his tone that took Kyla by surprise.

She bristled. "That's not what this is about. Not anymore. If there is plague coming, we need to get Valora back—" Max shook his head, but Kyla ignored him. "—to the healing circle."

His eyes flashed defensively and he opened his mouth to speak, but Kyla didn't want to discuss it further. She raised her voice so Valora could hear and said, "Let's take a few hours, then we can be on our way."

Valora was wiping tears from her cheeks with the heel of her hand as Kyla approached her. "Do you think you will be able to ride your own horse? We would make faster progress that way."

Valora nodded, "Yes, I think so. Yes. But I need to bind my hand first."

Kyla tapped her boot against the bag of medication, where it lay next to Valora. "Have a look in there for something to use. Duncan packed it with enough supplies to treat an army of ailments."

Leaving Valora rifling through the bag, and Max staring uncomfortably at his own feet, Kyla marched towards the horses.

It wasn't until the following afternoon that they reached the Great Plains. The forest trees grew thinner, as if the soil changed from one moment to the next and they ceased to grow. There was an odd feel to the place, and the formation of the land itself did not seem entirely natural.

The sight of open sky was invigorating, but the heat of the sun beyond the cover of the trees hit Kyla like a wall. It blistered, harsher than it had been back in Palantar. The air was dense with warmth that needed to be broken, and far off across the Great Plains dark clouds were rolling towards them.

"Thunder's coming," said Max. "We should find somewhere to shelter before it gets dark."

"Do you see any shelter out here?" said Kyla, spreading one arm in front of them, where there was nothing but bare rocks in the distance and mountain peaks to the north.

"Maybe we stay in the woods. At least the trees provide cover," Max said, his horse tossing its head, ready to back up into the forest.

Kyla wasn't going to delay longer. She urged her horse onwards with a sharp yell that echoed out into the emptiness of the Great Plains. She felt her body pulse with each beat of the horse's hooves. They could cover the ground across the plains faster than they could wheedling through trees in the forest.

It hit her then, galloping across the plains, the wind beating her skin, just how encumbered she felt by all that had happened. The burden of responsibility of getting a girl who could barely stand up straight, let alone ride a horse at any decent pace, all the way back to Moriya seemed too much.

Out here, she felt free.

A horn blew.

It was hard to make out over the thundering of the horse's hooves, but the sound exploded again and this time Kyla crouched low on her steed, expecting something to shoot over her head. An arrow perhaps?

She glanced backwards, but saw nothing other than Max and Valora, who were, surprisingly, not too far behind, clouds of dust raised in their wake. For farm nags, their horses ran surprisingly well, but all of them were panting, frothing at the mouth, and Kyla realised that in her eagerness to make progress they might have pushed them too far.

She pulled on the reins of her horse, which kicked its hooves and came to a stop.

"Did you hear that?" she called to Max.

He nodded, slowing his horse to a trot as he approached her. "Someone's following us."

Valora joined them, their horses grouped together, puffing hard-earned breaths from flared nostrils, shifting their feet on the dry earth beneath their hooves.

They turned to face the way they had come. A rider was speeding towards them on a sleek dark horse. To Kyla, it looked like death himself, come to claim them all.

"What is it?" asked Max.

Kyla squinted. "A man. A rider from Palantar."

"Are we going to wait for him? What if he's going to attack us?" asked Max.

"Why would they send one man alone to attack us?"

Lightning sparked in the distance over the mountains to the west, and the thunder soon followed, but it was still too far away to drown out the approaching sound of the galloping horse.

The rider, who Kyla now saw was no monster, but a man dressed in nothing more than a simple shirt and trousers, was gaining ground.

Valora gasped and covered her mouth with a hand.

"Kyla..." Max sounded unsure, and his horse felt the same. He was having to pull on the reins to stop the horse moving away.

"Hold your position." Authority rang in Kyla's voice and she was glad of it. She wasn't going to run from one lonely rider.

"It's Marlowe." Valora's eyes were bright, and her horse too was pawing the ground excitedly, infected by the girl's sudden enthusiasm.

Kyla squinted, trying to see what Valora had seen. How could it be Marlowe? Hadn't he been locked up?

As the rider drew close, Kyla saw his face. It was indeed Marlowe, and in that brief moment of recognition, her body betrayed her. Her heart, that she now realised had been almost numb since Marlowe had been hauled from the throne room, gave a traitorous, joyous leap. He was alive, and he was here.

She felt hollowed out, as if that small, irregular beat of her heart had stolen all the blood in her body. She took a breath, stilled herself, forcing her face to reveal none of what had just flashed through her mind, despite not knowing, nor wanting to know, exactly what it had been.

She focused on Marlowe. His dark hair was sweat-soaked and plastered to his forehead, just as his shirt was plastered to his chest. Pink stains spread across the white linen. Blood, but not his own. He was moving too well for someone who had lost that much blood. A hunting horn hung from a cord that was looped around his shoulder. His eyes flashed with the anger and resentment that Kyla realised she had come to expect from him. She felt a hardening sensation pass through her body, as if her muscles were morphing into armour, and whatever warmth the sight of him had aroused began to cool.

Marlowe's horse tossed its mane and shook its tail, great ribs heaving from the long ride. Beneath the saddle would be the white froth of sweat and dirt.

"I won't let you take her." Marlowe gasped the words as he tugged on the reins of his agitated horse, pulling it to a stop.

"They let you out of the cells then?" Kyla's voice was pleasingly cool and detached.

"Something like that."

For a few moments their horses danced around one another, and Kyla stared at Marlowe and he back at her. There was a world inside his gaze that Kyla knew she could slip into, as though his loathing might engulf her, but before she slid over the edge she said, "That's a fine horse. Did you kill someone before you stole it?"

The ripple of shame that flickered over Marlowe's face, quickly replaced by a defiant arrogance, let Kyla know that whatever had happened, Marlowe wasn't proud of it, but neither was he going to tell her about it.

The horse, however, was certainly stolen, and for a moment Kyla wondered if Lord Aralorn would send guards from Palantar, seeking to arrest Marlowe for theft of the horse, and whatever other crimes he had committed.

Marlowe moved the reins to one hand and dismounted. He led his horse towards Valora, taking the bridle of her horse in his hand too and stroking its blaze.

"Get away from her," Kyla said.

"I'm taking her with me."

Kyla jumped down from her horse. "Oh no. You are not taking the acolyte anywhere."

Marlowe turned on her. "Is that all she is to you? An acolyte? She's my sister!"

The clouds grew darker and rumbled overhead, closing out the last of the light.

It was only then that Kyla realised just how pale Valora was. There was no way she could ride further. She looked about to pass out.

Marlowe too had noticed, and his anger dissipated, his voice softening as he attended to the needs of his sister. "Are you all right? How is your wound? Can I see?"

Valora nodded and Marlowe helped her down from the horse. He untied the front of Valora's dress, revealing the bandages just below her neck. Even the fresh ones Kyla had replaced earlier that day were no longer white, but blotted pink and yellow with blood and pus.

Marlowe spun round, thumping the air with his fist, shaking it at Kyla. "How could you have agreed to travel with her like this? It's infected. She could *die*."

Max dismounted and stepped towards Valora. He reached out to her but she flinched from his touch.

Marlowe pushed him away. "What are you doing?"

"She can ride with me."

"You think I came all this way to make sure she had a strong soldier to help her ride?" Cruel laughter sparked from his lips. "I'm taking her with me."

Marlowe put an arm around Valora's shoulders, obviously intending to lead her away, and Max, his eyes wide, turned his confusion to Kyla. *Do something.*

She pulled her sword from its sheath and stalked towards Marlowe, pointing the blade at him.

Marlowe raised one hand in a gesture of surrender, and one black eyebrow arched over a dark eye. "That's hardly fair."

Kyla blinked. Had she heard a hint of mockery in his voice?

He tilted his head to one side. "I've an idea. In the interest of fairness... I'll fight you for her."

Kyla wasn't sure she had heard him correctly. "We outnumber you, two to one."

"I don't propose to fight both of you." Marlowe looked directly at Kyla. "Just you. An honest fight. No swords."

As he looked at her, Kyla felt something shift, as if some force had moved through him and into her. She felt her body respond, and some other part, something non-physical, tangled up with the same non-physical part of him. The edges of his lips, which were full and red, curled upwards. An unwelcome heat rose to Kyla's cheeks, yet in the same instant she realised that Marlowe knew the effect he was having on her, and knew that he had had such an effect on many women in the past.

A flare of outrage rippled through her, but she held her face in neutral, lowered her sword and sheathed it. "I'll take you on, if that's what you want. But I warn you, humiliation is hard for a man to take."

"Oh, I've had my share of humiliation. It doesn't frighten me."

"You won't win," said Max.

Marlowe dismissed the statement with a flick of the head, shunting his dark hair back from his forehead. "I'll take my chances."

Kyla could see flickers of movement in Marlowe's jaw. He planted his feet and pushed his shoulders back, holding out the reins of his horse to Max, who took them from him unthinkingly, like Marlowe was the Lord and he the stable boy.

"And if you win, what then?" Kyla asked. "If she goes with you, she'll die. You have no way to treat her wounds."

Marlowe's answer was fast, much faster than Kyla had expected. "That's not something we need to worry about."

Why not? Kyla tried to keep the question from her eyes, but promised herself she would find out why later. "And where will you go? You can't go back to Palantar, not now plague has broken out—" She broke off, seeing on Marlowe's face that he hadn't heard about the sickness that was spreading in the slums. She nodded at the blood on his shirt. "You've stolen a horse and who knows what else you've done. You're a fugitive. Even if you could go back, Palantar wouldn't take you, and Lord Aralorn would send Valora right back to Moriya."

"At least I wouldn't have to suborn her to you." His lips spasmed as though he was about to spit, but he held himself in check and swallowed instead, and then he pulled out a knife that Kyla recognised. It was the one from the healing, the one Max's father had given him before they had left Moriya.

"Stealing Moriyan weapons is a crime," Kyla said.

"I don't think it's stealing if you're so careless as to leave them behind."

It was then that Marlowe did something surprising. He smiled, not just the hint of a smile, but a full smile that showed his teeth. It wasn't a smile of joy or happiness, but a smile that showed he had the measure of her. Almost that he was laughing at her, but not quite.

It was unnerving. Kyla rolled her head to loosen the tension from her neck and looked him up and down. He was tall, but so was she. His shoulders were broad and she could see the strength in his arms. It wasn't going to be easy to fight him. She steadied herself.

And then she moved.

Her body, lithe and taut from months of training, sprang towards Marlowe, that strange smile still curling over his lips.

With one arm she pushed and with the other she twisted, yanking his shoulder round so his back was to her.

His body, soft and pliable because she had taken him unawares, yielded easily. She pushed him to the ground, dust puffing up around him as he fell. She held him there with one knee pressed into his lower back, one arm pulled right behind him, the shoulder twisted at an awkward angle.

He groaned and shouted out, but whether in pain or surprise she couldn't be sure. She twisted his arm yet further and dug her knee into his back. His fingers released the knife and Kyla picked it up.

"Still want to fight me?"

Marlowe turned his head to one side and spat the dust from his mouth.

"Yes."

Kyla pulled harder on his arm and twirled the knife before pressing it to the side of Marlowe's neck.

"Now?"

"Yes."

She pushed the blade against his skin until a drop of blood welled up.

"Now?"

"No!"

But the voice was not Marlowe's. Kyla turned to see Valora, a blur of pale dust-covered fabric, scramble to where her brother lay in the dirt. She dropped to his side, her hands hovering in the air over Kyla's, eager to guide the knife away from Marlowe's neck.

"Please. We'll come with you. We'll come."

"We will not," said Marlowe, his voice choked and bitter. Spit flew from his lips, landing on the ground and turning patches of dust dark as he spoke.

Valora knelt closer to him, her head dipped to the ground and her mouth pressed to his ear. She began to whisper, and Kyla, realising the words weren't meant for her and that the girl was likely trying to talk sense into her ass of a brother, stood up.

She pushed the knife into her boot and dusted herself off, watching Valora talk as Marlowe lay on the ground recovering his breath.

There was no way of knowing what they might decide, but the influence the girl had over him was impressive, and Kyla could only hope she would make him see reason.

When Valora had finished speaking, her tiny crippled body hunched over, she tried to pull Marlowe to his feet. But still he lay on the ground, winded and unyielding to Valora's efforts.

Kyla offered him her hand. He stared at it for a moment before grasping it in his own and letting her help him up, but he didn't rise evenly and Kyla had to slide a hand into his arm-pit where the fabric of his shirt was damp. Once Marlowe stood on his own two feet Kyla wiped her hands on her trousers.

"Didn't think you the type to be bothered by a bit of sweat," Marlowe said, glancing at her hands.

Kyla raised an eyebrow. "I think we can say I won."

"You cheated."

Kyla snorted dismissively. "We'll be on our way. You had best go wherever you are going."

Valora hobbled towards her. "Can't he come with us? If he stays out here alone he'll die."

Marlowe looked momentarily unnerved as he scanned the vast expanse of the Great Plains. The sky chose that moment to crack and raindrops began to fall, large and plump, exploding onto the dry earth.

"Don't leave him, please," Valora said. "Let him come."

Kyla looked him over once more. His scuffed boots, his wild dark hair, his stained and sweat-damp shirt that showed the shape of him beneath it. Part of her wanted to agree immediately, but she was so used to denying her own inconvenient longings that she snuffed this one out like a candle-flame. "We don't need another mouth to feed."

"He's my brother." Valora's lips began to tremble. "Please."

Kyla was about to say no when a memory speared her intention and left it limp and dead. Kyla's brother, Dain, had disappeared six years previously. It had broken her heart, and somehow, standing there, the rain falling around her, she was reminded of that pain. If there was a chance she could save Valora from such heartache, she would take it.

The rain was falling fast now and Kyla nodded, quickly, before she changed her mind, then she directed her instructions to Max but flicked her fingers at Marlowe. "Tie him up. Stop him trying anything."

Marlowe pushed wet hair off his forehead with one hand. "If you tie me up I'll slow you down. Better let me ride freely."

His thighs were strong, and given the horsemanship she had just witnessed as he had raced across the plains, she was sure he would have no trouble staying on the horse.

"You were raised as Lord Aralorn's heir, weren't you? Before your parents' execution required him to disinherit you." She waited for a nod of acknowledgment from Marlowe, whose gaze pulsed with bitterness and loathing. Kyla continued nonetheless. "Any nobleman could ride with his wrists bound. I wager you're no different." She turned to Max. "Tie him up. And hold the length of rope. Then he can't ride too far."

Obediently, Max moved to his horse and slipped his hand into the saddlebag, pulling out a coil of rope.

Kyla watched as Marlowe, a belligerent scowl marring his handsome face, held out his wrists and let Max tie them. He didn't once turn to look at her, but his shoulders were tense and he held them higher than was natural. He was, she was sure, entirely conscious of her gaze, just as she was aware that his avoidance of it was deliberate.

6

KYLA

THE GREAT PLAINS

The rain had eased off, but not before they were all soaked through. They travelled slowly across the plains, stopping every so often to eat, to change Valora's bandages and to rest.

For several days they saw no one other than each other. Kyla kept a close eye on Marlowe, making sure to keep him separated from Valora. He said very little, other than to complain about the rope that was tied around his wrists.

One morning they awoke in a camp they had set up under a rocky outcrop of the lower mountains that bordered the plains to the north.

"Look what I've got." Max threw down the carcass of a scrawny looking hare. It landed with a lifeless thump on the damp dirt.

Kyla raised her eyebrows and began to nod. "Impressive. How did you get it?"

"I set traps last night whilst you were all sleeping. About time we had some meat." Max crouched before the wild hare, pulled one of the knives from his boot and began to prepare it.

The fire was already burning steadily; Max must have started it before going off to check his traps, and for a few moments the only sound was that of the crackling flames and the wrenching of Max's knife through the skin of the hare.

"Your sword." He held out his hand to Kyla.

"What?" She grabbed the hilt. "No."

"I need to skewer the hare. To roast it."

Kyla glanced around. The plains were deserted; she wouldn't need her sword anytime soon. It was one she had purchased in Palantar and it held no sentimental meaning. She unsheathed it and gave it to Max, who forced it through the now skinless, gutted hare and then propped it up horizontally on some rocks on either side of the fire so the meat itself dangled over the flames.

Every so often he turned the sword to let the other side of the flesh cook, and within the hour the scrawny meat was beginning to look edible.

Meanwhile, Kyla lifted the leather bag containing the ointments and medicines. She hooked it on her shoulder and approached Valora, who was perched on a rock. Huddled up that way, she almost looked like one herself.

"Do you want anything? How is your pain?"

Valora didn't look up.

"Better?" Kyla probed.

"Yes. Better."

Kyla hesitated, unsure whether to ask the question she wanted to ask, but decided to go ahead anyway. "You can't heal yourself, but you can blast away a thousand eels as if they never existed. I don't understand how that's possible."

Valora looked up, and although she didn't speak, Kyla saw in her eyes a flash of defensiveness, as though something inside her was recoiling. There were no answers in that glimpse of expression, only more questions: the sort of questions a person had when they had spent their life being mocked and persecuted, looking for the next thing that was going to tear them down, or even kill them.

A shadow shifted over the ground. Marlowe must have known Valora was uncomfortable, for he had come to stand in front of her like a guardian. "Why do you need to understand it? Why can't you just accept it? She saved you. She saved everyone. Stop attacking her."

"Why do you assume I'm attacking her? I only want to know what use it is to have such gifts, if she can't heal her own wounds." Kyla waved a hand in the air to encompass the whole of Valora's disfigured self. "Her—"

"If you call her a cripple, I swear I'll—"

"Marlowe, stop." At Valora's interruption Marlowe pressed his lips tightly together. "There is no need for you to fight all my battles. I am quite capable, you know."

Kyla waited until she was sure Marlowe wasn't going to speak again before she asked, "What else can you do?"

But still it was Marlowe who replied. "Mother taught us to make ointments, salves, potions, sleeping draughts. All that sort of apothecary-physician stuff."

"Both of you?"

"Yes."

Ah, so that was why he had been so quick to respond that he didn't need to worry about tending to Valora's wounds if they were left alone on the plains. Kyla pulled the bottles from the bag that Duncan had given her. She popped the cork and held it up to let Marlowe sniff the contents. "Better than this?"

He shrugged, his hands still bound before him. "I can't tell. That's probably better than what I could make, but it wouldn't be superior to what Valora can produce."

Kyla contemplated this, eyeing Marlowe as he stood before her. He had a brazen expression on his face, daring her to judge him. The hair on his chin and jaw was thicker now than it had been when they left, making his dark eyes look even deeper, like twin abysses that could swallow her whole.

Kyla shuddered, shaking the thought away. "Are you bad at it, or is Valora good?"

He raised an eyebrow. "What do you think?"

Something about the way he posed the question made Kyla want to smile. There was a quality to it, a teasing, that was softer than mockery. She turned to Valora. "And do your potions work on you?"

"Not in the same way that they work on other people."

"Can you show me?"

Valora frowned. "I can make them, but it's hard for me to gather the ingredients. Marlowe always did it for me."

Marlowe held out his bound hands to Kyla, and nodded at the rope around his wrists. "You could untie me and I could go looking."

Kyla laughed. "Not likely." She turned back to Valora. "If you can make something that will help your wound, I can get whatever you need. Will you describe it to me? I can find it."

"You won't find it out here in the plains. Maybe in the forest—"

Kyla stood up and looked towards the western border of the plains, where she could see the trees, dark and thick. "A day's walk. Tomorrow we'll be there."

"I have this." Valora tapped a little pouch that was attached to a belt fastened around her hips. She unclipped it and opened the flap. Inside were what looked like dried herbs. "It's useless on its own. But if you could find some Valerian root to add to it, and steep it in hot water, it would make a very soothing drink."

"Soothing?" Marlowe laughed. "Valora's herbs are potent. It would probably kill us."

Kyla couldn't conceal the alarm on her face.

Valora quickly held out her hands. "No, no, he's exaggerating. It wouldn't kill anyone. It would put you to sleep. It would be comforting. Like the alcohol you keep giving me, but without the rotten feeling when I wake up."

Kyla weighed this up and, deciding she wasn't being tricked, said, "We'll find some then, when we get to the forest."

"Valerian for Valora," Max called, smiling as he turned the hare once more.

Kyla handed the bottle of lotion to Valora, so she could apply some to her wounds. "And for your hand," she said.

Marlowe shot Valora a questioning glance, but Valora shrugged in response, trying to affect a nonchalance that Kyla suspected was for her benefit. Leaving the two siblings trying to communicate without speaking, Kyla went to join Max.

He was bent over, poking the flames with a stick. He looked up, over his shoulder, distracted by some noise. In the sky above huge Nilari birds were circling, like vultures.

"I don't like it," he said. "They don't do that in Moriya."

Kyla squinted up at the birds. It was odd, the way they were hovering around, but perhaps it wasn't unusual out here. "The birds get fed in Moriya. These ones are probably looking for scraps."

Max stood up and turned back to the fire, but his lips folded in on one another and he shook his head gently. "What if they're like those ones at the river? I swear they're following us."

"They're probably hungry. That hare smells—"

"Disgusting," Marlowe called across the fire.

"You don't need to eat it," Max shouted back. He poked the roasting hare with the end of a knife and looked up at Kyla, speaking more quietly now. "But really, those birds have been after us since the storm cleared."

Kyla frowned. "I hadn't noticed."

"It's creepy." Max gave a shudder. "I don't like it."

"Ignore them then," Kyla said.

"If we knew where they were nesting—" Marlowe got up and moved towards Kyla and Max. "—we could find the eggs. They're delicious, Nilari eggs. You can sell them for a fortune too."

"We're not eating Nilari eggs," Kyla said. "They're sacred. The birds have royal protection in Moriya. You can't eat their eggs."

There was a glint of amusement in Marlowe's eyes, and a twist to his lips. "Don't tell me you really believe no one in Moriya eats Nilari eggs? They're a delicacy. I bet even the Sages eat them, right before they slaughter the birds and turn their feathers into dust and sell it to the poor and needy."

Kyla gasped. It was almost as bad as having said the God-Sage himself ate the eggs or made the dust. "What an outrageous thing to say. Of course no one eats the eggs in Moriya."

Marlowe, still smiling, turned to Max. "What do you think?"

Max, who was once more poking the hare, paused to look over his shoulder. "I think people will do anything for money, and those with too much of it always need something else to spend it on. Eggs, feather dust... whatever."

Marlowe nodded at Kyla, a satisfied smirk on his face. "At least someone around here knows how the world works. And a puff of feather dust is just as good as a Nilari egg. Better, maybe." Marlowe's eyes were gleaming, and Kyla realised with a jolt that he was enjoying himself, deriving pleasure from teasing and shocking her. "If we find a dealer you can buy some with all that gold you're carrying around." He nodded at Edmund's coin purse, which was still attached to her belt.

Kyla put a protective hand over it. "I don't want to smoke feather dust. I've no need for it."

Marlowe opened his mouth to speak, when Max said, "Meat's ready."

Max used both his knives to carve the meat from the hare. He tore it in strips, handing it out.

"Mmm." Marlowe ate like a squirrel, with his hands bound, holding the meat to his lips and nibbling at it. He wiped a trail of grease from his lips with the back of one hand. "Better than the rats I was catching for us back home."

Max stopped, mid-slicing, and looked again at the birds flying above. Kyla followed his gaze, wishing he wasn't so bothered by them. She could feel his anxiety as if it was lice that crawled on her skin.

The horses had begun to whinny, scraping the dust with their hooves, and Kyla was thankful they had already tied them up. They looked worked up enough to try and run.

The Nilari birds were closer now. There were three of them, impossibly large, with wingspans as wide as Kyla's own outstretched arms, and beaks as big as a man's hand and as sharp as the knife in her boot.

"They want—"

Max didn't have time to finish his sentence. One of the birds swooped down, claws out.

Kyla jumped up, looking around for her sword, forgetting it was impaled through the dead hare. She grabbed the hilt. It was still warm, but not so hot that she couldn't hold it. She tried to swing the sword, but it was heavy and off-balance, weighted strangely with the carcass on the blade.

One of the birds grabbed the hare, still smoking, and sank its golden talons into the meat.

Kyla yanked her sword and, with only a little resistance, it slid out of the meat, dripping in grease and fat.

The bird flapped at her, crowing wildly. She swiped at it, but other birds came to its aid and flew at her, air blasting her face from the thumps of their wings.

Max jumped up and tried to grab the meat back, but the bird was strong and fast. It rose into the sky, and others took its place, forming a barrier of claw and beak, squawking horrifically. The noise was deafening. Valora crouched over, her hands covering her ears.

One of the birds dived at Max, pecking at him, feathers flapping, great wings like evil shadows pounding the air. Max tripped back, and hit the ground like a dead man.

Kyla swiped her sword over his head. The bird flew backwards, sending up a flurry of dust and feather: a storm that beat at Kyla's body.

Marlowe was beside her, holding out his bound wrists. "Untie me!" he yelled.

If there was a moment to free him, this was it. She couldn't fend off the ravenous birds herself. Holding her sword in one hand she began to pull at the rope with the other, but Max had tied it so tight, it was difficult to loosen. She couldn't do it. A bird swooped down, its beak tearing at her cloak.

Marlowe disappeared behind the great wingspan of the bird. Kyla's cloak was still in its beak. She tugged it back.

"Great God-Sage," she cursed.

The bird fixed her with bulging eyes. It was looking at her, seeing her, as if it was more than animal, more than bird. She elbowed it away and swung her sword again.

She glimpsed Marlowe, her vision flickering where feathers obscured her view. He had given up on getting his wrists free and was moving towards Valora, batting the birds away as best he could. He scrambled, low to the ground, picking up rocks and hurling them over his shoulder. One struck, thumping a bird on the head. It fell to the ground, flapping, twisting, and then up again, sending gusts of dirt into the air.

A bird came at Kyla, claws out. She raised her arm, elbow up, to cover her face from the attack. Scratches like fire ripped her skin.

The bird meant to do more than scratch. It was fighting to the death. Kyla struck out with her sword.

She hit the bird across the wing. Feathers exploded. Blood spurted from some part of the bird Kyla couldn't see. There was a flapping, a squawking, a screaming – but whether from the bird or one of the group she couldn't tell – and then a heavy thud. The bird had fallen to the ground and lay on its back, one wing badly damaged, fluttering in a circle, talons scratching at nothing.

Then it was up again, its beak viciously sharp and its damaged wing trailing blood that mixed with the dust. It was bigger than any Nilari bird Kyla had ever seen, and it was coming at her again.

She stumbled backwards, tripping over a rock, her sword tumbling to the ground. The bird was on top of her, foul-smelling feathers smothering her. She couldn't open her eyes, she could hardly breathe.

She could do nothing but hold up her arms, shield her face. She tried to reach the knife in her boot but she couldn't, not without exposing her face to the claws.

A yell cut through the screech of the bird. She saw her blade arc through the air. Marlowe. He stood, eyes blazing with rage, the sword clasped in his bound hands. He smashed it down across the bird's back.

With a thwack, an explosion of feathers and an arc of blood that sprayed like a fountain, the bird fell. Dead.

Kyla rolled onto her knees, her heart pounding, her breaths coming quick and fast.

The other birds, both of them, were attacking Valora. One of them had a chunk of her long dark hair in its beak, yanking it upwards, dragging Valora almost off her feet. Max was holding her around the ankles, trying to pull her back. The other bird was clawing at Valora's neck.

Marlowe, Kyla's sword still in his hand, turned to Valora. He slashed the sword through the air in great curving, mindless sweeps.

Kyla stumbled to her feet. Marlowe's movements were so frenzied, he was just as likely to hit Max or Valora as he was the bird.

She pulled a knife from her boot and flung it, hard, fast, quick as an arrow.

It hit the bird in the back, between the wings, the blade sinking deep up to the hilt.

The bird reared back, the rhythm of its wings becoming uneven. It fell, still thrashing, bright blue feathers sweeping the dusty ground.

Marlowe yelled, bringing the sword down on the bird's neck, slicing right through it. Blood spattered the ground and the bird lay still.

The other bird, the one that had Valora's hair, began to flee, flying skywards.

Its rising squawks grew fainter, the gusts of wind blown back by the thrust of its wings growing less. Then it was gliding in the air, high over the bodies of its mates, which lay dead around Kyla's feet.

The silence that followed its departure was shocking: an emptiness where before had been chaos.

It took several moments for Kyla to catch her breath, to register what had happened.

Max, exhausted, lay on the ground, clutching his arm where the birds had scratched him. Not far off lay the carcass of the roasted hare, severed by the talons that had scraped through the meat. "I knew it." Max puffed and tried to sit up. "I knew there was something wrong with the birds."

Marlowe was standing utterly still, blood dripping from the blade of Kyla's sword. The sacred bird blood, dripping in the dirt. He dropped the sword and turned to Valora, who was lying on her back, her hair strewn on the ground, clumps of it lying detached from her scalp.

Kyla picked up a clump of the hair, letting it trail in her fingers before allowing the breeze to take it. The strands filtered away. She crouched beside Marlowe and helped Valora sit up.

"Are you hurt?" she asked.

Valora raised a hand to her scalp, touched it gently, her fingers coming away bloody. She winced but said, "It's not much."

Marlowe was trying to inspect the damage, his wrists still bound, his fingers running over Valora's head.

Kyla left him to it, picked up her sword and looked at the blood on it. Horror shot through her body, landing heavy and bilious in her stomach. "You killed two Nilari birds!"

Marlowe paused his inspection of Valora's injuries to look over his shoulder. He nodded at the bird that had Kyla's knife still impaled in its back. "Maybe you killed it."

Marlowe had clean sliced the bird's head off with her sword; whatever her knife had done, Marlowe had finished the bird off. She stooped to pull the knife out. "You meant to kill," she said. "I only meant to stop the attack."

"And then what?" His brow furrowed, his upper lip curled away from his teeth. "Nurse the bird back to health? Don't lie."

Kyla felt frustration, anger, everything, boiling up in her chest. She wanted to shout at him, to scream at him. How dare he speak to her like that? She was conflicted too, because she *had* meant to kill the bird, to do anything to get them away, to save them from more attack. But Nilari birds should never be killed; only sacrificed in the name of the God-Sage himself.

At least that was what she had believed before she had seen them swooping across the river, dropping deadly eels on the crowd.

She closed her eyes to shut out the sight of the dead birds, whose bodies served only to remind her how she had failed to sacrifice the bird back in Moriya during her initiation ceremony. And now here she was, in the middle of nowhere, miles from Moriya, surrounded by blood and feathers.

"They're sacred. The birds are sacred." As she opened her eyes the words exploded from her mouth like a reflex. Who did she mean them for? Perhaps it was only meant for the God-Sage himself, to let him know that she *knew* the rules even if she couldn't follow them.

Marlowe, his hands still bound, had shifted his attention from Valora to his own shirt. He was busy biting the sleeve, tugging it up with his teeth. When the skin was exposed he brandished his forearm at Kyla, displaying scars, three bold stripes of thickened tissue, too uniform to have been made by anything other than talons. "You're deluded. I've stolen my share of Nilari eggs, and even the mother birds aren't as vicious as the birds I've seen over the past few days. I don't care how sacred you think they are; those birds were out to draw blood, just like the ones at the river."

Kyla didn't want to think about it, didn't want to question something she had always accepted without question, but Marlowe wasn't ready to stop.

"Have you ever wondered why the birds are sacred? You think it has some religious meaning? Some significance? Some memory of those Moriyans lost in the Sage Rebellion? It's not. It's nothing other than the fact that the Sages are at the heart of a heaving and lucrative feather dust trade!"

Kyla gasped. "The Sages wouldn't touch the dust. How dare you? I won't listen to this... this... sacrilege! And you would be as well to keep your mouth shut if you want to keep it on your face." Her heart was hammering in her chest, but she tried to regain some semblance of equanimity as she sheathed her sword and turned to Max, who was toeing the piece of discarded hare meat with his boot.

He looked up at her, one side of his mouth pulled down, one eyebrow raised. "Think we could still eat it?"

"I don't have much appetite anymore."

Marlowe, however, was undeterred by the filth on the meat. He picked up the remains of the hare and bit into the dust covered flesh, tore a chunk off with his teeth and chewed laboriously before choking it down. He held Kyla's gaze and she felt a challenge in his eyes, but one so casual as to be almost insulting. He held out his wrists to her. "Untie me now?"

Kyla shook her head. "I don't have much appetite for that either."

7

MARLOWE

LEAVING THE GREAT PLAINS

Marlowe had soothed the raw patches on Valora's scalp and neck as best he could, but he had rejected any attempt on her part to heal the scratches on his own skin, and had violently repelled any attempt by the Moriyans to exploit her talents, despite Valora's desire to help. Max and Kyla, accepting that Valora was too weak to heal anyone, had receded to the far side of the fire to tend their wounds, which, like his own, were superficial.

"You showed them the burn on your hand?" Marlowe was seated on a rock, his elbows on his knees. His hands, wrists still bound, were clasped before him. He kept his voice hushed and glanced at Kyla and Max through the haze of the heat from the fire. They were talking quietly, cleaning their scratches with the contents of some bottle from the medicine bag. They were paying him less attention than they had done since he had caught up with them. If there was a moment to question his sister, this was it.

Valora shot a look towards Kyla and Max. "Wait. They'll feed the horses in a moment, and then we can talk."

Marlowe sat quietly next to Valora, listening to the crackle of the fire and watching it spit bright sparks into the night air, which were swallowed by darkness a moment later. As Valora predicted, once Max and Kyla had tended their wounds, they went to attend to the horses, turning their backs to where he and Valora sat.

"Why did you show them?" Marlowe said.

"It was painful. I couldn't keep it hidden. It was difficult to ride."

"So they know about the crooked wheel?"

"They know I had it, they know it burnt me and they know I don't have it anymore." She brought her bowed head closer to his, her eyes alight with urgency. "Where is it now?"

Marlowe looked towards his pocket. "I still have it. But I think we ought to get rid of it. If anything's going to get you hanged, it's that little piece of metal."

"How can you want to get rid of it? You don't know what it is yet, or why Mother kept it. It's powerful. Tremendously powerful—"

"Is it? How do you know it's not you that's powerful? I tried to use it to get out of the prison, and it did nothing. Nothing. It was as useless as a lump of mud."

"There was no Nilari priest there, though, was there? When you touched it?"

Marlowe narrowed his eyes. "No."

"Then of course it did nothing." Valora clamped her lips together and crossed her arms over her chest.

"What are you trying to tell me?"

Valora shrugged. "I know that wheel has something to do with Kyla too. We should ask her. She's as interested in it as we are. I'm sure she'd tell us—"

"Are you mad? We can't ask Kyla Tarthwen for anything. She'd kill us." Marlowe glanced across to where Kyla was standing, stroking the blaze of her horse. It was nuzzling into her chest. Her face was serious, her lips drawn tight and her brow furrowed. How did a person so young become so stern? And yet, as she focused on the horse, Marlowe was sure he could see another aspect to her, a caring, softer side. She might, even, if she smiled, be attractive.

"Marlowe?"

He snapped back to Valora, who was looking at him with a peculiar expression on her face, her eyes flitting from Kyla and back to him again. Then her eyes widened with the understanding that he was looking at Kyla with an emotion that was less than hatred, and perhaps even approaching admiration. "You—"

Marlowe felt shame and heat flicker in his belly. "Shhhh. Whatever you're about to say—" Marlowe glared at her. "—don't. Just stop."

Valora smiled and looked away from him. "Oh, pretend all you want, but I've seen that look on your face before. I remember—"

"Stop. Kyla's father killed our parents."

Valora's smile vanished and Marlowe wondered if his reaction had been too severe. He hadn't meant to frighten her, only to stop her reeling off a list of times he had been smitten with some woman or another.

Valora twisted a chunk of her dress between her fingers and then let it go. She held out her hand to him. "Give me the wheel. It's mine."

Marlowe glanced at Kyla and Max to check they weren't looking, saw that they were still occupied with the horses, huffed, stood up and shuffled his bound hands towards his pocket, fishing out the wheel with the tips of his fingers. "There. Take it."

Valora slipped it into the pouch around her neck. Kyla and Max were finishing up with the horses, and they were walking back towards the fire, back towards where he and Valora were sitting, but they were deep in conversation and paying no attention.

Marlowe felt a tug on his sleeve, and he turned back to Valora, who was looking at him anxiously, warily, like she expected him to snap at her again.

"Yes?" he said.

"I've been thinking about that day down at the river. About how the wheel got hot and burnt me."

Marlowe waited. Valora looked as though she was struggling to choose the right words. "Go on."

"I don't think it was me. I mean, I don't think I activated it."

Marlowe frowned. "Who then?"

"That Nilari rebel. Yarmon Sacfron. From across the river. It was... I can't explain it, but it felt like he was... calling it. And it replied, at first with heat, which coincided with the appearance of the eels. Only after that was there the first burst of light. I know it wasn't me, because I hadn't done anything." She sighed again, recognising that Marlowe wasn't following. "When I heal, I have to form some intention, hold some desire in my mind, of what I want to happen. And when it is strong enough I can feel it move through me into the other person's body. Even with Max, although it was an entirely different type of healing from what I'm used to, I still held that intention when I grabbed hold of that knife. I put all of my will into it. I wanted his suffering to end." She glanced up at the sky and sighed, letting her hands fall into her lap. "I can't explain it, other than to say I wasn't exerting any sort of power over that piece of metal."

"So you didn't rescue us all from the eels?"

A crease appeared between her brows. "Oh, yes. That final blast that made the eels and the birds disappear, and even Yarmon... That was mine. But I only used the power that was already there. It was as if it had been charged... by someone else. By Yarmon. I was only able to turn his power against him, forcing my intention over the power that I felt emanating from the wheel. I didn't create anything myself. At least I don't think I did."

Marlowe took a moment to absorb this, and then fear shuddered through his bones. "Give it back to me. Right now. We cannot keep it."

Valora shuffled away from him. "No. Don't you want to know why he wanted it? Maybe that Nilari priest who came down from the mountains, the one who got Mother and

Father killed, maybe he didn't come to heal me at all. Maybe he came for this." She tapped the pouch around her neck.

Marlowe was about to demand again that she give him the piece of metal when something occurred to him. "Those birds too, the Nilari birds that attacked us out on the plains…"

Valora was nodding, eagerly. "Yes. They're watching me. You. Us. They want it. They know we have it." She clutched his hand in hers. "Mother never gave it to the priest."

Marlowe nodded slowly, as all the information began to slide into place. "She kept it hidden, and she gave it to you."

Valora nodded earnestly. "Exactly. I knew it didn't make any sense, back when Duncan said Mother had sought out the priest so that he might heal me. They would never have done that, not without asking me first. They weren't traitors, Marlowe. They were never on the side of the Nilari."

Marlowe pondered this for a moment. It was convincing… possible even. He longed to believe it, longed to cling to some proof that his parents really were innocent. He felt it in his heart, but still the doubts crept in. He shook his head. "We have no way of knowing. We're guessing. We have no proof."

Valora was quiet, and Marlowe wondered if she too was feeling the sadness that engulfed him unexpectedly, every so often, since his parents had died. Sometimes it took almost nothing to be reminded of that loss and to feel the violent pain of it in his entire body, almost out of nowhere.

Finally, Valora whispered, "I don't need proof." She spoke without meeting Marlowe's eye.

"I'm sorry," he said. "I don't mean to doubt our parents. I want them to be innocent as much as you do, but they're dead. It makes no difference either way."

"It does to me."

They sat once more in companionable silence. Although he hadn't agreed with her, he felt no resentment or anger from her. She was simply stating the facts as she saw them, and if she had convinced herself of their parents' innocence, then he saw no reason to disabuse her of that conviction.

She interlaced her fingers with his. "I'm glad you're coming with me. I was so afraid that I would have to go to Moriya without you."

Marlowe slid his fingers from hers and averted his gaze. He couldn't bear to see the way she would look at him when he said, "I can't come with you to Moriya."

"What? But Marlowe, why not? I need you there. You must come! You have to."

Marlowe closed his eyes and bit the inside of his bottom lip, fearing that if he didn't pin it in place, however briefly, it would begin to tremble. "I killed a man. In the cells. One of the guards. Grandfather might have sent people out to find me already, to exact punishment. And I know he will have sent word—"

"To Moriya." Valora finished, her face creased with worry. "Oh Marlowe." A strangled noise, a thwarted sob, sounded in the back of her throat. Marlowe spoke quickly, worried that if she began to cry he might too.

"Yes. They'll arrest me at the gates. I can't come with you. I'll come as far as I can, but I can't enter the city alongside you. It's too dangerous. For now, I can stay with you. Kyla doesn't know what happened. She doesn't know what I did. If she did—"

"*Murder must be paid in blood*," Valora quoted the oft repeated words from the Book of Wings.

Marlowe hung his head. "Exactly. And I don't think Kyla would hesitate to exact the punishment."

Valora placed her hand over his. For a few moments they sat like that, silently, and Marlowe wondered how much more pain he could bear in one lifetime.

A flicker of movement drew Marlowe's attention and he looked up. Kyla was pacing towards him, the medicine bag slung over one shoulder, and he could feel the speed of his heartbeat increase with each of her steps.

"What's going on?" She halted right before where he and Valora were seated. "I've a good mind to keep the two of you separate."

Kyla's eyes glistened in the light of the fire, and for a moment, as he stared up at her, Marlowe was speechless. She didn't wait for an answer before she unslung the bag from her shoulder and thrust it towards him. "Here, you can tend to your sister's wounds. I need to sleep."

Marlowe balanced the bag on his forearms and pinned it in place with bent elbows. "I can't... Untie me..."

But Kyla had already turned away and moved off, raising one hand higher than her shoulder so that he could see it from his vantage point behind her. Then she flicked her fingers back towards him in a silent *Work it out yourself. I don't care.*

He shrugged, and turned disbelieving eyes on Valora. "Charming."

Valora, who was already digging into the medicine bag, gave a snort of laughter, and Marlowe returned her smile, feigning ignorance. "What's funny? I take great comfort in the fact that, when she kills me, I'll be dying at the hands of a truly lovely woman."

When they reached the forest beyond the Great Plains, death was heavy on Marlowe's conscience. He had been joking when he had spoken to Valora about dying at Kyla's hand, but he couldn't help recalling how he had sworn he would be the one to kill *her*. Was the feeling mutual? Perhaps she too was biding her time, waiting for a moment to dispose of him. But even if that were true, now that he had taken a life and knew how it felt to slide a blade between a man's ribs, he wasn't sure he could do it again.

He tried to shove the thought out of his mind, focusing instead on the task in hand. He and Kyla had gone in search of the herbs and plants Valora had requested, leaving her and Max to set up camp for the night.

Beneath the heavy foliage the air was rich and moist, unlike the dry dust of the plains. Marlowe was glad to have left that barren landscape behind, and directed his attention to the pleasurable sensation of his boots sinking into the softness of the forest floor.

Kyla was crouching at the side of a shallow stream. The water sparkled with dappled light and she leant forward to fill a leather flagon, drinking deeply from it before filling it once more. As he watched her, the reflected light glinting across her face, it struck Marlowe that the trickle of running water was one of the most melodic sounds he had ever heard, and the sight of Kyla was no less enjoyable. He shook his head to release the thought, thankful that Valora wasn't here to see his face this time.

Her father killed our parents, he reminded himself.

Kyla, oblivious to his observation of her, forced the cork into the flagon and turned to look at him as she stood up, dispelling his daydream. "We'll be able to turn south soon, avoiding Traitors' Lake entirely."

Marlowe nodded, but he didn't want to discuss the progress of their journey, not when it meant he was getting closer to losing Valora forever. Instead he kicked at the clump of Valerian at his feet. The green stalks were so tall that they brushed against his thighs, and the frothy white flowers bounced back and forth like happy children.

"Here, this one." He kicked again at the flowers. "That's what we want. The root."

Kyla hesitated. Wasn't she going to help at all? Marlowe grunted and stooped, his hands still bound, to tug up the valerian himself. He began to tear off the roots.

"Do it like this," he said.

Kyla began to copy him and he instructed her, as best he was able, on how to prepare and store them. She stuffed what she could into Valora's herb pouch, which was hanging on her belt, next to the heavy coin purse that clinked every so often.

For a few moments they worked in silence. Then Kyla said, "Could Valora really make a potion that would kill someone?"

Marlowe bit off some of the flowers and began to chew on them. "Are you worried she'll try it on you?"

Kyla held his gaze a moment too long, as though she was trying to work out the right answer to the question. Finally she said, "No."

Marlowe shrugged. "Valora's never killed anyone, not as far as I know. Not even by accidentally brewing something for too long, or applying the wrong ointment." He glanced down at his shirt, wishing he could forget the murder he himself had committed. The blood of the guard he had killed back in Palantar had faded, mixed with rainwater and sweat, but the stain was still visible. He hoped Kyla hadn't noticed his momentary pause; he didn't want her to think he cared about a bit of blood, and rushed to keep speaking. "But then I don't think she ever tried. I didn't really mean it when I said she could kill you with a potion."

"I'd be annoyed if I asked for a sleeping draught and died instead."

Marlowe gave a sharp snort of laughter. Kyla was almost amusing, sometimes. "I only meant her salves and potions are more powerful than anyone else's, even if they're made in the same way. They were more powerful even than our mother's, and she was as good as any apothecary. People in Palantar came from the other side of the city for her healing salves. Nothing magic – Mother didn't have any powers, not like Valora does.

"Anyway, Mother taught us both how to make the creams and such, but mine never did much. I mean, they did what they were supposed to, but Valora's were... special. All she had to do was think about the reason she was making it, the effect she wished it to have... and it did." Marlowe paused to look at Kyla, who was watching him eagerly. "Mother had to stop her making them. It was too dangerous. Once an old woman came with aching hands... She had knuckles that were swollen like olives, and mother sold her one of Valora's salves. The woman came back the following day asking for more, asking for all of it. Her hands were healed. Not just comforted... but healed. They looked twenty years younger."

"Was your mother worried?"

"Terrified. I remember her and my father discussing it. Wondering if they should poison the old woman, kill her before she could tell everyone."

"What happened?"

"She was tremendously old. She died not long afterwards."

Kyla raised an eyebrow. "Naturally?"

"Are you asking if my parents killed her?"

"Did they?"

Marlowe shook his head. "No. They might have been executed as traitors, but they weren't murderers." He paused to spit out the chewed Valerian flower. "I don't know why I'm telling you all this. Let's go back to the others." He nodded at the clump of roots Kyla was holding. "That's more than enough. Put them in there." He nodded at the herb pouch on Kyla's belt.

He watched as Kyla squashed the roots into the tiny leather pouch. There was something strange about seeing it hanging around Kyla's hips, next to her sword, and Marlowe was suddenly struck by how different Kyla and his sister were. One made her way in the world with a sword in her hand; the other made magic with her hands and potions with plants.

A thought occurred to him then, one so obvious he couldn't believe he hadn't asked her before.

"What happened to the other acolyte?"

Kyla straightened. She stood almost as tall as he was, meeting him eye to eye, but there was a wariness in her glance. "What acolyte?"

"There are ten, aren't there? I assume you aren't adding Valora as an eleventh, so what happened to the previous acolyte from Palantar?"

Kyla paused for a moment and then spun quickly on her heel, storming back in the direction of the camp.

"Wait, stop." Marlowe called, tripping over shrubs and fallen branches as he ran to catch up. With his hands tied he was strangely off-balance.

Ahead of him, Kyla stopped. She turned quickly. "She was killed. Murdered. During my initiation ceremony."

"Murdered?"

He had caught up to her now, and had his hands been free he would have grabbed her, shaken her, pushed her. Something to release the anger that had begun to swirl in his chest.

"Why? Who murdered her?" His voice was strained and tight.

Kyla merely stared back at him. "I don't know."

Marlowe's jaw dropped, but he collected himself instantly and began to shout, hardly able to restrain himself. "You don't know? You don't know who killed her, and you want to bring Valora to Moriya to replace her, like a sacrificial lamb? By the burnt-isle, you're insane! I swear it! If you think I'm going to stand by and let you—"

Kyla's hand crashed against his cheek, sending him stumbling backwards. Unable to break his fall or regain his footing, he fell backwards into the bushes. Kyla stood over him, a knife in one hand, and looked down at him, calmly.

"What exactly do you think you can do?"

"I'll kill you, I swear, as soon as your back is turned, I'll—"

Kyla knelt over him, crouched low, pinning him to the ground. Her knife was to his throat. He could feel the pinch of the blade against his skin.

He slid his eyes sideways to the knife, then up at Kyla, and felt a smile tug at the corner of his lips, knowing it would be the thing that would annoy her most. "I could get used to this."

She shook her head in disbelief and he felt the slightest tremor of the knife at his neck. "There's a plague spreading from the pestilence in Traitors' Lake," she said. "People are dying. Our only hope is to get Valora back to Moriya, so the healing circle can heal the sick. You would do well to get your priorities straight. This isn't about Valora. It's about—"

"What is it about? Is it about you? What do *you* get for your trouble? What's your reward?"

Kyla's eyes were as cold as a winter morning, and Marlowe felt her gaze chill his soul. "I take up my place in the Sacred Core."

She might as well have slid the knife into his neck, her words so knocked the life out of him. Marlowe barely breathed the words. "The Sacred Core?"

That she was Lander Tarthwen's daughter was one thing, but that she was to join the ranks of the legendary Sacred Core, the brutal men who enforced the oaths of the God-Sage and had sent many a traitor to their deaths... Why, the Sacred Core were responsible for seeking out every illegal healer and exposing them, delivering them to the healing circle and ensuring their demise.

Marlowe didn't move. "They're evil. The Sacred Core are evil. Do you know how many innocent people have lost their lives because the Sacred Core claimed they were breaking the oaths?"

Her knife moved to his cheek, and he felt the sting as she cut his skin. "Ow, what are—"

She didn't let him finish. "The Sacred Core are agents of the God-Sage. They are trusted by the Sages themselves, the elite—"

"You expect to join them and yet you haven't killed Valora." Marlowe edged out beneath her knife, and when he was sure she was going to let him move without cutting him again, he pushed himself up to a sitting position. She never once took her eyes off him. He kept his voice curious, but not aggressive. He wanted to understand, not to fight. Not right now. "You've witnessed her breaking oath after oath, and you're still determined to bring her back to Moriya as an acolyte. Why?"

Kyla must have sensed that the fight had gone out of him, for she pocketed her knife and then grabbed his bound hands at the wrists, heaving him up to standing. "Your sister is marked for the God-Sage. My duty is to bring her to his glory."

She was already half-turned away from him when Marlowe pulled her back round. "And if she hadn't been branded? What then? What would you have done?"

The air fell still, the only noise the soft rustle of the leaves in the trees overhead. Kyla's brow flinched, drawing low over her eyes.

"You should thank the God-Sage that the matter was taken out of my hands."

Then she turned and moved ahead of him, so quickly that he couldn't catch up, but this time he didn't want to.

Several hours after they had settled to sleep, Marlowe awoke to find that the darkness of the night had crept closer. The fire was little more than glowing embers, and what heat it had given out earlier that evening was almost non-existent.

Max, wrapped in his red army cloak, was seated, his back propped against the trunk of a large oak tree. His head drooped at a funny angle and occasionally he gave a startled snort: he was sleeping.

Marlowe shivered and wished he too had a travelling cloak to cover himself with. He sat up and looked around, comforted to see Valora sleeping peacefully, despite the fact that she wheezed with each breath. Her lungs were weak, and in the slums back in Palantar Marlowe had been worried that the weakness might kill her. But now, even crackling as it did, her breathing sounded better than before. The wound on her chest was healing too, and Marlowe was feeling more confident that Valora would be all right.

There was no sign of Kyla. Perhaps she had taken the watch, but if so where was she? He held his breath, but could hear nothing other than the sounds of slumber and the occasional call of an owl.

He stood up, needing to relieve himself, and stepped away into the woods. It was difficult to loosen his trousers with his hands tied, but he managed it with a little tugging here and there. When he was done he bent down, awkwardly lopsided, to hook his trousers back up and fasten his belt. Then he stood still, listening to the night. There was a noise, not close, but also not far off, that caught his attention. A splashing of water. Not a steady stream of urination, but a flicking and slapping, as though someone was playing in a pool. Suddenly he realised how long it had been since he had had something to drink, for Kyla had not shared her flask with him back in the forest. He was overcome with thirst, and the sound of water was impossible to resist.

Was it foolish to pursue such a noise with his hands tied? Probably. But it was dark enough that he could conceal himself in the shadows of the trees. He followed the sound, the scent of dampened earth growing more potent and the metallic tang of wet rock sharp in the air as he approached.

There, between the trees, he caught the reflection of a jagged moon, half-concealed in cloud, on a rippling surface.

He caught his breath. In the middle of the pool stood a woman, immersed to her waist in water. She stood so still that the water's surface became a darkened mirror through which she rose, her arms raised and her fingers tangled in loose brown hair that fell down her back.

Kyla.

The realisation that it was Kyla was a strange one. It had been so long, too long, since Marlowe had seen a woman's body, and yet here, now, he wanted to look away. Shame coursed through his veins. It felt wrong to watch from the shadows.

But, try as he might, he couldn't look away. His breathing grew shallow, his movements small, hoping she wouldn't notice him. What would she say, to see him standing there gaping at her?

He watched as she combed her fingers through wet hair. Great God-Sage, she was barely a woman... Wasn't that what he had thought until that moment? That she was some unfeeling, inhuman being. A soldier, a member of the Sacred Core. A woman forging her way in a world made for men. And yet suddenly he knew that of all women, this one here before him now was more desirable than any other woman he had ever known.

He felt torn in two by desire and loathing.

The moon passed out from behind a cloud and only then did he see the scars on her back. Scars like he had never witnessed, even on his grandfather's slaves. They crisscrossed this way and that like cart tracks at a muddy crossroads. They were grotesque, the tissue thick and raised. Who had done that to her? How old had she been? Little more than a child, surely?

Suddenly the pieces came together in his mind and he felt them with certainty, as though he had known them all along. Her father, Lander Tarthwen, had done it to her. He had maimed his own daughter.

Anger seethed beneath Marlowe's skin. Just as he thought he could no longer contain it, another emotion surged up, quelling the fire. This one was altogether softer, gentler and yet more distressing. He had never expected to feel it for Kyla Tarthwen, and he was loath to name it, but the sensation dredged the word to the front of his thoughts. Pity, swiftly followed by an almost overwhelming urge to protect her. To save her from a life that made scars like that acceptable.

As he watched, Kyla became very still, reminding him of a deer, caught in the hunter's line of sight. His heart thumped.

Had she heard him? Just as he was wondering whether he should retreat or reveal himself, she gave an alarmed yell, her arms flailing over her head, and plunged beneath the surface of the water.

Marlowe's muscles tensed. Had she slipped, or been pulled? Was she drowning as he stood there like an idiot? Who knew what creatures lurked in the woodland pools...

Just as he was debating the merits of saving her, he noticed her weapons lying beside her boots and a pile of clothes. The knife too was there. If he could only reach it, he could cut through the rope that bound his wrists and free himself.

He dashed to the water's edge and lowered himself down in front of the knife until he could lift it and place it between his knees.

His fingers shaking, nervous that Kyla would resurface and see him, he held it between his knees and prepared to work at sawing the coarse rope. The blade was sharp, and he was free faster than he had expected to be.

His hands sprang apart and the rope fell away. The knife tumbled to the ground. He stood and turned to run, but there was still no movement from the water. He waited a few more seconds. The silence was eerie. Could Kyla hold her breath that long? It had been too long, surely. He began to grow nervous.

What if he was standing watching as she drowned? He couldn't leave. He scuttled to the water's edge and waded in, gasping as the frigid water hit his skin. He could see nothing. The water was black. Only the rippled reflection of the moon above broke the monotone surface. His leg slipped from under him. He yelled, sliding, slipping, deeper into the pool.

Only he wasn't slipping... he was being pulled! Dragged. He plunged into the water until only his head was above the surface.

He struggled, kicking, but something held him round the ankles. Something strong. He screamed out, thrashed his arms. He didn't want to die out here in the middle of nowhere. What would Valora do? Who would care for her?

His head was suddenly under the water; the shock of cold stung his face. Something tugged on his ankles and he kicked out into the blackness of the water below his feet. It was dark. He could barely see the moonlight above now; the pool was deeper than it looked.

Fighting to get to the surface, a tightening in his chest took hold. There was no air in his lungs, but if he opened his mouth to breathe, he would only take in water. His lungs, his chest, began to burn with the need for air.

The fight began to leave him and he was sure he would die.

He was going to drown in water that had looked so still.

He kicked one last time. The pressure on his ankles loosened, disappeared, and he rose towards the surface. Something was still touching him, hands on his legs, his arms, holding him under the water.

Kyla.

Her body was pale, unclothed, like some soft underwater creature in the watery moonlight that blurred his vision. She rose until she floated before him.

Time paused, hanging in that airless moment beneath the water, his lungs aflame, as he took in the sight of her; the vulnerability of her exposed skin, hair that hovered around her face.

He burst upwards. Chill air hit his skin as he broke the surface, simultaneously shocking and pleasurable. Each breath was a gasp, painfully tearing at his chest. He spluttered, splashing, unable to believe what had just happened. What *had* happened?

Kyla's head popped up in the water and she slicked her wet hair against her scalp with both hands.

"You? You?" The stupidity of the repetition, the weakness of his voice, echoing in his ears, made Marlowe feel like a child.

He splashed to the side of the pool, dragged himself onto the mud and collapsed, still struggling to breathe.

He rolled onto his back, aware that Kyla was rising out of the pool, grabbing the clothes she had left on the side. None of her movements betrayed any shame, any embarrassment. He cursed her silently. What game was she playing?

He kept his gaze directed upwards, focusing on the leaves and the starlight that sprinkled through them from the sky above. He had only to look at her and he would see... really see...

He covered his eyes with his hands.

"Great God-Sage, woman," he said. "You could have killed me."

Kyla's voice was calmer than his own, but it quivered with restrained anger. "Perhaps I should have. Do you know what the punishment is for spying—"

"Spying? I was doing no such thing. I heard the water and wanted to drink!" Marlowe spluttered the words, hoping they rang true despite the flash of guilt that heated his skin.

"I hope you got your fill." Her voice was flat, yet steeped in heavy disdain, and Marlowe gave a hopeless groan at the sound of it.

She moved off into the trees and hopped into her trousers. He could hear the flick of leather as she fixed her belt, the dull clatter of her sword against her thigh.

He heard her step towards him and he closed his eyes beneath his hands, a double layer of protection from this strange woman, but even in the darkness he couldn't get the sight of her body from his mind. It was like a bright light, imprinted on his eyelids; the scars that had spattered her back, the paleness of the skin over her spine, the contrasting darkness of her face, her hands, where the sun had tanned her skin.

He opened his eyes and sat up, speaking faster and louder than he meant to. "I only went in the water because I thought you were drowning."

Her face was taut, her mouth drawn into a thin line. Then she turned her eyes to the starlit sky and smiled, but not at him. It was so unexpected that Marlowe looked away; the urge to echo the smile of a woman who had toyed with him in the water, a woman who had almost killed him, threw him into confusion.

She bent down to pull on her boots and fixed her cloak around her neck. "Was it because they raised you to be some kind of gentleman at that hall? Some sort of pretend nobleman? Must have been hard, losing all that. And to think—" She picked up the knife Marlowe had used to cut the rope that had bound his wrists, tossed it in the air, caught it and slammed it into her boot. "—you could have made a run for it. Cut yourself loose—" She toed at the shredded bits of rope. "—grabbed Valora, and left. But instead you stopped to save a damsel in distress."

Marlowe scowled at her. "I didn't say I was trying to save you. I was going to keep you down there. Make sure you didn't come back up."

Kyla rolled her eyes and he knew she didn't believe a word of it, or perhaps doubted he would even have been capable of it. He had a sudden urge to get up and throw her back in the water, but he balled his hands into fists instead.

"You'll have to dry off your clothes if you don't want to get sick." She held out a hand to pull him up. He let her drag him to his feet, his head still light, his thoughts somewhat detached from his physical self. "Are you going to try and escape? Because if you are…" She left the rest of her sentence unuttered and flipped her knife out of her boot and pointed it at him, spearing the air between them with it.

Damn. The knife. Why hadn't he taken it and run? What had compelled him to wade into the water after her? He must have been staring, for Kyla waved the blade at him again to get his attention. He shook his head.

"Good." She tapped him on the shoulder as she pushed past him. "Because I really do want to get back to Moriya sometime soon."

He watched her move, so sure-footed. There was nothing delicate about her. It was all hidden; all the femininity that made her a woman. But it *was* there, and now he knew it for certain and that changed things, or at least it felt that way to Marlowe. He had seen her unclothed, even if it had been underwater, and with that came a subtle shift in his feelings towards her.

He cursed under his breath. He loathed the way his body and mind reacted to her presence. It wasn't new. He had felt it the first time he had seen her, in the moment their eyes had locked. He had sensed the person beneath the gaze, as if some unseen part of her had reached out and touched him. He felt alive with it, as though she pulsed in his bloodstream.

It made her so much harder to hate.

"Your scars," he said, remembering.

Marlowe found he had no more words to add, and Kyla stopped so abruptly that he had to pull himself up to avoid slamming into her.

"Just because you've seen them doesn't give you the right to ask questions."

"Did your father do that to you?"

Kyla swung round so fast that Marlowe hadn't time to blink. She had his arm locked and twisted, pressed against his back, pulling on sinew and tendon. Somehow she was behind him, her chin almost resting on his shoulder.

"A man who is surplus to requirements should know when to keep his mouth shut."

A shiver ran down Marlowe's spine as her breath hit his neck. And not an entirely unpleasant shiver. But a hard tug on his arm, threatening to pull it inside out, hauled him back into reality. He winced, letting a whimper of air escape his lips: a shameful, weak sound. He flopped forward as she released him, and he clutched his shoulder with the opposite hand, rolling it in the socket. By the God-Sage, she was strong. Much stronger than he thought any woman could be.

Had there been a threat in her words? Yes. Would she harm him if he got in her way?

Undoubtedly yes.

But if so, and his heart gave an infuriating and yet simultaneously hopeful flutter, why hadn't she done it yet?

"Take your drink and hurry up."

She nodded at the pool before turning and stalking back to where the others were sleeping under the trees. There was an arrogance in her step, in the set of her shoulders, that suggested she knew she didn't have to worry about turning her back on him.

Marlowe knelt at the side of the pool and drank his fill, although having nearly drowned in it, the water did not slake his thirst with the satisfaction he had hoped for. He wiped his mouth with one hand, scrambled to his feet and hurried to follow Kyla.

He had nearly caught up with her when she stopped, one foot raised in midstep, and crouched lower to the ground until she was as low as the bushes that grew on the forest floor. She turned her head and, with a twitch of two fingers, beckoned him towards her.

Marlowe felt panic rise in his throat like something he could choke on. Men shouted and whistled, talking with an accent Marlowe didn't recognise. But one thing he did know: it was coming from where they had set up camp.

Marlowe made a sound that was the beginning of a question, but Kyla cut rigid fingers through the air and he fell silent, dropping down to her level. She had one hand on the hilt of her sword.

"Slavers," she whispered.

Marlowe peered through the leaves, watching as several men, their clothes so dark they seemed to melt into the shadows of the forest, kicked the ashes of the fire and stamped on the embers. Max, his face slow and puffy with sleep, but his eyes alight with fear, stood, his wrists bound and mouth gagged. Valora, her feet and hands bound, was slung over the shoulder of the tallest man. Blood trickled down from her hair and across her temple. She had been knocked unconscious.

"What's here?" said the man, looking at Max. "Moriyan soldier out in the middle of the night? What's brought you so far from home?" He shunted the shoulder bearing Valora upwards, but still she lay lifeless. "Not this little thing?"

Max stumbled forward, angry, muffled sounds coming from his gagged mouth. Another man stepped forward and wrenched him back with one hand, thwacking him across the back of the head with the other. Max jolted, lost his balance and fell in the mud. He squirmed, pushing himself up with tied hands, the red of his tunic dark with dirt.

The man holding Valora looked down at Max. "Is she really worth all that?" He laughed, a grotesque chuckle, and bounced her on his shoulder like a sack of grain.

Anger rose in Marlowe, and just as he was contemplating revealing himself and threatening the man, he felt the warmth of human touch on his thigh. Kyla must have sensed his intention to move. She was still looking fixedly ahead, but her hand was on his leg, pinching it in warning. Tomorrow there would be bruises where her fingertips had crushed his flesh.

"Look how many of them there are." Kyla pointed first to a group of shadowy figures to the right, and then to more to the left. There were men on all sides, each with a curved sword slung from his hip and, Marlowe supposed, any number of other knives concealed beneath their cloaks.

"We can't let them take her," said Marlowe.

He slid his fingers into the damp earth in an effort to contain the urge to make war with the men in the clearing. Mud clumped against his hands.

"Don't move," said Kyla. "We have more chance of helping if we stay put. Watch where they go. They'll head for the nearest city. You can hide anything in a city."

"Palantar?"

"Not now. Perhaps Vixar or Turlento. Whichever is closer."

"They've got horses. Four of them," came a voice, strong in the darkness.

"Four horses? For two of them? There must be more of them nearby, soldiers maybe. Spread out. They won't have gone far."

Some of the men began to crash through the bushes, swiping their peculiar curved swords through the leaves.

Other men were untying their horses, claiming them for their own. They were taking Marble! Marlowe's own horse!

Before Marlowe had time to register his outrage Kyla cursed aloud. "If they take our horses we'll have to follow on foot."

A cart creaked forward into the clearing, a cage of wooden bars propped on top. Inside were several sorrowful figures, emaciated, slumped against the sides.

"No we won't," said Marlowe. He crept forward keeping his body low, letting the branches scratch at his face. Kyla tugged at his shirt to keep him back, but in her effort to make no noise she must have judged it wiser not to resist him.

He looked over his shoulder. She was behind him, moving so silently that he hadn't been sure she was following. The cart was only yards away now, the men distracted as they unlatched the cage on top.

"This one's in uniform," said one of the men, announcing his quarry to the others as he pushed Max harder than necessary into the cage. Max stumbled and fell, landing against one of the other bodies. He grunted as he extracted himself from the clutches of the almost lifeless form. "Bit filthy, but you can still see that symbol on his chest. God-Sage, that is. It'll make him even more valuable at the sale."

"Sale?" Marlowe mouthed at Kyla.

"And this one's a cripple." The tall man slapped Valora, but she still hung limp on his shoulder, which was so wide that she nestled neatly into it with little overhang. He paced to the cage and flung her into it. "Got to be something special. Why else would she be guarded by Moriyan soldiers?"

"Cripple sacrifice," shouted one of the men. "Got none grown cripples in Moriya. Pure city and that. Probably going to offer her up to the God-Sage."

Marlowe felt his cheeks burn; he hated to hear Valora talked about that way, as if a cripple was all she was. This was his moment: the men were distracted, saddling the horses and preparing to leave.

He rolled out from the cover of the bushes and went under the cart. Kyla followed him, and they lay on their backs, side-by-side, in the dirt beneath the cart.

"What in the name of the God-Sage are you doing?" Kyla's eyes flashed dark in the shadows.

Marlowe gripped the beam of the underside of the cart. "Going with them. What are you doing?"

Marlowe watched as an array of visible but incomprehensible thoughts flickered over Kyla's face. Then she said, "Going with you."

He was about to heave himself up when Kyla's hand clamped around his arm.

"If they're going to Turlento you'll have to hang on all night and most of tomorrow. It's not possible."

"And walking would be more efficient?" He raised himself up, twisting his arms and legs into the frame of the underside of the cart. Kyla muttered and shook her head, but had curled her hands and feet onto the beams next to him, and with a soft grunt raised herself up. Her sword was dragging on the mud beneath.

Marlowe nodded at the sword. "You'll have to lose it."

Kyla cursed, unfastened her belt and wedged the whole thing, sheath and all, into the beams on the bottom of the cart.

Well, that was probably a better solution than his idea had been. The ground was so wet, the mud so thick after the downpour of rain, that the sword would no doubt have sunk in the oozing earth, to be lost forever. He tilted his head in what he hoped was an appreciative manner.

Boots squelched around them. The slavers were still moving around, searching for them. Marlowe held his breath.

"You found those others yet?" came the deep voice of one of the traders.

"Nope."

"No matter. That's enough. Round up. Let's go. We want to make it to the sale, we've got to move."

The wheels of the cart creaked and Marlowe could just make out Kyla's whispered words, "This is insane."

"You didn't have to follow me."

"I did. I can't let them take the acolyte."

"And I can't let them take my sister."

8

KYLA

JOURNEY TO TURLENTO

Kyla had known it was a bad idea to try and cling to the bottom of the cart, although it hadn't been as bad as she had anticipated. The cart had stopped at least twice on its journey and they had been able to drop down onto the ground, unseen, and stretch their arms and legs. But even so her muscles burnt and cramps whipped up her calves, and it had been a long time since they had eaten that roasted hare out on the plains.

Marlowe was stronger than she had realised. He hadn't trained as she had, but he made no complaint as they bumped across the rocky ground of the path that ran through the forest. Nor had he shifted the position of his arms from where they hooked onto the wooden ruts, even when the wheels of the cart splashed through puddles and splattered them with mud.

Late on the second night the cart juddered to a halt. Kyla could hear someone, above, stepping down. The driver perhaps.

"Don't leave the cart," came a voice.

"I got to take a piss," came the response.

Footsteps moved off and faded away, and when Kyla was sure the man had gone she turned to Marlowe. "I can't do this any longer," she whispered.

"Thank the God-Sage. Me neither." Marlowe let himself down and lay quietly in the mud beneath the cart. Kyla did the same.

Marlowe held a finger to his lips. "Shhh." Then he scrambled out from under the cart.

What was he doing?

She held her breath and listened. The cart creaked and listed as someone climbed up. She could hear indistinguishable whispers. Had Marlowe climbed into the cart? Or had he just gone to relieve himself? She tried to hoist herself closer to the base of the cart, to press her ear against it, but she hadn't enough strength left. What if the cart moved off and she couldn't hold on any more? She would be exposed.

A moment later Marlowe's face appeared in the gap between the ground and the cart. He smiled at her and slithered back beneath the cart.

"Where did you go?" she asked.

"My bladder was full enough to drown a pig. When you've got to go..."

"Someone could have seen you."

Marlowe grinned. "But they didn't."

She gave a shake of the head to both acknowledge and ignore his self-satisfied smirk. "Did you see the others?"

He nodded. "Cart's locked, but they're in there. Come." He shifted back the way he had come and beckoned her, but Kyla shook her head and pointed up to the cart above, where she could hear the driver taking his seat again.

They waited until the sounds of the night were quiet and they could hear snoring, before they crawled out again.

Marlowe crept out first, looking around to make sure no one was awake. Kyla followed, crawling out, dragging the sword with her.

She stood up, not even bothering to dust herself off. She was coated in mud. She fixed her belt and sword in place.

Marlowe gripped her hand, and pointed. "There."

The slaves were all crammed into the cage on the back of the cart. There were men and women, children, all sleeping.

Valora was asleep in one corner, curled up against Max's chest. He was also sleeping, but he had one arm around her, holding her close.

The sight of them snuggled together made Kyla's heart ache. They might have been in a cart, caged and chained, but there was something so tender about the way they slept that Kyla found she had to blink and look away.

Marlowe crept right up to the bars of the cart.

"What are you doing?"

"Like you said, I can't cling onto the cart any longer." He nodded up at Max and Valora. "Let's get them out."

"Now?"

"Why not?"

Marlowe hopped up to the cart, clinging onto the side, fiddling with the large padlock.

"I could pick this if I had enough time..."

Suddenly the eyes of one of the slaves, a man, sprang open. His cheeks were covered in dirt, his skin was grey in the moonlight and his gaze, which he turned first on Kyla and then Marlowe, was wild and frightened.

There was a short moment where they all looked at one another, shock and fear bouncing between them, and just as Kyla was about to motion to the man to stay silent, he looked sideways, eyes widening in alarm.

"Watch out!" he yelled.

One of the slavers was coming out from between the trees across the clearing. Something, too fast to see, flew through the air. With a thump, an arrow impaled itself into the wood of the cart, right next to Marlowe, who sprang backwards onto the ground beside Kyla.

The slaver held a bow and arrow in his hands. He stared at them, nocked another arrow in the bow and continued to march towards them, all the while shouting to the other slavers.

"Moriyan soldiers! Moriyan soldiers!"

Max, awake now too, looked around frantically, searching for the source of the noise. His gaze came to light upon Kyla, and for a brief moment their eyes locked. But before she could communicate anything more than her presence, Marlowe's fingers wrapped about her arm and pulled her away only seconds before another arrow sailed towards them, flying through the bars of the cage and lodging into the boot of one of the slaves, who wailed in agony, clutching at his foot.

Men were shifting in the darkness around them, closing in. The archer had another arrow poised and ready, and with each step he came closer to his targets. There was nothing to do but run. Marlowe's hand was tight about her own as they crashed through the woods, breaking through the lower branches, raising their arms to protect their faces.

Kyla's heart was thumping, its pounding punctuating the noise of the slavers as they shouted to one another, their boots thundering through the undergrowth, breaking branches and crunching leaves as they ran to catch up.

They ran and ran, Kyla wasn't sure how long, but by the time they stopped, they could no longer hear the voices behind them. The men had given up. Kyla was dizzy with exhaustion. She stopped, laid a hand against the trunk of a nearby tree, leant into it and took a few deep breaths.

"I think we've lost them," she said.

Marlowe cursed and dragged both his hands through his hair, holding his fingers tense against his scalp for a moment. He let out a wild groan. "We've also lost Valora."

"We'll find them. We need to head west. That's where they were going. When the sun rises we'll know which way to go."

They had rested only briefly, but it was sunset the following day by the time they came to the edge of the forest and had a view across grassy plains to a city in the distance.

"Turlento. It must be. It's the largest port on the western shore," Marlowe said, his eyes lighting up as some realisation dawned on him. "It's the city with the largest slave market in all of Tolinaye. That's where they're headed!"

Kyla nodded. She had heard of the slave market at Turlento. It had a reputation for attracting unwholesome characters.

"That haze in the background..."

"The sea. The Half-Sewn Sea."

Kyla had never seen the sea, but she had heard of it in the stories Aida used to tell her. A memory, of balmy afternoons back in Moriya, seated with her cousin Leanna beneath a shady tree, drifted back to her. She could see Aida as she was then, her face swollen with pomposity as she paced back and forth, thrusting her arms in the air, enacting some long-forgotten battle as she regaled them with tales of foreign lands beyond the Half-Sewn Sea.

Aida was Princess Leanna's nursemaid and the woman who had accompanied Kyla's mother, Virien, and the Queen across the Half-Sewn Sea from Varo to Tolinaye, when they were delivered as peace offerings to be married to the King and Lander Tarthwen. Kyla felt strangely overwhelmed at the thought of reaching the city where her mother must have come into port all those years ago.

"Let's go," Marlowe said.

As much as she admired his determination, Kyla wasn't sure continuing when they had barely slept and eaten only nuts and berries, along with a few foraged mushrooms that Marlowe assured her weren't poisonous, was a good idea. "Now? It's going to be dark soon."

Marlowe looked up at the sky. "No clouds. It'll be a clear night and we'll be out in the open. It'll be easy enough. Besides, we'll be a long way behind the cart already. We need to know where they are. If we don't get there in time, they'll have sold Max and Valora on, and then we'll never find them."

Kyla, although she was exhausted, didn't object, and they began the long walk towards the distant city.

The sun was only just beginning to rise as they passed through the gates alongside market vendors carrying their wares. Sounds of a city waking filled the air: horses' hooves clipping against stone, men and women shouting to one another, the rattle of carts, the rumble of wheels on stone. The air smelt like human endeavour, the bitter reek of sweat coated in freshly baked bread. It made Kyla think of home and she longed to be back in Moriya, down at the alley market bargaining for a loaf or a cut of fresh pork.

She longed, most of all, for a bed to sleep in.

Great seagulls squawked in the air overhead, their strangled calls unlike any sound Kyla had heard before. They were far smaller than Nilari birds, but just as loud.

She could smell the sea. Or at least what she thought was the sea. Salt sparked in her nostrils and dried her tongue. Beyond the hum of the market, the buzz of vendors setting up their stalls, was the rhythmic wash of waves.

Marlowe snatched an apple from a stall, in a movement that was spectacularly slick, and bit into it.

"Did you steal that?" Kyla snapped before she turned back, fished into Edmund's coin purse, and pulled out a small copper coin to pay for the apple.

The vendor, who obviously hadn't even noticed Marlowe's theft, blinked at her in confusion but she forced the coin into his hand anyway.

"Want me to put my order in with you instead? So you can buy my food for me?" Marlowe raised an eyebrow and Kyla was about to tell him that yes, he ought to do exactly that if he had no money of his own, when he raised his other hand, now holding a large piece of dried meat. He grinned at her as she looked around, trying to work out where he had swiped it from. Then he bit into it and held it out to her.

"Go on," he said, his mouth full. "Admit it, you're starving."

She nodded, but didn't take it from him, and stopped instead to buy bread from a stall they were passing.

She split the bread and gave half of it to Marlowe. Kyla ate ravenously, feeling the strength seep back into her bones.

As they paced the winding streets of the city, they drifted into an amiable silence, each letting the movement of their body fall in time with the other's. Kyla was surprised to find that she was comfortable in his company and, for the moment at least, she was glad to have him as an ally, although the unease at not knowing the whereabouts of Max and Valora never left her.

"Know where we're headed?" she asked.

"The docks. That's where the slave auction is. At least, that's what I've heard."

"Let's ask someone where it is," Kyla said.

Marlowe shook his head. "No. Enough people keep looking at you as it is. Someone's going to recognise you, and then word will get to those traders, wherever they are. They saw you." Marlowe looked her up and down, his eyes narrowing. "It's the uniform. It's so... red. I think you should lose it. Get rid of that cloak and those trousers, those military boots. Then you'd be just like any other woman."

Just like any other woman. What did that even mean? What did it mean to *Marlowe*? Had there been a flirtatious lilt as he had said the words? Or had she imagined it?

Kyla felt heat rush to her cheeks and willed it to cool. "That doesn't sound good to me."

Marlowe, unexpectedly, winked. "It sounds good to me."

Kyla felt a bizarre flutter in her heart, swiftly followed by a wave of outrage. So she hadn't imagined it. He *was* flirting with her. Was it possible, too, that she had actually, briefly, enjoyed it? "A Moriyan uniform is a symbol of—"

"Tyranny?"

Kyla inhaled sharply. How dare he speak that way about the Moriyan army? She turned to reprimand him, only to find him smiling at her, his eyes bright, his lips pressed together to hold back laughter.

"Is something amusing you?"

"Oh no. Not at all. Not in any way. No. Absolutely not."

Still he smiled, and Kyla felt a cloud of confusion descend around her. "Don't talk that way about my uniform then. It's disrespectful. Moriya is the home of the God-Sage. The Moriyan army are the soldiers of the God-Sage. This uniform is a sign of divine blessing, not tyranny."

Marlowe's smile disappeared. "You don't know me at all, do you?"

Kyla looked away. Her first thought was that she had somehow disappointed him, her second that she didn't know why. And the third was a rush of anger that took her unawares, flaring through her. She swung back to face him. "Why do I need to know you? You're the brother of the acolyte. I don't need to know more than that." She pointed her finger in his face. "But I'll tell you what I do know. You smiling like that, like we're sharing some kind of joke, pretending you haven't just insulted the most important thing in the world to me, it's..."

She struggled to think of the right word, and in the hiatus Marlowe blew out an exhalation. "Woah." For a second Kyla thought he was about to apologise, and then, more quietly, he said, "Your uniform is the most important thing in the world to you?"

She shook her head, not as an answer to his question, but to let him know that she didn't think him worthy of her conversation, not on this topic at least. She kept her gaze straight ahead, and they walked side by side in silence for a few moments.

Marlowe took another bite of the piece of dried meat, and then, his mouth still full, said, "You're not entirely what I expected."

Kyla felt something twist between her heart and her stomach. She kept her eyes low, wanting to ignore him, but the desire to know what he thought overwhelmed her. "What did you expect?"

Marlowe paused, his upper lip bulging where he was using his tongue to unstick something caught between his teeth. When he had finished, he said, "I expected you to be more like your father."

"Did you expect me to kill you?"

He laughed, a low and pleasant sound. "Actually, yes. I'm continually surprised that you haven't."

Kyla, unable to stop herself, laughed in response. "I still might."

But Marlowe shared none of her amusement, and he turned the full force of his gaze on her. His eyes narrowed. "I don't think you've ever killed someone."

And with those few short words Kyla felt as though he had hollowed out her insides. She huffed, puffed her chest, tried to seem affronted. "Well, no, I…"

His eyes were serious, scanning her face for some sign of the answer he wanted. Tension creased his brows and Kyla realised he wasn't merely gossiping or being intrusive. He was seeking some kind of comfort, some reassurance that he wasn't alone.

"And you have?" she said.

Marlowe glanced briefly at the pale rust-coloured stains on his shirt. The blood he had never explained. The flick of his eyes to his shirt was so quick Kyla almost missed it, but she knew from the expression on his face, as if he had been caught and might suffer the consequences, that he had taken a life.

"Sometimes you have to. When it's you or them."

Kyla said nothing. She didn't want more details; if he confessed explicitly, she would be obliged to hand him over to the Sacred Core when they reached Moriya, so that they could exact the punishment for taking a human life.

Marlowe kept his head down. Shadows lanced his cheekbones.

Kyla felt the strangest desire to do something, anything, to make him smile, as though a smile might somehow undo all of the grief he had suffered, all of the pain her own father had inflicted on him. It felt like a bubble within that threatened to burst if she didn't act on it.

She shook herself. It wasn't up to her to make him feel better, or to apologise for her father's actions. Or to forgive him for killing a man, or a Nilari bird for that matter. The God-Sage would judge him, when the time was right. Besides, Marlowe's parents were traitors and, harsh though the punishment was, they deserved it.

She kept walking, indicating that Marlowe should follow her, but when she looked round she realised he wasn't following her at all. Instead he had stopped, taken off his bloody shirt, thrown it to the ground where it lay in a heap at his feet, and was pulling a clean one from a low-slung washing line that hung between the buildings on either side of the street.

Kyla stared, and he flashed a smile that she found totally disarming. For a moment she was too stunned to move, aware only of the rapid beating of her heart.

He pulled the fresh shirt over his head and tugged on the bottom of it, pulling it tight for her inspection.

"How's this?" he said.

And then, "Hey, thief, hey!"

A woman was leaning from the window, pointing at Marlowe, who looked up and turned his glorious smile on her. The woman paused, momentarily taken aback by the sight of such a handsome face looking up at her. Marlowe performed an elaborate bow.

"Thank you for the fine shirt," he said.

The woman shook a fist, her fat arm jiggling in rhythm as she said, "Why, you cheeky little..."

Marlowe began to run, laughing all the while. As he passed her he grabbed Kyla's hand and together they dashed through the streets, the woman's calls of 'thief, thief' growing ever fainter, until they could no longer hear it.

They turned a corner and the narrow street opened out onto a wide vista of the sea. All of a sudden it was there, brisk and salty, washing against the walls below. They must have climbed steadily, for now they were far above the waves.

The sight left Kyla choked and breathless. The horizon was long and straight where sea clashed with sky, and the sun sprinkled the water with flashes of light. She hadn't stood at such a distance from the ground since she had last visited Gregor, up in the Star Tower back at Moriya. She had missed the elation that came with being so high, and without stopping to think, she hopped up and swung her legs over the sea-side of the wall. In that brief but glorious moment, the warmth of the sun striking her cheeks, she allowed herself to forget everything else.

Marlowe didn't climb up, but stayed street-side. He propped his elbows on the wall and looked out. "Get down. Look how high we are."

She turned a questioning gaze on him and raised an eyebrow. "Are you frightened?"

He shook his head, but his eyes were wide with alarm. She was tempted to tease him, as he had teased her, but instead she offered him her hand, and when she spoke her voice was more inviting than she had expected it to be. "You might never see the sea again."

Marlowe held her gaze a fraction of a second too long, searching for something, but what, Kyla had no idea. He looked away before she could tell if he had found it. "We need to get to the docks," he said. "They could be setting up the auction any minute now."

Kyla stretched her arm towards him, still offering her hand. "You'll be able to see them from up here. We can work out where we are, and how to get there."

A furrow formed between his brows as he considered his options, and then he nodded. He waved her hand away and pulled himself up onto the wall, hanging his legs over the edge. The movement was bold and fast, but his fingers clutched at the stone beneath him, betraying his fear.

Kyla glanced at him, taking in the distance he sat from her, wondering if she dared get closer to him, and then wondering why she even wanted to.

Marlowe nodded across the sea. "Maybe we could escape. Steal a boat and sail away."

"That's a terrible plan. I'm not escaping from anything. I'm going home. And you're coming with me."

Marlowe was quiet, and Kyla listened to the beat of the waves and watched the white foam smash against the rocks far beneath her feet. She began to count the crashes... one, two, three, four...

"I don't see the docks. We need to head back down." Marlowe swung his legs back over the wall and stepped down onto the street, taking a few steps towards where Kyla sat. She had her back to him, but she could feel his increasing proximity as if each of his steps squeezed more air from her lungs. She kept her gaze on the horizon, but when he spoke he was so close she felt his breath on her skin.

"Can I ask you something?" he whispered.

Her voice was soft, almost yielding, when she answered. "Maybe."

"Will you tell me about your scars?"

A prickle of uneasy heat rushed over her skin. "No."

She brought her legs up and stepped up on the wall. She walked along it slowly, placing one foot carefully in front of the other, arms stretched out to either side for balance.

Marlowe looked up at her, then out at the sea and then back to her again. "You're making me nervous."

She stared out at the water, listening to the gulls swooping overhead. "Do you care if I fall?"

"Not really."

Kyla turned to face him, looking down from her much higher vantage point on top of the wall.

Then she took a step towards where he stood, her foot hovering in midair for a moment before she dropped right down before him.

"What the—" Marlowe exclaimed, but he put his arms out, instinctively, and grabbed her as she fell.

Kyla felt her boots hit the ground, but it was Marlowe's hands around her waist, on her hips, that she was most aware of.

They stood like that for a moment, longer than necessary, his hands on her hips, moving softly, as if his fingers dared not hold on too long. His eyes, at first shocked, were now calm, still, and darker than any eyes Kyla had looked so long at. She felt a strange heat rising through her body, pleasurable and uncomfortable all at once, and shifted away, out of his embrace.

"We should go," she said, shattering the intimacy that had been created between them.

Marlowe nodded, taking a step back himself and brushing his hands down on his trousers. "We should hurry."

9

— · —

KYLA

THE CITY OF TURLENTO

By the time they reached the port, it was thronging with people. Boats were moored, hulls gently thumping the jetties to the beat of the sea. The tang of salt was sharp in the air, the sound of seagulls piercing.

From their elevated approach, running down a narrow cobbled street that opened out to the sea view, Kyla could see a raised wooden platform set up near the water, a little apart from the boats.

"This is it." Marlowe pointed to a man in a blue tunic and loose trousers, who was marching back and forth across the platform, waving his arms dramatically. He was too far away for them to hear exactly what he was saying, but it was clear he was rallying the crowd.

The audience was mostly men, a mixture of sailors and off-duty soldiers, peasants in dirty clothes and nobles, robed in velvet and satin. There were a few children too, bare-footed and dirty, scarpering through the crowd. Near the front sat a group of old women with wrinkled faces and hardly any teeth between them, but they were smiling nonetheless, eagerly anticipating the action.

"There!" Marlowe clutched Kyla's arm with one hand and pointed to the stage with the other, where three cages were set up, each containing several people.

In one of them Kyla could clearly see Max's red uniform, and next to him the small huddled form of Valora in her grey dress. Off to one side of the erected stage were more cages, more slaves, and other traders who had come from all over Tolinaye, their carts lined up along the port-side. Some of the carts displayed sigils from the various major cities throughout the country, and Kyla even thought she could see one from Moriya itself.

"Look." She nudged Marlowe and pointed at the image of the God-Sage on the side of the Moriyan cart. "Maybe they'll help us."

"It's probably stolen." Marlowe was right. Someone had gouged a knife though the image of the God-Sage and carved the words *death to all Moriyans* in the middle. "No one's going to help you here. People come for the bargains. Stolen women. Children. Men from across the seas. It's about the show, the entertainment. Why are you looking at me like that?"

Kyla shifted and lowered her gaze, feeling oddly guilty that he had caught the look of confusion on her face. Why was he so conversant on the topic of the illegal slave trade?

Marlowe sighed. "When we were banished to the slums, you know, after our parents were executed..." His eyes slid away, briefly drawn inward to the painful memory. "I saw the markets first hand there."

Before she could ask any further questions Marlowe had moved, ducked down and pulled her with him, crouching behind one of the carts. His mouth fell slightly open as he tilted his head to look upwards. His gaze darted back and forth across the sky, watching something overhead.

There was a flutter of wings followed by a loud caw. A Nilari bird was circling up above. It was the first Kyla had seen in Turlento, which, unlike Moriya, seemed to be dominated by seagulls instead. Why, then, was there a single bird here, by the sea?

Marlowe was still staring up. Kyla noticed that his breathing was faster, and his whole body had taken on a rigid alertness, which she felt a need to pacify. "It won't attack us, not here."

Marlowe lowered his gaze and nodded, slowly. "Yes. You're right."

She hadn't realised the birds had struck such fear into him. Just as she was pondering if there could be some other, more sinister reason for his fear, the scent of feather-dust, acrid and mildly unpleasant, drifted from the crowd. Who here dared to smoke feather dust out in the open?

Marlowe sniffed. "Illegal trade auctions attract all sorts."

Kyla searched the air for the distinctive blue smoke. At first she saw nothing, but then it caught her eye. A slow curl of smoke, blue and quickly dispersing, rose from a pipe held by a man dressed exclusively in black, who stood almost a head taller than everyone else. His cloak was of thick velvet with a fur trim, beneath which he wore a short jacket of black leather. He was dressed for winter and he must have been sweltering, yet he showed no sign that he had even broken a sweat.

Around his neck he wore a chain of silver wings.

Recognition hit Kyla like an arrow to the heart. It was the same Nilari rebel she had seen at the riverside, back in Palantar. Yarmon Sacfron. Now that she was closer to him, she could see the fine detail of the tattoos that traced his cheeks, a feathered wing spread wide inked on each one. He was quite unlike the priests of the God-Sage in their pale, ethereal robes that Kyla was used to, and she understood why Verbun had taken such offence at sharing the title 'priest' with a man such as this.

What was he doing here? Nilari rebels were hunted all over Tolinaye by the Moriyan army, yet here was this man, in plain sight, not even bothering to disguise himself. And people were moving around him as though he was any other man! Outrage surged through Kyla's limbs. If he were to show himself this way in Moriya he would be strung up faster than he could run, but here no one paid him any attention.

His eyes were pale brown, almost yellow, but that wasn't the most remarkable thing about them. They were sharp and focused; his mind was alert. In Moriya, smoking feather dust tended to have the opposite effect. Or perhaps he had smoked so much of the stuff that he was immune to its power. Kyla quickly pulled back out of sight.

"There's a man out there. The one smoking. A Nilari rebel. The one from the funeral."

Marlowe peered round the cart. When he caught sight of Yarmon Sacfron his entire body jolted, but he tried to conceal it by immediately shifting position before he answered her. "I see him," he said. "Dressed as though he just crossed the northern mountains."

"Why do you think he's here?" asked Kyla.

Marlowe cursed under his breath. He looked uneasy as he said, "Same reason everyone is. Either for entertainment, or because he has money he wants to spend."

Kyla shook her head. Marlowe's tone was off. He was concealing something from her, but she sensed there was no point pressing him further. "It's a big coincidence though, isn't it? That he was at the river and now he's here? I don't like it. Not with the others coming up for sale."

Another voice cut through the buzz of the crowd. It was the man wearing the pale blue tunic, whom Kyla had noticed earlier storming across the stage rallying the crowd.

"Ladies and Gentlemen." There was a burst of laughter at the deferential address. "Thank you for joining us here tonight, at Turlento's most infamous auction. I, Atrimus Deegeld, have some very special offerings for you today. Oh yes. Very special." He smiled, rubbing his hands over one another, his eyes gleaming with greed. "Yes, we do indeed."

He was smaller in stature than the tenor of his voice suggested. He was thin and wiry, with hair that hung in greasy strands to his shoulders. His skin was dark with dirt, but his clothes were clean and fine. He was a man, Kyla imagined, who played two roles in life. He was a ruthless slave owner, but here, now, he was about to play auctioneer to the wealthy men in the crowd.

"He's Varoan," Kyla said. "I can hear it in his voice."

Marlowe nodded, the curl of his lip telling her he found the man repulsive. The crowd, however, held no such objections and began to roar, their appetites thoroughly whetted.

Atrimus strode to the other side of the stage, and it was then that Kyla noticed the roughly erected gallows, from which three nooses hung side-by-side. They were empty, but they dangled with the promise of death. The sight of them transported her back to Moriya, and the bodies that had hung in the square the day before her initiation ceremony.

Marlowe must have seen her staring, for he spoke in her ear. "If someone wants to pay a lot of money to see a particular person hang, they'll do it here. For the right price."

Kyla felt her stomach plummet. Rescuing Max and Valora was one thing, but preventing a hanging was another entirely.

Atrimus waited for the crowd to settle before he reached up and rested one hand in a noose. "And perhaps even a hanging or two," he added. The crowd roared in anticipation, feet stamping, arms punching the air overhead, demanding the auction begin.

First up was a young girl, sold as a kitchen serving maid, but bought by a man who looked like the local brothel owner, pompous and well fed, his purple coat made of a garish brushed-satin. The young girl squirmed as the man dragged her away. Kyla felt utterly powerless: it would be impossible to save all these people. Not even Edmund's coin purse would hold enough gold to buy every slave.

Yarmon Sacfron bought nothing and made no bids, but he smoked constantly and watched proceedings with narrowed eyes. He looked to be waiting for something, and a chill rippled through Kyla's veins.

Marlowe nudged her. "There." He pointed to where one of the slave traders was opening a cage and hauling someone out. Max. Kyla thought she caught a glimpse of Valora before the cage was locked again, but she was swallowed up by the other slaves, who swarmed to the front to get a better view.

Max's Moriyan uniform was such an unexpected sight that the crowd gasped in unison. Someone near the back threw an apple, but it didn't reach the platform, and a woman yelped as it struck the back of her head. It rolled to the ground and a scavenging child sprang upon it, picked it up and bit into it in one smooth movement.

"Here we have a Moriyan soldier. Highly trained. One of the elite. We start the bidding at five gold tucks."

No one moved. Then Yarmon stepped forward. "And what if the wrath of Moriya falls on us for this purchase?"

"Wrath of Moriya's going to fall on *you* anyway," someone shouted, and a few people laughed.

Atrimus tilted his head and considered the question. Then he reached forward, grabbed Max's tunic and tried to yank it, as if hoping to tear it. Max, a panicked look on his face, pushed him away.

"Ooh, he's a feisty one." Atrimus laughed nervously and turned back to Yarmon. "Someone like you, Sir, a believer and worshipper of the Nilari race, I see, would no doubt take great pleasure in owning a Moriyan soldier. Think what you could do with such a prize, Sir."

Yarmon crossed his arms. "And how do we know you haven't just dressed him up to sell?"

Atrimus prodded Max in the back. "Where are you from?"

Max stumbled forward a step, but he was gagged, a dirty piece of fabric tied around his mouth. Atrimus yanked it out.

Max gasped. "Moriya."

Atrimus fixed the gag back over Max's mouth.

Yarmon laughed and the wings on his cheeks appeared to flutter. "Hardly convincing. A bit of berry juice would turn any pair of trousers red."

"Death to all Moriyans," shouted a voice from the back.

"Hang the Moriyan," shouted another.

Max's eyes opened wider, alarmed and fearful.

Atrimus raised his hands in the air and smiled as though he was offering the greatest gift of all. "Pay up and you can see him hang!"

Someone at the front spat at Max's feet. Max backed away and the crowd began to shout and jeer, calling for his death.

"Five tucks for this one." Atrimus pointed to Max. "Ten to see him hang."

Yarmon had refilled his pipe and the smoke was thicker and darker this time. It sank in the air when the man exhaled and obscured the faces of those who stood nearby.

"Eleven, for the soldier," he said.

Atrimus' arm paused mid-gesticulation, hovering over his head. His brow creased in mock-confusion. "You mean you don't want a hanging this week, Sir?"

"I could use a soldier."

"But surely, Sir, a man such as yourself, to have travelled all the way from..." Atrimus' face went blank and he hurried to continue. "Wherever you have come from... Surely you want something to speak of when you get home?" He waved his arms, rolling his wrists theatrically. "A spectacle. A little entertainment?"

The crowd babbled in agreement.

Yarmon shook his head. "I would rather something to show for my money."

A woman, dressed in orange velvet she looked to have borrowed from someone half her girth, bowled her way through the crowd until she was right at the front, her chin almost resting on the platform. Standing beside Yarmon, who was taller and more elegant, the little woman looked positively rotund.

"Twelve gold tucks, to see him hang," she said.

A roar of appreciation went up like a flame, but Atrimus was calm as he looked to the competition.

"Have you any advance on that, Sir?"

Yarmon nodded, and the feather in his velvet cap bobbed. "Thirteen."

"Fourteen, to hang," shouted the woman.

Kyla's heart sank. It was too much. No one would pay more than fourteen gold tucks to save a stranger, let alone a Moriyan stranger.

Yarmon waved a hand in a gesture that said he was done, and would bid no more. The woman climbed the platform and extracted a leather pouch that hung on a thong between her breasts. She rattled it vulgarly and smiled, revealing a mouth with wide-spaced teeth.

Max looked around, as though hoping to find someone in that hostile crowd who might save him. Two men took Max's hands behind him and bound them. He struggled but could not overpower them. Muffled curses came from beneath the gag.

The men dragged Max across the platform until he stood beneath the noose. With a flick and tug they forced his head down and fixed the rope around his neck.

Kyla's body tingled with an urgent fear. "We have to do something." She moved forward but strong hands pulled her back. Marlowe.

He clasped her tight to him, his body warm through his shirt. "Stop. What are you going to—"

She shook him off. "They're going to kill him."

She forced her way through several more rows of observers, who looked at her at first with irritation and then, when they noted her red uniform, her indisputably Moriyan cloak, with surprise. Marlowe followed in her wake. She could feel him tugging at her cloak, trying to hold her back.

"Kyla, this is madness—"

She stopped, swung round to face him. He was so close to her, the two of them crushed together in the crowd, that she could feel his body against hers. She could smell the scent of him; musk, sweat and earth. She shoved him away.

"If you aren't going to help me, then go."

He stumbled backwards and Kyla noted a flash of confusion in his eyes as he looked at her before he was engulfed by the crowd. People pushed back at him, irritated at the sudden weight of his body crashing into them. Leaving him arguing with those nearest, Kyla turned and shoved through the heaving mass of bodies. She was near the front now, approaching the stage.

The countdown to Max's death had begun. Two men were forcing him up onto a wooden stool, the noose already looped about his neck. Any moment now they would kick the stool from under him and Max would fall. And then she would have... how long? One minute? Two? How long would it take for Max to die?

Her heart hammered against her ribs and her thoughts were rampaging wildly through her mind. She could make no sense of them, but she knew she had to do something.

Gold! There was still plenty of gold in Edmund's coin pouch. She could buy Max!

"Wait!" she shouted. But as soon as the word was out of her mouth, she realised the weight of the coin purse had gone. She reached for it, finding nothing but the frayed ends of the thong that had attached it to her belt. All that hung there now was the pouch containing Valora's herbs.

People had turned to look in her direction, and those nearest her were moving away, clearing a path from her to the raised platform, where Max, his eyes nervous, his legs visibly shaking, still stood with his head in a noose.

She had no money but it was too late to turn back. She couldn't hide, not now, and especially not dressed as she was in the glaring red of her Moriyan uniform. She was close enough to the stage to mount the steps, which she did without hesitation, her sword clinking as she went.

Atrimus turned to her. "Hold up, wait here... What's this?"

Kyla planted her feet on the stage, legs apart. "I'm Kyla Tarthwen, of the Moriyan army."

There were a few gasps, a few titters of laughter from the crowd, but most people were silent, watching. Kyla's heart thumped so hard in her chest she was surprised that the sound wasn't booming out like a drum.

"And I'm the God-Sage." Atrimus, a skeptical grin on his face, flourished his hand before him and doubled over into a bow.

There was genuine laughter now, rippling through the crowd.

Kyla looked at Max. She could see the worry in his eyes, the fear that he was about to die. Worse still, she sensed that any faith Max had that she might be able to save him was draining away as the laughter of the crowd grew louder.

"I command you to take him down." It was hard to maintain her dignity given the jeers coming from the crowd behind her.

"My dear," said Atrimus, one thin, hairless eyebrow arching over a dark eye. "That's not how this works. As much as I respect your uniform—" Atrimus paused to pull a face over his shoulder for the benefit of the crowd, who howled with united laughter. "—we're many moons from Moriya, and it doesn't look like you have any backup. So if you don't want to become part of the act, I suggest you leave. Unless of course, you happen to have an awful lot of gold." He paused, stroked his chin. "Do you have gold?"

The crowd had begun to jeer again, calling for Max's death. He tottered on the stool, his hands tied before him, beneath the makeshift gallows, rabid panic in his eyes. Kyla looked away. What if she couldn't save him? If her uniform, her name, wasn't enough to stop this, what options did she have? She glanced around, searching for inspiration.

Coins clinked onto the stage. "Here, here."

It was the woman in orange, throwing more coins from her purse at Atriums' feet. "I have more if you want to string her up beside him."

The woman reached out for Kyla's cloak, taking hold of it, and Kyla tugged it away. Would they string her up with Max? There was a noose hanging there, empty, waiting.

Panic roared loud in her ears and she shouted to drown it out. "I am a soldier of the Moriyan army! I command you to stop this!"

"Moriya, Moriya, Moriya." Atrimus flicked his wrist, dismissing the entire city with the motion. "We're not in Moriya now, dear." He turned his attention to the crowd and threw his arms wide. "What shall we do with her?"

"Hang her, hang her," began the chanting.

Kyla thought her uniform, her name, might have been enough to stop the shouting, but it wasn't. There was one last thing she could do... She drew her sword.

For a moment there was silence, a breath of quiet, and then more laughter, jeering, shouting.

The sword made no difference.

Still they laughed.

One of the guards approached her, a cruel grin across his lips. His intent was written on his face: he would string her up in an instant and delight in doing so. In her peripheral vision she could see other men creeping towards her. She was penned in.

The first man took one step closer, and Kyla swung her sword. For a brief second she thought she would kill him, but he managed to raise his forearm to parry the blow. Skin and flesh parted, and blood ran from his elbow to his wrist, dripping from his fingers. His scream of pain silenced the giggles from the crowd, and Kyla was glad of it. He scuttled from the stage, clutching his arm, and disappeared.

Suddenly a huge guard, the one who had been watching Valora, stepped up and grasped Kyla's arm. She felt his fingers begin to crush her elbow. He had enough strength to break the joint with his fist, she was sure of it. She held the sword as long as she could, but eventually she had to drop it, letting it clatter to the ground.

The guard grabbed Kyla's arms, holding them behind her back, and Atrimus himself picked up the sword and twirled it in the air, feigning admiration for the blade. The crowd laughed at his antics.

Suddenly he held the sword very still, blade vertical before his face, and then peeped around it, playing the comedian. "Who'll pay to see her hang?"

More coins were thrown onto the stage. Atrimus began to pick them up, pocketing the gold and silver, but when he inspected the smaller lower value ones, the tiny bronze ones, his face contorted with mock disgust.

"You'll have to do better than that!"

Another spatter of coins flew from the crowd and hit the stage. The woman in orange emptied her bag of silver too, letting the coins fall and roll around Atrimus' feet, but still he paraded across the stage.

"I can't hang a Moriyan soldier for this!" Atrimus gestured to the coins that were clinking onto the stage. "Lander Tarthwen's daughter?" He smiled at Kyla and his lips split apart, showing two missing teeth. "Oh, yes, we all know who you are! Lander Tarthwen! He'll have my head on a pike, my balls on a pyre." He waved his arms in the air at the crowd, as if they were flames he could fan. "You've got to make it worth my while, ladies and gentlemen. Gold, I need gold! Who will pay gold to see her hang?"

Kyla's heart was racing. She tried to pull against the guard who pinned her arms, but there was no point. She could never resist his strength. He was huge. Without her sword she was helpless.

She looked at Max, visibly shaking, the noose around his neck. What hope was there? She searched the crowd for Marlowe, but couldn't see him anywhere.

Someone threw a bag of coins onto the platform. "Hang them."

More coins followed, and Kyla covered her head with her arms as copper and silver rained down around her. The crowd began to throb, their energy pulsing like a living creature. Kyla could feel it through her feet, and up her entire body.

"Come on! Do you want to see her hang or not?"

A violent roar pounded across the docks as the crowd screamed their agreement.

Atrimus smiled broadly. It was sickening. "I will endeavour to give you what you wish, but I need more gold. Who has gold?"

A moment of silence. Then, "I do."

The voice was loud. A man, dark hair, tall, was forcing his way to the front. People were moving out of the way.

He held up a coin purse. "I have gold."

Strangely, it was the purse Kyla recognised first. It was Edmund's. She looked again at the man holding it and cursed under her breath. Marlowe. When had he taken it from her?

He stood there, holding the stolen purse aloft. Kyla knew there was more in Edmund's purse than any of these people would have put together. More gold in that one purse than everything else that had already been thrown onto the stage, but what difference would it make, now the crowd were set upon an execution?

"Hang them, hang them, hang them." The chant rose from the crowd like an angered beast. Nauseous panic roiled in Kyla's stomach as she realised there was no way Atrimus would, or *could*, deny so powerful a demand.

"You, Sir." Atrimus flailed a floppy hand in Marlowe's direction. "What do you have?"

"Enough," said Marlowe.

There was a strange smile on Marlowe's face, and Kyla stared in confusion, waiting for him to give some sign that he was joking, that this was part of some grand plan to save her and Max. That perhaps, despite the vehemence of the crowd, he meant to use the gold to buy them, rather than kill them.

Marlowe didn't look at her, but kept moving forward, holding the coin purse high in the air. He shook it, and the sound let everyone know it was full of metal.

Marlowe was on the steps now, mounting the stage. He paused to tease open the purse, prising a single gold coin through its still-tight neck.

He approached Atrimus, holding the purse open for the man to peer into. "There's more." Atrimus licked his lips, keeping his gaze on the money as Marlowe continued speaking. "It's all yours, every last gold tuck I have on my person—"

Atrimus bent towards him, one eyebrow quirked upwards. "Yes?"

"If you allow me to kill them myself."

Kyla spluttered and choked as if Marlowe had squeezed his hands around her throat. Had she heard him correctly?

Atrimus' face seemed to elongate as his eyebrows rose and his mouth hung open. "That's somewhat irregular but—"

Marlowe made an elaborate show of intending to pocket the money. "If you don't want it—"

The crowd screamed and Atrimus' hand shot towards the purse. "No, no. Sir. Wait. Of course you can. Of course."

Marlowe dangled the purse, almost dropped it into Atrimus' hand, and then snatched it back. "I want to do it myself."

"Yes, yes, I said yes..." Atrimus was still holding his hands out for the coin purse.

A cold unease was spreading down Kyla's neck, through her chest. She remembered the hatred in Marlowe's eyes when he had first seen her, the grief in Valora's face after the branding, the way Marlowe had screamed when he had been dragged to the cells.

Suddenly she remembered his words out in the forest. *I'll kill you, I swear, as soon as your back is turned, I'll—*

A wave of comprehension flooded her. He loathed her. He had every reason to want to kill her, and none to keep her alive. All this time, his smiles, his teasing... He had been playing her, waiting for his moment to strike.

"I want to do it with the sword. Not the noose." Marlowe pointed to Kyla's own sword, the one that Atrimus was still holding.

The crowd, at least those at the front who could hear what was being said, began to thump on the stage with clenched fists, stamp their feet, shout for it.

"The sword, the sword, the sword..."

Atrimus looked around nervously, as if searching for some kind of authority figure that might punish him if he allowed Marlowe to do what he asked. "Err, we're really not set up, that's really beyond what..."

Again, Marlowe made to put the coins away.

"Wait, wait, I am sure we can do it."

Atrimus made a few hand gestures, waving to a few of his men, and they began to scuttle about. One rolled a barrel up the steps and onto the stage until he stood before Kyla. Then he tipped the barrel upright so that it stood on one end and stepped back, so as not to block the crowd's view of her.

Atrimus handed the sword to Marlowe, who took the hilt in his hand, bounced his arm up and down slightly, feeling the weight of the sword. Kyla stared at him, willing him to look at her, to provide some kind of reassurance, but he didn't.

She studied the serious expression on his face, the tension in his jaw... hoping to find some small sign that he didn't mean to kill her. But she found none.

"Wait," she said. "No, stop, Marlowe—"

Atrimus, on hearing a name, paused and gave a low whistle. "You know each other?"

Marlowe looked up at her, but his eyes were dead. Kyla searched them for some hint of his personality, some spark of recognition she could latch onto, but found nothing. It was as though he didn't even see her, as if all the time they had spent together ceased to exist, and she was once more just a soldier. A uniform.

"What is this? Some lovers' tiff?" Atrimus was goading the crowd further. They yelled and clapped in response.

Marlowe's voice cut through the laughter. "Her father killed my parents."

A chill blasted through Kyla. He meant to do it. Marlowe was going to kill her.

"Well, all right then." Atrimus clapped his hands and then gestured to the large man still holding Kyla. "Bind her hands."

Another came forward with a coil of rope.

"No, no." Marlowe held up one hand. "I prefer her free, but powerless."

Someone far back in the crowd jeered. Atrimus raised an eyebrow and swept a hand, palm-upwards, through the air in front of him. "As you wish."

The man with the rope stepped back.

Atrimus held out his hand for the coin purse. "Let's see what you've got."

Marlowe plopped it into his waiting palm, and he opened it up, peered inside and poked through it with one finger to count the coins. His eyes grew wide. He'd probably never seen so much gold in one coin purse.

"Why, sir. How generous. You must really—"

"Get on with it." Marlowe swiped the sword through the air, once, twice, as though testing it. He walked the few paces towards Max, who stood on the stool, his mouth bound and gagged. Some muffled, desperate sounds came from Max's direction, but Marlowe paid no heed. He pointed the sword at him instead. "Hang him first."

"Right, as you wish, Sir." Atrimus nodded towards a guard who was standing at the edge of the stage. The guard kicked the stool beneath Max with his dirt-crusted boot, and Kyla saw Max drop, the loose rope over his head snapping taut.

"No, No!" Kyla screamed. She struggled, tried to free herself, but could do nothing against the man who held her. He was too big, too strong.

Max was going to die, and she was forced to watch, completely powerless. Just as Marlowe wanted her.

The crowd was roaring, screaming, yelling for the fall of Moriya, for the death of all Moriyans.

Kyla felt a huge hand, fingers splayed, press against the back of her skull. The guard forced her head down on top of the barrel that had been set up before her. She could see Max, his legs kicking the empty air. She yelled, tried to move, but it was no use.

Her legs were trembling, but she swore she would not collapse. She would not fall to her knees. Behind her, the guard pinned her in place, one of his large hands on her back.

She could do nothing but breathe her last shaking breaths. There, suddenly, was Marlowe, standing at her side. She held his gaze, and spoke as loudly as she could.

"May the God-Sage damn you to the dead world."

The guard slammed her head against the barrel, and pain shot from her temple all around her skull.

Her vision blurred, but she could still see Marlowe, who tilted his head in silent acknowledgment of her curse, and raised the sword. The crowd began to settle, their jeers and shouting grew dim.

Kyla closed her eyes, knowing that in moments she would feel nothing. All of this, everything, would be over.

She waited, but the moment was too long. Longer than she'd prayed for, and rather than the swish of the blade racing towards her neck, her body was shunted from behind, crushed between the barrel and the guard holding her. She felt the weight of him against her, and then it lifted. He had released her! She heard him step back.

No, he hadn't *stepped* back. He had stumbled.

The crowd broke out in screams. Chaos erupted on all sides. Kyla's stomach lurched. What had happened? Was it Marlowe? Was he dead?

She pushed herself off the barrel, only to see the guard who had held her moments before clutching his belly, blood running between his fingers. And something else... something pale, small and pointed protruded between his hands.

The tip of a sword.

He looked down at the blade where it had forced its way through his tunic. His mouth was wide, gaping, and he blinked as blood bubbled up over his lips. He had been run right through from back to belly.

He was dying.

It was then that Kyla saw Marlowe. He stepped towards her, appearing from behind the bulk of the stumbling guard. His face was grey, his hands empty, held out before him. He looked like a helpless child, caught breaking the rules.

She understood. Rather than use the sword to slice her head off, he had skewered the guard from behind, just as they had skewered that hare out on the plains.

Her heart exploded with relief, but fear raced behind.

The crowd, their darting, frightened eyes drawn to the dying guard and his murderer, began to surge like panicked pigs in a pen. Screams grew as they pushed and swarmed against one another, men trampling women, women trampling men, bones and bodies crushed alike.

It was only a matter of time before someone called for Marlowe's blood.

Kyla glanced at Max. His body was jerking, twisting on the rope. How long did it take someone to die from hanging? Suffocation? Three minutes?

She looked back at Marlowe. He was hovering behind the guard, trying to pull the sword out from where it was lodged near the spine, but the man was staggering around, and although Marlowe had his hands on the hilt, it was slippery with blood and he couldn't get the grip he needed. Then, still impaled on the sword, the man tottered backwards. Marlowe let go, dodging out of the way just in time.

People were screaming, but Kyla saw only the wounded man. Blood was running from his stomach, but he wasn't dying. Not fast enough. He swung back, his arms pounding the air, swinging uncontrolled.

Kyla leapt out of the way, but Marlowe didn't move. He was staring at the huge guard, who was turning, slowly, his boots in a puddle of his own blood. The red liquid poured from his mouth, and his slabs of hands reached out for Marlowe...

Kyla looked again at Max, whose body hung more limply than before, and then back at Marlowe. For a moment she was torn between the two of them. Then she moved, grabbing Marlowe, hauling him out of the way of the guard.

"Quick, help me," she said.

She ran towards Max, Marlowe following close behind. She knelt down, slid a knife from inside her boot and leapt up at the rope. "Grab him!"

Marlowe took hold of Max's legs, holding him up. Kyla worked at the rope with her knife, but it wasn't slicing through. Max was heavy, the noose still tight around his neck.

People were climbing on the stage, swirling around her. One man grabbed at her ankle, screaming for her blood, but she kicked out with her leg, only just managing to hold onto the rope above Max's head. Her foot slipped free and she thrust it forward, her boot colliding with the man's chin. The impact sent him flying backwards, knocking others behind him to the floor and falling on top of them himself. Beneath her Marlowe too was elbowing people away as he struggled to hold Max up.

Atrimus Deegeld was on his knees, scrabbling about for the coins, thrusting them in his pockets. "The gold, get the gold," he shouted at his men. "Forget them, forget them." He waved at Kyla and Marlowe. "Get the slaves and the gold!"

Kyla hacked at the rope again and relief swelled inside her as the rope split and Max's body fell, thumping into Marlowe's waiting arms. Marlowe staggered with the weight of it and Kyla fumbled to loosen the noose that was still around Max's neck.

The huge man was still stumbling about the stage, his hands around the blade where it poked through his stomach. He grabbed at Atrimus, leaving bloody swathes of fingerprints across his tunic.

Atrimus pushed him off and the man fell with a great thud onto the wood. People scattered, no one daring to get too close to him as he lay dying.

"Here, you take Max," Kyla shunted Max's weight to Marlowe, before dashing towards the huge man, who had fallen down face first. She placed one boot on his back to keep him in place and tugged the sword out. It was dripping with blood but she didn't wipe it, instead trailing droplets all over the stage. Men and women alike gasped and drew back, allowing her to pass back towards Marlowe and Max.

Max, his neck red and raw, was choking, coughing, and Marlowe was holding him.

"Come on, Max," urged Kyla. "We have to move."

Already people were pushing at them, grabbing at them. Kyla wasn't sure how they would make it through the thrust of the crowd that had become a vast swell of uncontrolled momentum. With Marlowe's help she hauled Max to his feet. With her other hand she swung her bloodied sword, threatening to slice anyone who got too close.

The sword was too heavy to wield one handed for long. "You need to hold Max alone." Without waiting to check Marlowe was ready to bear the weight of him, she let go of Max and took her sword in both hands.

"What about Valora?" Marlowe said. "We can't leave her."

Kyla looked around, taking in the rabid faces of the people thronging around them, baying for the blood they had been deprived of. If it hadn't been for the fact she was waving a sword, she was sure she, and Max and Marlowe too, would have been torn apart by the bare hands of the crowd.

She thrust her sword towards an aggressive looking man with a thick beard. He moved backwards and she took the moment of respite to shout across to Marlowe, "You killed a man. If we don't leave now, we won't make it."

Marlowe shot an uneasy glance over his shoulder, back towards where Valora had been. He didn't move, and for a moment Kyla thought he would forge back into the throng, and surely lose his life for it.

"There, there he is!" Atrimus' hoarse voice sounded surprisingly shrill as he rallied his guards. He was standing on the stage, pointing down at Marlowe. "Don't let him get away!"

The guards that had been scattered around the stage began to gather, their faces streaked with their friend's blood and grim with determination, forging one purposeful path through the crowd towards Marlowe, their curved swords raised in the air.

People began to scatter, but Marlowe stood like a rock, balanced on the precipice between risk and chance. Max still clung to him, his gaze shifting from the guards to Valora, trapped in the cage. Kyla was sure there was no chance of saving her, no chance of all of them leaving alive, if Marlowe turned back.

A look of unwavering focus crossed his face and Kyla realised he was going to throw his life away in a moment of impassioned rage. If she didn't do something now, he would die...

In the same moment he let go of Max and stepped towards the guards' waving swords.

Max stumbled and clutched at Kyla, a desperate look on his face. "Do something."

Kyla felt panic rip through her. She shrugged Max off and stepped between Marlowe and the guards, raising her sword and pointing it at Marlowe's chest. "Turn around, now. Or I'll run this right through you."

"Get out of my way," he said.

They locked eyes, and Kyla tried to still the wicked beating of her heart. If they stood here much longer, it wouldn't just be Marlowe who would die. Behind her she could head the roar of the guards. They were close.

She held her ground, her blade touching Marlowe's stained shirt. Just as she thought she had lost him his eyes flicked away from hers, drawn to the approaching guards over her shoulder. All at once his rage turned to fear, his shoulders dropped and he grabbed her, pulling her with him.

"Run."

10

Marlowe

The City of Turlento

Marlowe was numb. He was moving without thought, his body responding to some base survival instinct. He stumbled through the crowd, elbowing and shouldering people out of their path, pulling Max along with him. Kyla was yelling, screaming, ordering people away. Most scuttled out of her path like rats before a wolf, but if they didn't she thrust her sword towards them.

Would she actually stab anyone with it? Marlowe felt sick at the thought of the sword he had rammed through the guard, the feeling of it sliding into his flesh, the force he had had to apply to get it to go through, more than he had expected at first and then softer, yielding, like slicing a loaf of bread after breaking through the tough crust.

If Kyla didn't know what that felt like, then he envied her.

People around them were streaming away from the stage too, escaping the chaos. In the tangle of bodies, the thrusting of limbs, Marlowe was sure the guard he had killed wouldn't be the only man to die.

They broke free from the crowd. The sun was setting, red and violent, over the sea. The evening air was sharp with salt, and beyond the shouts from the auction he could hear the smash of the waves against the docks.

They rounded a corner and stopped in a quiet alleyway, where there were few windows and no noise. The buildings were tall and close together, and the last of the day's light barely fell between them. They were cloaked by the cover of darkness.

Marlowe leant against the wall, and put one hand to his forehead before dragging it down his face. "We left her. We left Valora."

"We had to." Kyla put Max down, letting him rest against a wall, but she did not relax. She stood, facing the way they had come, holding out her sword in case anyone had followed them.

Max rubbed a hand at the rawness of his neck and looked up at Marlowe, his eyes narrowing with suspicion. He flicked his gaze to Kyla and then back again to Marlowe before he spoke. "I thought you were going to let us die."

The statement lingered in the air, and Marlowe was sure they all heard the unuttered question that followed. *Why didn't you?* And in that instant he understood the implication that hung beneath it: that there was some reason, some *feeling*, connected to Kyla that had prevented him from following through with the threat. Max knew it, and he was prodding at it like it was an open wound. Marlowe clenched his jaw and looked upwards, avoiding Max's gaze. "I considered it."

Kyla swung round, pointing her exposed sword at Marlowe's chest. "You more than considered it. You wanted to do it. I saw it on your face."

In the dim light of the sheltered street her eyes flashed with a fierceness that made him want to back away, even more than the blade itself did. But he held his space, looked her in the eye and said, "I didn't though, did I?"

Max let out a stifled guffaw, his eyes rolling so far skyward that Marlowe wanted to punch him. "You had the gold. You could have bought us."

Marlowe could hardly contain the snarl that rose to his lips. "They wanted you to die. Both of you. I would have needed ten times the gold to buy your freedom. I did the only thing I could think of, and it worked. You're alive."

Kyla didn't look like she was going to accept this, but after a moment her features relaxed. She sheathed her sword and said, "Thank you."

Her gratitude was unexpected, and Marlowe flinched as if she had struck him with it. Those two words, a simple *thank you*, were a burden he didn't feel worthy to bear. He sniffed and, unsure what else to do, ran his fingers through his hair. It was thick and slightly matted with sweat.

"Thank you," continued Kyla, her voice suddenly dripping with sarcasm, "for deciding not to kill me *when my back was turned*."

Max made a noise, halfway between a gasp and a groan, and looked anxiously between them.

Marlowe stiffened. She was quoting the words he had said to her back in the woods, the day they had collected the Valerian root. The expression of thanks that had so stunned him only moments before had been nothing but empty words. She wasn't thankful at all!

He felt the cold hand of guilt crushing his throat, and it became harder to breathe. He had saved Kyla rather than his own sister, and even now Valora was still down there in a cage. He had deserted her, but when Kyla had been up on that stage, *her* life at risk, he had acted on impulse. And for what?

Kyla's gaze was unforgiving yet invasive, as if she was trying to see beneath his skin and bones to the content of his heart. What she hoped to find there he didn't know, but it didn't matter. He didn't care what she thought. It was Valora he needed to worry about... Valora and that lurking Yarmon Sacfron and his bird.

"We have to go back," he said. "We have to get Valora."

"And we will. But if we go back now, they'll kill us." Kyla loosened her hair, letting it fall about her shoulders before tying it back tightly again. Marlowe looked away, as though the sight of her hair was as improper as what he had seen at the moonlit pool. "The gold," she said. "When did you steal it?"

Marlowe shrugged as he turned back to face her, striving to look as casual as he could. "When you fell off the wall."

Kyla's eyes widened. He saw, or thought he saw, her cheeks flush red. Was she too remembering that moment, how intimate it had seemed, his hands on her hips, their bodies pressed close together? She jerked her chin as if to dislodge the memory. "With what?" She pulled at the torn cords on her belt, from which the purse had previously dangled.

Marlowe pulled Kyla's knife from his pocket. It was the black one, with the twisted handle that ended in two clasped hands.

Without taking her eyes off him, Kyla put her hand into one of her boots and took out the knife she had used to cut Max free. Then she checked the other boot and found nothing. Her eyes, grim and dark, flashed up at him. "For the grandson of a Lord, you're an accomplished thief."

Marlowe twirled the knife in his hand, trying to appear calm. "When you have no gold you have to learn to steal." He cradled it gently by the blade, holding out the hilt for Kyla to take.

She snatched it and slammed it into her boot. "You could have used it to help me cut Max down. You could have done something with it—"

"I forgot I had it." The shock of running a blade through a man was hard to stomach. Marlowe had barely been able to walk straight, let alone remember he had a knife he could wield.

Max exhaled sharply through his nose. "How convenient." He paused to look Marlowe up and down, his gaze settling on his torso. When he spoke his voice was flat. "You have blood on your shirt."

Marlowe glanced down. Yes, he had blood on his shirt, again. Blood on his hands. He felt queasy. He had killed two men in the space of a few days.

Killing the guard in the prison had been one thing, but this was something else entirely. Hundreds of people had seen him do it.

He dragged a hand over his eyes and down his cheek. "I don't think there's any point filching a fresh one this time. I have a feeling that it's not the last time it will happen." He held out his hand to Max, intending to pull him up. "We have to go back for Valora. We have to do this together."

"You're not going anywhere. If there are still people down there, they'll kill you," Kyla said.

"I'm not waiting any longer," he said, pacing from side to side across the width of the alleyway.

"You have to. The only reason we're still alive is because of me. Because those people, whatever they might have said, still have respect for my uniform." She tapped on the emblem of the God-Sage embroidered on her tunic.

Marlowe scoffed. "It wasn't your uniform. It was your sword. Without that we would have been mauled to death."

Kyla looked momentarily affronted and he expected her to contest him, but she shook her head and said, "Either way, I cannot let you wander back down there."

"I wasn't going to announce myself. How stupid do you think I am?" Anger flared, burning between his ribs. He slammed his hand against the brick wall and immediately wished he hadn't. He gritted his teeth so Kyla wouldn't see him wince. "Do you or don't you want your acolyte?"

She stared at him. And then something in her broke, and words cascaded through the rupture, loud and all at once. "I don't want you to die."

Silence fell, hard and fast between them as they stood facing one another. Marlowe's heart thumped in his chest, slightly off the beat, struck from its rhythm by her words. Max, still seated against the wall, shuffled awkwardly, trying to pull himself out of the way, to disappear. Marlowe didn't blame him; the intensity of whatever was passing between him and Kyla in the instant of her admission was corrosively intimate.

All his urgency, his anger, drained away. For a split second Marlowe thought Kyla was going to step towards him, but she didn't. She moved back, and whatever force had sparked between them was broken. His anger swelled to fill the void.

He slashed his arm through the air. "We can't wait!"

He half expected Kyla to shout again, but she didn't. Instead, a furrow formed between her brows and she tilted her head.

"What are you not telling me?"

Marlowe began pacing back and forth again. He dragged one hand through his hair. Could he tell her that he suspected Yarmon Sacfron's attack at the river hadn't been random? That he was after the very object that hung in a pouch around Valora's neck?

Could he trust Kyla Tarthwen?

He took a deep breath. "Nothing. Nothing."

The tension dropped from Kyla's shoulders. "Good. We need to rest. You and I haven't properly slept in hours. Days. I'm dead on my feet here. We'll take turns watching the port, see if it calms down. If it looks like the slaves are leaving, we'll move. Immediately."

Her entire body sagged as she finished speaking, as if the mere mention of her exhaustion had left her weak and limp.

Marlowe nodded in begrudging agreement, but even as he did so he leant against the wall and felt his legs beg to crumple beneath him. He could barely stay upright. How much longer could he go on without resting?

"I got a bit of sleep in that cart," Max said. "Not great, but something. I'll take the first watch. You two look like you need rest."

Marlowe forced himself to stand tall and stared quite deliberately at Max, raking over the soldier's bloodshot eyes and the raw welts around his neck. "You nearly died. You need the rest more than I do—"

Max raised an eyebrow. "I'm not sure I do."

"I'm not walking away from Valora again." Marlowe felt the tension build in his jaw and the next words were barely more than a growl. "I'll take the first watch."

Max looked up at Kyla, waiting for her permission to agree. She nodded and Max, relieved, put up no fight and sank down, as if the exhaustion he had been denying finally felt free to burst through. "Wake me when—"

"I'll wake you when I can't stand up any more."

11

KYLA

THE CITY OF TURLENTO

Kyla wasn't sure how long she had been asleep, but it must have been a couple of hours at least, because night had fallen and she could see Max leaning against the wall, peering out towards the docks. He must have taken on the watch. A quick glance around told her she was right. Marlowe lay across the alley, tucked into a disused doorway. His eyes were closed and his chest moved in a slow rhythm that told her he was asleep.

Her body still ached with exhaustion, but now that she was awake once more she couldn't stop the unceasing thoughts running through her mind. She sat up, her back against the wall, the hard cobbles beneath her, and pulled her knees to her chest. The air smelt of stale urination and she reckoned they hadn't been the only people to seek shelter in this quiet, narrow alleyway. But she was past caring about the smell. All she really wanted was to quiet her mind, but it seemed impossible.

Max's voice cracked through her thoughts. His voice was a mixture between a whisper and a hiss. "He doesn't care about you. You know that, don't you?"

Kyla snapped to attention just in time to see Max nod his head towards where Marlowe lay curled on the doorstep. From where she sat, Kyla could look directly at him. He looked almost peaceful.

Max, by contrast, looked irritated, both arms crossed over his chest.

She felt an odd tightness spread through her torso. "Is this because I said I didn't want him to die?" She took a breath and tried to sound as nonchalant as she could. "Honestly, Max. I don't want you to die either."

"It's not the same." Max looked awkwardly down at his hands but his voice was still tinged with bitterness. "You're enjoying him being with us."

Kyla's heart began to race in the most peculiar way. She shot a look across the alley. Marlowe's eyes were still closed, but she didn't want to risk him waking up so she hissed the words she spoke. "What are you talking about? You think when I point my sword at him I'm enjoying myself?"

Max still didn't look at her. "Something like that."

Kyla exhaled in a burst and spoke too loudly. "Stop it. Don't be ridiculous. I'm not *enjoying* him. He's been useful."

Max looked up, darting a glance at Marlowe to see if her outburst had woken him. When he was satisfied it hadn't, he said, "I just don't want you to get hurt. That's all."

The compassion in Max's eyes, so delicately balanced against the knowledge that his words would anger her, took Kyla by surprise, and a sudden need to weep crawled up her throat. For a moment she said nothing, but the tension in her chest was almost unbearable.

"Me, get hurt?" She forced out a laugh, but it sounded awkward and hollow. "If it weren't for Marlowe, neither of us would be here. You would have died with your neck in a noose—"

"I didn't mean that kind of hurt." Max bit the words, and even in the dim light Kyla could see the colour rising in his cheeks. He hung his head and shook it gently, and Kyla realised he was almost as loath to have this conversation as she was. "It doesn't matter—" His head jerked up, his thoughts having charged ahead on another path. "—but Marlowe didn't save me. You did. He wanted them to hang me first!"

"Shhhh. Keep it down." She jerked her head at Marlowe. "He wouldn't have let you die."

It was Max's turn to let out a bark of humourless laughter. "Are you sure about that? Didn't you see the pleasure on his face when he was prancing over that stage? Using Edmund's gold to offer to buy your death, like he was some kind of prince and you were some kind of criminal?"

"Shut up, Max. I need some sleep. You're alive, aren't you? Thank the God-Sage for that."

Kyla was about to lie down, to try and find some position to sleep in, when Max paced towards her. He didn't speak until he was right in front of her, and then his voice was calm and deep.

"Do you remember that day, when we were children? When we stepped into the healing circle?"

Kyla held her breath, her heart beating faster than ever. A coil of anxiety roiled in the pit of her belly. What sort of question was that? If there was anything she had expected Max to say at this moment, it certainly wasn't that.

She shook her head. She had never stepped into the circle. But even as she pondered it, a recollection surfaced. The memory was foggy, forbidden. Her father, beating her, screaming at her, all for a transgression she couldn't recall. Something so terrible that he had whipped her until she thought she would die.

She shook her head. "Not really."

When Max answered, his voice was so quiet that she could barely hear him. "Well I do. I cut my own hand with a knife, just to see what would happen when I stepped in the circle. It worked. We stepped into the circle, and it worked. The circle healed me. Without a Sage, without an acolyte. It worked, with just you and me."

Max's words tugged at a memory long hidden, unearthing it from where Kyla had buried it.

"No, Max. We never... I never—"

"We did. We stood in the circle, together. It's all lies, Kyla. That the circle only works with a Sage and ten acolytes. Here we are struggling to rescue Valora, to get her across the kingdom, and the circle doesn't even need her."

Kyla's whole body was alight. She had never told Max what had happened in the temple the night before her initiation. About the acolyte, who had dragged her into the circle and healed her.

That same acolyte had been killed during Kyla's aborted initiation. The long-held secret burnt in Kyla now, desperate to be shared. If Max had known all along that the circle had the power to heal without all the ceremony they had been led to believe was required, then maybe she could tell him...

But instead she asked, "Why didn't you say anything?"

Max was silent. Then, after a moment, "I thought you remembered too. I thought you knew. I tried to ask you, to question you, to see what you really thought, but you never answered me. I thought you were avoiding the whole thing."

"I remember nothing like that."

Max swallowed. "I was afraid to push you. I watched hundreds of people die over the years. Hangings. Beheadings. I didn't want to die. And I saw how your father beat you. I didn't want that either."

A shiver ran over Kyla's skin from her shoulders to the tips of her fingers. "And now?"

Max crouched down to her level. The intensity of his gaze surprised her, but before she could wonder what he might have to say, he pulled the sleeve of his shirt up on his other arm, revealing the black marks that still shifted over his skin.

His voice was no more than a whisper on the breeze, but the words were sharp. "You wanted to know when they hurt? Well, they hurt now. They're all over me, all over my entire body. I can sense things I never could before. I can touch this wall, this brick—" He put his hand against it. "—and tell you who made it. Who laid it. Everything swirls in my mind, just as the marks swirl on my skin. It's like with Valora's rings, back in your room at Aralorn Hall. I thought I was going mad, but whenever I did it, whenever I touched something with the intention of learning from it, these marks—" He glanced at the black scrawls on his arms. "—would move more rapidly. Sometimes they move so intensely that I can feel them inside me, squirming with secrets that don't belong to me. Secrets that belong to the dead."

Kyla tried to conceal the horror on her face, but her voice pitched upwards. "Max—"

He tilted his head, resigned to whatever his fate was, as he pulled his sleeve back down. "I can't do it every time, and it's not clear. It's never really, truly clear. But I've seen things I didn't know existed. I've witnessed them. I *am* them. And I'm frightened, but I can't pretend anymore."

Kyla was beginning to feel increasingly uneasy. "Pretend what?"

"Pretend that the God-Sage is all there is. Pretend that all we need to do is bring the acolyte back to Moriya, and suddenly everything will be all right again. It's not true." He looked across at her. "I knew there was magic. I've always known it. They lied to us; the priests, the sages, the soldiers – everyone told us there was no magic. That there was only the God-Sage. But there's so much more out there than we were ever allowed to know." He tapped his breastbone, his fingers crunching against the thick embroidery of the God-Sage that covered his tunic. "There's so much more in here."

Kyla's emotions were at war. She had held her faith all her life. It was the only constant. It had been her comfort when her brother disappeared, and each and every time her father beat her. It was her solace at every difficult moment, and here was Max asking her to give it up, to surrender it like it was nothing. She was determined to cling to it, even if it pulled her beneath the waves. But as she spoke the familiar words, she felt something inside her disintegrate. "*The God-Sage deserves a pure city.*"

They locked eyes for the briefest moment, but it was more than long enough for Kyla to witness Max's disdain. He had exposed himself entirely, and she had thrown the catechism back in his face. She wanted to yell at him, to grab hold of him and scream in his face *I know, I know, I know. I know all of it.* And yet she couldn't form the words. What, after all, did she really know for sure?

Max sprang up and moved back to his position at the end of the street, from where he could see the port. "Get some sleep, Kyla. I'll wake you when we have to go."

Kyla shuffled down against the wall and lay on the ground. How was she supposed to sleep now though, with even more to contemplate?

Just as she was trying to find a comfortable position to sleep in and was about to close her eyes, she looked straight across the darkened alley, right into Marlowe's eyes. He stared, unblinking, for only a moment, then closed his eyes. Kyla felt hollowed out, knowing that in that brief second Marlowe had seen more of her than anyone ever had. It was more than skin this time. He had glimpsed her soul.

How long had he been watching her? How much had he overheard?

Kyla shut her eyes, but even behind her closed lids she could see the image of Marlowe's shadowed face, his eyes glinting with reflected moonlight, staring right at her.

Lying there in the darkness she was overcome by the strangest urge to get up and run away.

There was no way she would be able to sleep.

12

MARLOWE

THE CITY OF TURLENTO

By the time the crowds had fled the dock, Marlowe was as anxious as a caged rat. What if Max hadn't been paying attention and Atrimus had loaded up his slaves and left already? What if someone else had come along to buy Valora? What if they had stashed her on a boat and sailed away? What if, and here he felt a cold sweat break out across his shoulders and down his spine, Yarmon had seen her, and recognised her as the girl from the riverbanks at Edmund's funeral?

Kyla kept shooting uneasy glances in Marlowe's direction, as though she expected him to go up in flames. Or perhaps it was because she had seen him watching her last night, but either way it was uncomfortable.

The three of them kept close together as they ventured back into the open. Lanterns bobbed on the boats, casting speckles of flashing light on the surface of the Half-Sewn Sea. It was quieter now, all sound muted by darkness, broken only by the soft thump-thump of boats hitting the jetties, the hushed chatter of sailors, the drunken moan of a lone man stumbling around the docks after drinking too much ale.

The three of them, Marlowe, Kyla and Max, crouched behind a clutch of barrels.

Kyla pointed. "Look, there."

Atrimus Deegeld was leaning against a cart that was parked near the water. The slaves were being escorted into the cart by his men.

Marlowe clenched his fist and thumped it into the palm of his other hand. "I knew we would be too late. They're moving off."

"Better late than dead," Max said, rubbing his neck with one hand, tracing the marks left by the noose.

Marlowe wasn't going to wait any longer. He lurched forward, but a hand on his arm held him back.

"Listen," Kyla said.

Marlowe held his breath, tuning his hearing to the voices by the carts. Atrimus' husky voice rose over the soft slap of the boats on the water. He was talking to one of his men, a youngish man wearing a dark cloak. Kyla crept forward, leading them all closer until they could hear exactly what was being said.

Atrimus was pointing a finger in the young man's face, irritated by whatever had gone before. "Do you know how much a cripple is worth?"

Marlowe's heart thudded. They were talking about Valora. His body jerked forward, but Kyla grabbed him to hold him back. He shook her off and scuttled closer, keeping low between boxes and boats. Kyla gave a disgruntled huff, but a moment later he could sense her following close behind him, although her movement made so little noise.

Atrimus was still speaking, his voice even rougher than before, as if his throat was raw from all the shouting he had done. "I'm not handing her over just because someone says he has gold. I need to *see* the gold. Where is this man anyway?"

"He was at the auction, I tell you. The man with the wings on his cheeks. He—"

Atrimus gasped. "The Nilari man?"

Bitterness rose in Marlowe's throat and he nearly covered his own feet with bile. He swallowed it down and tried to pay attention, despite the shivers coursing over his body.

"Yes, yes." The cloaked young man spoke quickly, to avoid angering Atrimus any more. "That one. He promised he would come back after everything settled down."

"Where is he? I can't wait much longer. If we don't leave now we won't get to Vixar in time for the next auction."

"Atrimus, I swear, he said he wanted her."

"I'm not waiting for gold that might not exist. Especially not after what went down this afternoon. It's too risky. Load up. Let's go."

The young man looked unhappy about it, but he clambered up beside one of the drivers. Atrimus began checking the fastenings on all the cages. The men and women inside were mostly quiet, either sleeping or having long ago given up hope of freedom. Where was Valora? She had to be in there somewhere.

Just then Kyla pinched Marlowe's thigh again and, when she had his attention, pointed off to the right where a figure was striding purposefully towards Atrimus, a huge Nilari bird fluttering just behind him.

Marlowe cursed under his breath. They were too late. It was Yarmon Sacfron, come to claim his prize. Marlowe tried to stand up but Kyla's grip on his leg was harder than ever now.

"Don't move. You killed one of their men. They see you, they'll kill you."

Marlowe sighed, and the sound that came from his mouth was laden with frustration. She was probably right. He shook his head. He watched Yarmon cross the docks, his footsteps silent despite the speed of his movement. When he was close to Atrimus, who obviously hadn't noticed him, he paused to drag on a long white pipe from which curled blue smoke. He blew the smoke over Atrimus' shoulder, causing him to raise his nose and sniff, his hands still on the lock of one of the cages.

It was then that Yarmon spoke. "Are you leaving?"

Atrimus jumped. "Oh, oh goodness. You mustn't..." He pressed a hand to his heart, bent over and rocked back and forward. "I can't be having any more surprises today."

"Stand up, man."

Atrimus straightened, gripping the side of the cart with one hand. He stared at Yarmon, raking his eyes from the velvet cap that sat on his head, all the way to his leather boots. His eyes settled on the large Nilari bird, now seated at Yarmon's heel like a dog.

The bird had its head under its wing, preening its feathers. It raised its head, jerked its neck until its beady black eyes looked in Marlowe's direction, and began to make short cawing noises as if it was hacking something up from the back of its throat. Marlowe held his breath, afraid the bird had seen him.

Yarmon ran his free hand over the bird's feathers, whispering, "Hush now, hush now." The bird made a soft clucking sound and settled comfortably at his feet.

Phew. Marlowe gave a silent sigh of relief, and hunkered down to listen to the two men.

"I left word with one of your men that I was coming back to buy the girl." Yarmon peered around Atrimus, pointedly looking at the slaves in the cart and the men round about who were loading slaves into other carts. "But it looks like you had no intention of waiting."

Atrimus clapped his hands together. "By my word, if I had known it was you I would have waited. But it's not good for business to be waiting for every man who says he intends to buy. Most men don't have the power to follow through. Nor the gold."

Yarmon slid a hand into his pocket and there was a clinking sound that could have been nothing other than a purse full of coin. He dangled it in front of Atrimus. It looked as bulging and full as Edmund's had been.

"I am not *most men*."

Atrimus' eyes grew wide, just as they had done when Marlowe had given him the gold for Kyla's execution.

"Oh I know, I know. You are the great Yarmon Sacfron, a leader of the Nilari rebels."

"You didn't appear to know me before."

"It is my business to know everyone of note in this great land of Tolinaye. But it is not my business to let people know what I know. Can't have people thinking I am listening to all the rumours about the Nilari and their supporters. Danger, if you don't mind me saying, Sir, lies that way..." Atrimus bowed, whilst simultaneously reaching out with a cupped hand to scoop up the coins that Yarmon still held out.

Yarmon wagged a finger in his face. "You first. Where is she?"

A sly look carved itself over Atrimus' face. "Saw your face at the auction today and I thought to myself, 'why, what could have brought the great Yarmon Sacfron down from the mountains? What could I possibly have that might have attracted the great man himself?'"

Yarmon flicked his fingers and the great bird beside him shot out its wings, giving a great caw as it did so. Atrimus backed away, pressing right up against the cage behind him.

"I don't have time for games!" Yarmon's voice cracked across the docks. "The cripple. I know you have one for sale. Where is she?"

"Oh, don't worry, don't worry yourself; the cripple is safe. She's locked up." Atrimus banged on the cart behind him.

Yarmon twirled his fingers between the necklace of linked silver wings that hung from his neck. "Did she have anything on her? Any jewellery?"

Atrimus drew himself up, puffed out his chest a little. "Let us agree a price first for the girl." He shoved his hand into his pocket and pulled something out, pinching it between finger and thumb and holding it up for Yarmon to see. "And then we can make arrangements for this."

Marlowe felt his heart leap into his throat. It was the crooked wheel, the little piece of metal that Valora had been determined to hold onto. Kyla saw it too, for she covered her mouth with a hand, as if she might have gasped had they not had to stay silent to remain hidden.

Yarmon, his jaw suddenly slack, stared at the piece of metal. "It's exactly as we thought it would be," he said, his voice far-off and dreamy. Then he snapped to attention, fully focused, and his eyes lit on Atrimus, who flinched at the sudden beam of the rebel's gaze. "I will give you four gold tucks for it, and not a bronze more."

Atrimus chuckled, and slid the wheel back into his pocket. "You forget, dear Yarmon, that I myself am Varoan. I know exactly what this is, and I know exactly what it's worth."

"It's worth nothing to you."

Atrimus grinned. "And everything to you. So tell me, what will you give me for it? How much was it you offered to pay for the Moriyan soldier who escaped? Twelve gold tucks, was it?"

Yarmon's grey eyebrow flickered. A small movement but enough to signify that he was unnerved. He stepped closer, towering over Atrimus. The bird at his feet flapped its wings and a burst of air hit Marlowe's cheeks, even from his spot beyond the barrels. "Extortion. That's what this is."

The two men glared at one another and then Atrimus gave a low whistle. Several large men jumped down from the carts, their gaits rocking with the size of their muscles. They had finished locking the carts, and began to gather around their master like a shield of human protection. Yarmon took a step back and Atrimus began to laugh, his mouth wide, the sound rolling out between his lips. "Extortion? For this?" He held it high in the air, admiring it like treasure. "Why, this is worth all the slaves I have to sell combined."

"It's worthless without the girl."

"The Dream Key? Worthless? I am not sure I know a man who would say he had no use for the key to his own dreams."

Atrimus gave a theatrical bow and his voice took on a high, false tone, as he spoke to an imagined audience. "Does anyone want to make their dreams come true? No one? No one? Ah, what a shame."

The men around him began to chuckle, low and sinister.

Atrimus pocketed the wheel and grinned at Yarmon.

Yarmon eyed him with great suspicion. "What do you want?"

A moment of silence. "I want everything you have."

Yarmon dragged on his pipe. He was clearly trying to remain calm, but his eyes burnt with rage. "Why, I could—" He raised one hand to strike Atrimus, but each of the guards shifted at once, swiping their curved swords into the air and pointing them at Yarmon.

"Use Nilari magic? Here in the middle of a city? That would be extremely unwise." Atrimus paused to nod at Yarmon's leather purse. "I will not deal with you until you bring me more than what you have in that purse. Much, much more."

The burly guards began to move in unison, a slow march towards Yarmon, who backed away, all whilst pointing one long-nailed finger towards them.

"This won't be the last you'll see of me, Atrimus Deegeld," he called. "I will find you."

Yarmon turned and walked away, the bird fluttering beside him for a moment before rising to the sky and flying over his head like a solitary raincloud.

When he had disappeared from view Atrimus slapped his hands together. "We're going to be rich, boys. Rich. I can smell the gold from here."

The men mumbled in agreement and took up their places on the carts again; the next moment the wheels gave a crunch and began to roll. They were on the move.

The moonlight hit the cages in such a way that Marlowe saw Valora, clinging to the bars, peering out, searching for someone. *For him.*

He dashed towards the trundling cart, jumping over stray sacks and barrels that scattered the port. He no longer cared if anyone saw or heard him. When he was close enough he cupped his hands about his mouth and called out.

"Valora!"

She looked up. He waved, knowing she would only be able to see him as a dark figure, a silhouette in the moonlight, but hopefully his voice, his outline, was enough to tell her who he was.

He ran, gaining ground, but the cart was moving at a surprising pace.

But he was faster.

He caught up, running alongside the cart for a moment, trying to see Valora, but there were too many others crushed in with her. Then he dropped back behind the cart so he could grab the bars of the cage. He leapt, seized the bars with both hands and pulled himself up.

He could see her! She was right there on the other side. She was alive! She touched his hands through the bars.

The cart jolted. Valora lost her balance, her hand slipped from his. Marlowe saw the fear and panic in her eyes.

"I'll get you out," he said.

Valora had no chance to respond before a voice yelled, "Oi, there's a stray on the cart."

They shuddered to a halt and Marlowe was nearly thrown to the street. He only just managed to cling on. From somewhere up ahead, a man jumped down. Footsteps approached, increasing in pace, getting louder, closer, but still Marlowe kept his fingers entwined with Valora's.

"Please... don't leave me," she said.

The man came into Marlowe's vision. He was holding a thick wooden stick in one hand. He thrashed it through the air, bringing it down on the cart around Marlowe, battering him with it, crushing his fingers where they gripped on. Pain shot through Marlowe's hand. He had to let go, and fell to the ground.

Valora's tiny fist reached through the bars. "No, Marlowe! No!"

The cart began to move off but the man with the stick didn't follow. He lingered, and Marlowe knew what was coming. He curled up, covering his head with his arms, but the blows crashed over his back, not ceasing until the cart was quite a distance away, when the man aborted his beating in favour of catching up with the cart.

Marlowe lay, his face in the dirt, his body throbbing, his mouth full of blood. One of his hands was starting to throb with swelling numbness.

The rumbling of the cart wheels died away.

Valora was gone.

A crunch, then another. Footsteps. Someone was standing over him. He felt their presence more than saw it.

"Well, that was stupid, wasn't it?"

Kyla.

But her voice wasn't entirely unkind, and when Marlowe rolled onto his back and looked up at her, pale in the moonlight, he fancied he could see a glimmer of concern in her eyes.

Winded, he spattered blood from his mouth, choking out half-breaths. When he was able to speak he said, "I think our definition of stupid might differ."

Shaking her head gently, Kyla held out her hand to him, and with the hand that hadn't just been smashed, he took it. She pulled him up.

A shadow blocked the moonlight that fell over Kyla, briefly casting her in darkness. Up above a large Nilari bird swooped across the sky, its wings wide, squawking into the night.

13

KYLA

LEAVING TURLENTO

Kyla was sure the carts were heading towards Vixar. It was the nearest city. At least Atrimus hadn't sold the slaves to a merchant or a sailor, who might already have sailed away. Valora was still on dry land, still in Tolinaye, and that meant they could save her.

Marlowe was in pain, and a lot of it. He wasn't moving well and one hand hung like a dead fist, curled up, barely moving. But he hadn't complained. He was angry, though; Kyla could feel it hissing off him like steam. He had wanted to rush in and save Valora at once, but it would have been a fool's mission. They had been lucky enough to get out of the auction alive, with a sword and two knives between them. The traders had taken all Max's weapons when they captured him.

They followed the road, keeping well behind the carts, on horses they had stolen. Kyla hadn't wanted to steal, but seeing as they had no gold now it seemed the only available option, and Marlowe was as good at thieving animals as he was at stealing knives, gold, items of clothing and pieces of dried meat.

How had she ended up in the company of a petty thief who had nearly killed her?

And was she really *enjoying* his company, as Max had suggested she was?

Marlowe's voice cut through her thoughts. "Stop looking at me."

Kyla hadn't realised she'd been staring, but she didn't stop. She deliberately looked him up and down as he sat astride his horse. "You look uncomfortable."

"I'm in agony. Unless you can do something to stop the pain, you can at least stop looking at me." He winced, then smiled. "Or do you want to point your sword at me again? That might be more—" He paused to give her a knowing look, and he drew the next word out, imbuing it with meaning. "—enjoyable."

Kyla turned away so fast he might have slapped her. So he *had* heard some of their conversation. Well, she had heard a few things too. "What did Atrimus mean by *Dream Key*? That little wheel that he held up, it was the same as the burn on Valora's hand. What did he mean by it?"

Marlowe shrugged and then groaned as if the motion had caused more pain. "I don't know any more than you do."

"If you expect me to believe that—"

Max's voice was a welcome distraction. "Look, we've caught them up. They're making camp. Up there."

Max pointed to a clearing amidst the trees, and sure enough three carts were stationed to one side. The traders and guards had descended and dismounted, and were setting up camp fires. There were more men than Kyla had anticipated. As she looked closer, she could see even more carts. This wasn't merely the men they had followed from Turlento. This was a meeting place of many slave traders on their way to Vixar.

"There are loads of them," Marlowe said.

"Let's leave the horses here," Kyla said. "We can move closer on foot."

Kyla jumped down from her horse. Max was staring at her as if he was trying to work something out, then he turned the same expression on Marlowe, who had trotted up behind them.

"What?" she asked.

"I'll stay here. With the horses," Max said.

There was something about the set of Max's mouth, the look on his face, that ruffled Kyla. She felt judgment in it, as if he would prefer to avoid sharing company with her and Marlowe *together*, like they had become two pieces of a whole that Max didn't like.

"Tie up your horse," she said. "You're coming with us."

The forest was dark aside from the moonlight filtering through the leaves above, and the bright flames of the slavers-' campfire.

The three of them crouched behind rocks and trees on the edge of the clearing. The crackle of the fire was comforting, despite the anxiety that bubbled in Kyla's stomach.

"That's the man who shot at us." She pointed to a man who was perched on a rock, a bow and quiver full of arrows at his side. "Back before we reached Turlento."

Marlowe stiffened. "There, look. Valora's over there. That cage, there."

Kyla looked where he pointed and sure enough Valora was there, crouching in the corner at the front of the cage.

"Look at the size of that padlock," Max said. "It didn't seem so big when I was inside the cage."

"Someone will have the keys on them," Kyla said. "One of the guards."

Next to her Marlowe crunched forward and she reached out to grab him. "Do you ever think before you move? You can't go now. Unless you want a repeat of what happened at the docks." She glanced down at Marlowe's hand, which he held strangely, close to his body, fingers cupped, as though it hurt to flex them. He saw her looking and pulled it closer.

"You've done your fair share of rushing into danger. You were the one who got up on that stage in the first place—"

"Both of you, stop," Max said. "What we need is time. Time where no one will see us, for at least a few minutes."

Marlowe's eyes narrowed as he cast his gaze over the encampment, before he turned to Kyla. "If you kill them all, we'll have ample time. You have your sword?"

Kyla placed one hand on the hilt of her sword, realising she hadn't cleaned it since Marlowe had thrust it through that enormous guard. If she didn't do it soon the blade might rust. "You want me to kill them?"

Marlowe nodded. "Get in there. Slice them all up."

"*Slice them all up?*" Kyla looked at him, surprised to see that he was entirely serious. "These aren't just any men. They're slavers. You think I can just walk in and *slice them all up?*"

Marlowe shrugged. "I'll do it if you don't think you can."

"You're an idiot." She pointed across to the right of the campfire, a little way away, where a tent was pitched, glowing as if lit by a flame inside it. The tent opened and a man stepped out. It was Atrimus Deegeld himself. He surveyed the camp and, obviously satisfied, bowed down to re-enter his tent. "It's not just the men we can see. There are more. There's got to be another way."

"What about the herbs?" Max asked.

"Herbs? What herbs? What good are herbs right now—" began Marlowe.

Kyla realised what Max meant. "You mean Valora's herbs? I have them, and the valerian too." She turned to Marlowe. "Can you make a sleeping potion?"

Marlowe looked askance at her. "What do you want to do? Put them all to sleep? Is that your big plan?"

"It beats carnage and bloodshed."

Marlowe gave a quirky little smile and shook his head. "And you, a Moriyan soldier and everything. You continue to surprise me."

"I don't want to kill anyone unless I have to. And I don't think we have to right now." She unhooked Valora's herb pouch from her belt and held it to Marlowe. "That's it. That's everything we collected, and everything she gave me."

Marlowe peered into the bag, reached in with his good hand and pulled out a few droopy roots, flattened and dull.

Max waved his hand in front of his nose. "Whew, those stink."

Marlowe held up one of the roots and looked at it, tilting his head to one side. "It won't be potent. We didn't dry them properly. Squashed and limp like this..." He flapped the plant, wafting the foul smell in the air. "Hmmm. If Valora made a potion with this, they would be asleep all night, but if we do it... it won't be the same. They wouldn't sleep for long. It wouldn't give us much time."

"Valora prepared some of those herbs." Kyla tapped the pouch. "Half of it was hers. It's got to be worth a try. We only need a minute or two. Maybe less if one of those men has the keys to the cages on him."

Marlowe lowered the roots, staring over them at Kyla. "I still think we should kill them."

Was he mocking her? It was hard to tell, but at this very moment it didn't matter, so rather than retort she tutted and shook her head. "I don't want to start a war in the woods."

Marlowe huffed. "We can hardly build a fire and brew a potion. We would be seen. And even if they didn't see us, it would take too long. And we don't have a pot to use."

Max raised his eyebrows and pointed to the men, who were seated around the fire. There was a large pot set over the flames, and one of the men was filling it with water from a nearby stream. "We don't need a pot, or a fire. All we need to do is get the herbs into *their* pot."

Kyla watched the men as they ceased their milling about and came to settle around the fire. Just as she was wondering how they could slip the herbs in, Max pointed upwards. There was a large tree overhanging the slavers' camp, with one huge leafy branch that grew directly over the pot of soup.

"I'll climb up and drop it in. It'll fall right in the pot."

Marlowe looked deeply sceptical and Kyla couldn't help agreeing.

Max turned both palms upwards. "Do you have a better idea?"

For a moment they were quiet, and then Marlowe said, "All right, give me the herbs. Seeds. All of it."

Kyla hurried to empty the pouch of all the little plants they had collected, the roots mixed with Valora's dried herbs and seeds, pushing them into Marlowe's cupped palm.

Marlowe grabbed a rock, a good hand-sized boulder, and began grinding the roots and seeds between it and another large rock. Kyla offered to do it, but he belligerently refused any assistance, despite working with only one hand. He pounded the limp herbs harder and faster, pummelling the dried pods and seeds until it was all mashed together.

Kyla kept glancing up to look at the men, but they were sharing a flagon of ale and singing so loudly that they were unlikely to hear any noise Marlowe was making.

When he was done Kyla scooped up the little pile of mash with a large leaf, which she folded in on itself, putting a stone inside the parcel so that it would fall straight into the pot when Max dropped it.

"Here." She went to hand it to Max, but just before she let it drop into his palm, she hesitated. He looked at her questioningly.

"Kyla, what—"

She pulled her hand back, squeezing the little parcel tighter. "I'll go. I'm a better climber. I'll be faster, and the quicker we are, the sooner we'll be able to get Valora back."

Without waiting for either Max or Marlowe to object, Kyla spun round and headed into the trees.

She could hear the men singing traditional Varoan songs. So Atrimus wasn't the only Varoan among the crew then. The journey across the Half-Sewn Sea was not known to be an easy one. What were these Varoans doing so far from home?

She scaled the tree quickly, the bark rough beneath her fingertips, fixing the toes of her boots into the nooks between branches.

She crawled out over the branch that hung above the pot and peered between the leaves of the trees. How could she drop something into the pot now? They were all sitting around it, looking right across it. They would see anything that dropped into it instantly.

Suddenly the singing stopped. Kyla held her breath.

One of the men stood up and waved his arms. "What's the noise?"

"Heard a ghost, did you?" Laughter followed.

Kyla clung to the branch, sure the foliage was thick enough to conceal her, but she felt the tingle of fear spread through her arms and legs, making it harder to stay steady. What if they found her?

The man looked up. He tilted his head this way and that, squinting up into the thick leaves. "Must be one of them giant squirrels. Swear I heard it."

"Leave it, have a bit more," One of the men held out the flagon to him. He threw one last puzzled look up at the tree before taking the flagon, raising it to his lips and swallowing deeply.

Kyla, relieved, shifted her position. Her boot caught a branch, shaking it. Something fell from the tree. A chestnut, large and fat, fell to one side and the men turned to look.

"What's that?"

Some of the men sprang to their feet, searching for the source of the noise. Then the others were up, moving around. If she didn't drop the parcel of herbs now, it would be too late.

As she was about to drop it she caught sight of the archer, his bow lifted and arrow pointed up into the tree, right at her. He couldn't see her, not with the leafy coverage that was obscuring her from view, but if he loosed an arrow now, he would kill her. She pressed her body as close to the tree branch as she could and mumbled a prayer.

Leaves rustled, torn and forced aside. A thud followed. When Kyla was sure she felt no pain, that the thud had not in fact been the arrow piercing her thigh, she creaked an eye open. The arrow, quivering, was embedded in the very branch to which she clung.

"There's nothing there, leave it," came a husky voice.

"I swear, there was something..."

The archer was still staring up into the tree. Another man placed an arm on his shoulder, but he shook it off.

"Got the fear, have you?" said the man who had touched the archer's shoulder. "Worried someone's going to run a sword through your belly too?"

The man with the bow turned on the other man, pointing an arrow right at his nose. "What happened at the auction was no joke."

Jeers and arguing began, and then men began to lash out. This was it. They were distracted, focused on each other. Kyla lowered her arm as far through the branches as she dared and released the little bundle of herbs.

It plopped right into the pot as the men were arguing below. Not one of them noticed. She scuttled backwards along the branch and clambered to the ground as fast as she could.

Max greeted her first, his face pale and his brow creased with worry. "When he shot that arrow... I thought you were—"

"You didn't need to start a riot," Marlowe said as she approached, but his lips were stretching into a smile, his eyes alight with hope. Then his lips split into a smile so wide and warm it took Kyla's breath away. "You did it."

She clenched both her fists and shook them in the air. She saw her excitement mirrored in Marlowe's eyes and he raised his arms to embrace her. But as their eyes locked an energy shot through her, and the intensity of their entangled and simultaneous triumph became unbearable. She looked away, leaving Marlowe no choice but to sheepishly lower his arms again.

"We have to hope it works," she said, serious once more.

They settled down, hidden by the bushes, to wait.

The pot continued cooking for another hour, and even after the men had resolved their differences and begun to eat, Kyla was beginning to suspect the potion wouldn't work. None of the men looked remotely sleepy.

They were laughing, joking, slurping their soup like there was nothing wrong with it, which was a wonder given how disgusting those herbs had smelt. In fact, the soup smelt wonderful and Kyla couldn't help remembering how hungry she was herself. If they had offered her a bowl right then, she would almost certainly have eaten it too.

Maybe Marlowe was right. Maybe they couldn't make a potent potion with bashed up herbs that had their juices squashed out of them. Or at least they couldn't if they didn't have Valora's power.

The thought of Valora's power sent a shiver crawling up Kyla's spine. What was it, really? Magic, or some unknown blessing from the God-Sage? She hoped, prayed, that it was the latter and determined to put the entire matter out of mind until she had Valora back, safe, at her side.

Finally one of the first traders began to doze off. He lay in front of the fire and began to snore. The others laughed, kicked at his legs, pulled at his boots, but he didn't move.

Kyla waited, listening to the crackle of the campfire and the crowing of the men. Bit by bit, the voices died down as the men fell asleep, one by one, surrounding the fire.

"It's starting," Marlowe whispered.

Soon the men were all either splayed on the ground or slumped against trees and rocks.

"Let's go," said Kyla. Beside her Max moved to follow but she held up her hand. "Not you. Go back and wait with the horses. We'll need to be ready to flee when we have Valora."

Max looked doubtfully at Marlowe's swollen hand. "But Kyla—"

"I'm sorry, Max. It has to be Marlowe who comes with me. Valora trusts him."

Max looked about to object, but then he nodded, and Kyla, keeping low to the ground, led Marlowe forward, creeping towards the rocks on the edge of the clearing.

They were so close now that Kyla could smell the scent of unwashed men, and she wrinkled her nose.

Amidst all this filth, there was something, no, *someone*, so precious that the idea of losing her forever was unthinkable.

Valora. Valora Tide.

14

MARLOWE

THE SLAVERS' CAMP

It was only moments before they were creeping between the sleeping bodies around the fire. Marlowe could hear the low muttering of voices from the other tents further off. People were awake elsewhere in the encampment, people who hadn't eaten the soup.

Marlowe darted from man to man, searching their belts, looking for keys that might open the cage. His body still ached from the battering he'd received at the docks. If he saw the man who did it, he'd kill him.

Valora had noticed Marlowe immediately, as if she had been expecting his arrival. She stood in the cage, her hands clutched about the bars, watching him with anxious eyes, following his hurried movements across the camp. He wished he could search without her watching; every time he searched a body and came up with nothing he felt he was letting her down.

"By the burnt-isle, where are the keys?" he cursed.

Kyla, bent over one of the sleeping men, stood up. "They aren't here. We've searched them all." Her voice was a hoarse whisper.

Marlowe scanned the rest of the encampment. There were two other carts, and one tent, the one Kyla had pointed out earlier, where Atrimus Deegeld was stationed. A low hum of voices was coming from it, but Marlowe couldn't work out anything they were saying.

"And look, over there—" Kyla pointed towards another fire further off between the trees, where even more men were camped with more carts. "Perhaps one of them has the keys." She gave a desperate sigh. "What can we do?"

"I can pick the lock."

Kyla put one hand on her hip and looked him up and down. "What other hidden talents do you have?"

"I need the knife."

Kyla, hesitant for only a moment, reached into her boot and handed it to him. She was watching him intently, a curious mixture of disapproval and awe on her face.

He gave the smallest smile and said, "How do you think I got out of the cells back in Palantar?"

He moved to Valora's cage, Kyla close behind. He lifted the lock in his good hand, feeling the heft of it.

A groan came from behind. He looked over his shoulder at the guards lying in the dirt. One of them was tossing in his sleep.

"Quick. Hurry. They're stirring," Kyla said.

His hand was in agony. It throbbed like a heartbeat. He couldn't hold the lock. "Kyla, psst." She looked over. "I need you to hold it still. I can't... my hand."

She stepped towards him, taking the lock in both hands so he could direct the knife. But it was still harder this way than if both his hands had been functioning, and having Kyla breathing down his neck, so close he could feel her warmth, was distracting. It was worse, even, than having Valora's doleful eyes staring at him from above.

Another of the men gave a drowsy yawn. Marlowe cursed under his breath. He could pick a lock, but he had never done it under pressure like this. He slid the tiny knife into the lock, turning it ever so slightly until he felt the tip of the blade pinch and shiver. He had it. The movement had to be slight, or the blade would lose its hold on the pin within the lock.

One of the prisoners in a cart nearby gave a husky, gritty cough. "Hey, you there, with the knife, I'll scream if you don't do ours too—"

"Shut up," Marlowe spat. "I can't concentrate. Be quiet, or no one's getting out."

The lock clinked open and Marlowe gave a sigh of relief. Kyla took her knife, slipped it back into her boot and then unhooked the lock from the bars and opened the gate. Valora at first didn't move, staring from her hunched position like a rabbit that expected to die. Marlowe held his hand out to her. "Come on."

Hope flooded his chest as her fingers gripped his own. She jumped down and Kyla took hold of her as she hit the ground.

Marlowe tried to close the cage behind her. It squealed on rusty hinges, and before he could push it all the way closed one of the men inside shoved against it. Marlowe was forced backwards and the slaves fell out one after the other, clambering to get to freedom.

The guards were stirring even more now and Marlowe hissed at the freed slaves. "Keep it down."

One of them, a scrawny looking middle-aged man wearing little more than rags, turned at Marlowe's words. "Don't tell me to keep it down. You were going to lock us all up and leave us."

The man's feet were bare. He lifted a large rock, and for a moment Marlowe thought he meant to hit him with it, but instead he held it over the head of one of the sleeping slavers. Marlowe's stomach plummeted as he realised the man's intention. He was about to stop him, when he took another look at the sleeping slaver. It was the one who had beaten him and crushed his hand! Before Marlowe could reach out the man brought the rock down on the slaver's skull.

It made a sickening crunch.

Kyla, who had seen it too, quickly put her arm around Valora and began directing her back to where Max was hiding.

Marlowe was about to follow when a banging started up in the cart next to Valora's.

"He's not doing us. He's not opening it." One of the slaves was yelling, and soon the others joined in. They began to slam themselves against the sides of the cage, rocking it. "He's leaving us, leaving us."

Marlowe moved towards the cart, determined to try to free these men too, but Kyla grabbed him. She pointed at the other slavers. "They're waking. With your broken hand it will take too long to pick the lock. We don't have time."

One of the largest slaves was clutching the bars of his cage, his eyes large and wild with rage "I'll yell so loud the whole forest will wake." He took a deep breath and began to count. "One..."

"Kyla," began Marlowe, realising that the man really meant to scream, and if he did the traders would all wake and all hope of escape would be lost.

Kyla must have understood too, because she foisted Valora onto him and drew her sword from its sheath, stepped up to the cart, raised the sword over her head, and brought it crashing down onto the lock.

The clang of steel on steel vibrated through the air. The lock fell in two pieces onto the mud below.

Marlowe whistled, staring at the pieces of metal on the ground as the slaves scrambled free of the cage and trampled about the campsite. Some were running for the trees, others had turned on their captors. "If you'd just done that in the first place—"

A hand gripped his arm, pulling him away. Kyla. "Lift your jaw out of the mud. We need to move."

One of the slavers, rubbing his sleep-swollen face, sat up. His eyes locked onto Marlowe's, and the sleepy confusion turned quickly to suspicion, and then full understanding. The slaver scrambled to his feet calling, "They're free, they're free – the slaves are getting away." He pulled at the limbs of the other sleeping men, hauling them into wakefulness. There were only a few moments left before every one of them would be on his feet.

Men from other carts, other camps, were moving this way too. There were too many of them.

"Go, go," yelled Marlowe, urging Kyla and Valora on. They were nearing the edge of the clearing when one of the slavers nearby began to rouse. He lay blocking their path.

For a split second Marlowe stood and stared, but it was long enough for the man to jump to attention. He was on his feet, pulling a knife from his belt. He glared at Marlowe, his upper lip curling into a snarl. "Going somewhere?"

He reached out to grab Valora, but just as he did something flew from behind, sailing over Marlowe's head, hitting the man square in the face. A large rock thumped onto the ground and the man stumbled back, one hand clutching his nose.

Blood poured between his fingers, and suddenly freed slaves surrounded them all, swarming past on their way to escape, knocking the man from his feet.

"They're killing us!" yelled the man, struggling to his feet and pointing at his companion, the slaver whose head had been smashed in.

The chaos was uncontrolled. Fear trilled in the air. A figure burst from the tent across the clearing and the acrid scent of feather dust spilled out into the night air. Atrimus Deegeld. He raised his arms, shouting, "Where's the cripple? The cripple! Get the girl, you fools! If you don't find her I'll kill you all!"

He began to stride around the camp, striking any one he could reach with a thick knobbled stick. The slavers lumbered more quickly now, shaking off the remnants of their drugged sleep to avoid a beating.

Kyla, panic streaking over her face, pointed off to the left, where the bushes grew thick. "That way."

Without waiting for a response she tugged Valora along beside her and ducked down, keeping to the shadows as she moved across the camp, Valora beside her, half-hobbling, half-scurrying away.

Marlowe followed, jumping over the fallen tree trunks and rocks that surrounded the campfire.

A hand reached out, fingers snaking towards his ankle. It was one of the slavers, still lying on the ground half asleep. Marlowe leapt, trampling the man's hand. The slaver yelped in pain.

Marlowe thundered through the bushes, catching glimpses of Kyla and Valora up ahead only when moonlight broke through the leaf canopy.

When he caught up to them, breathless and panting, Kyla was leaning against a tree, heaving breaths just as he was. In one hand she held a bow that she must have stolen from the sleeping slavers. The quiver was slung over her back.

He nodded at the bow. "We'll make a thief of you yet."

She didn't acknowledge the comment, but looked past him to the encampment they had just left. "We can't stop. They'll be coming after us."

Valora was crouched on the ground, looking even more alert and just as fearful as she had when she had first caught sight of him creeping towards her when she was locked in the cage.

"Quick, before they find us." He grabbed his sister's dress, tugging her away. "We need to find Max. The horses. Get out of here."

Valora snapped round, fierce eyes glaring at him over her humped shoulder. "Let go of me."

Marlowe released her dress as if the fabric scalded him.

She touched a hand to the spot around her neck where the pouch she kept their mother's jewellery in used to hang. It was gone. "He's got it. The crooked wheel."

For a moment the phrase meant nothing to Marlowe, and then it hit him: the delicate piece of metal that had been inside their mother's jewellery box. The Dream Key, as Atrimus had called it.

"That Varoan," Valora continued, waving towards the lit-up tent from which Atrimus had just appeared. "He took everything from me before the auction. He looked at that wheel like it was the most precious thing he had ever seen. He knew what it was, I'm sure of it. I won't leave without it."

A loud caw sounded, followed by the flapping of wings. It could only mean one thing. Yarmon Sacfron had beaten them here, bringing with him untold amounts of gold. Kyla's eyes slid sideways, catching Marlowe's gaze. She too understood.

"You take her. I'll get it," he said.

Kyla nodded, pausing only to draw an arrow from the stolen quiver on her back and nock it into her bow. Valora was about to protest, but Marlowe didn't stay to listen. Kyla could handle Valora's objections, he had no doubt about that.

Atrimus was heading back towards the tent, his face like a storm that had not yet reached its peak.

Where would he have put the Dream Key? It must be either on his person, or in the tent itself.

Marlowe crept closer to the tent, making sure to keep out of sight as he watched Atrimus lift the entrance flap and go back inside. Voices started up immediately. Atrimus was arguing with whoever else was inside. The words were unclear, but the tone of their voices, the anger that shot back and forth, was evident.

All of a sudden words rang out, clear as water. "Where is she? Where is the cripple? Have you lost her?"

The voice sent a chill right through Marlowe, leaving him empty. He had suspected it, but now he knew it, and the difference between suspicion and knowledge was unbearable. It was Yarmon Sacfron.

Marlowe approached the entrance to the tent, and knelt down. He was barely breathing. He lifted the two flaps of fabric that made the entrance so he could peer inside, making sure that he couldn't be seen.

The tent was larger than it appeared from the outside, and a small fire burnt in the centre, throwing out unstable bursts of light.

The two men were standing opposite one another. The Nilari bird sat at Yarmon's feet, its small black eyes bulbous and wary. Beside the bird were large sacks, one of which was open at the neck and flopping over, revealing piles of gold coin so copious that Marlowe blinked and rubbed his eyes to check he wasn't imagining it. He had never seen so much gold in one place.

"She's gone?" Yarmon's voice boomed, shaking the sides of the tent.

"We'll find her. We'll find her. And I still have this." Atrimus held up the wheel.

Yarmon struck out at him, nearly knocking the wheel from Atrimus' hand. "You blind fool. The key is worthless without the girl. The cripple. She is our saviour! The saviour of the Nilari! She is the only one who can unlock the Isle of Ashes. I will give you nothing until you bring her here."

What madness was this? Valora, the saviour of the Nilari? Marlowe's head swirled. And what of the Isle of Ashes? The resting place of the slaughtered Nilari souls? A legend, surely! Nothing but a story... But then why was Yarmon speaking about it like it was a real place?

Marlowe clenched his fists and dug them into the mud. He was barely breathing, so that he might hear what was being said.

Atrimus gave a hopeless whimper and Yarmon pushed past him. "I'll find her myself."

Yarmon's form was looming larger as he stormed towards the entrance of the tent. He was leaving! Yarmon was seconds from colliding with Marlowe, where he crouched on the other side of the entrance.

Marlowe took a step back, intending to retreat into the bushes. He glanced over his shoulder. Valora and Kyla had long disappeared.

A branch snapped under his foot just as Yarmon exploded from the tent. He whirled round, his strange pale eyes locking on Marlowe's. Barely a second had passed, but it was long enough for Marlowe to feel all of the man's power; it hit him like a wave and Marlowe had the sensation that this man knew everything about him, instantly.

"It's him! From the auction," yelled Atrimus, who was following right behind Yarmon. "Killed one of my men!"

"You!" Yarmon's eyes narrowed. "Where is she then? Where is your sister?"

A shiver of pure panic rolled down Marlowe's spine. The man knew everything, *everything*. He pointed one long-nailed, trembling finger at Marlowe, who could do little but answer, "I don't know."

"Liar." A knife, thrown with unexpected skill, flashed from Yarmon's hand, flying through the air so quickly that Marlowe barely had time to react. He tried to dodge, but the knife was faster. *Thud*. It lodged in his shoulder, spinning him off balance.

Marlowe stumbled, clutching out for something to hold onto. There was nothing but low shrubs nearby. He fell to his knees.

Yarmon stepped towards Marlowe, coming to stand over him.

Marlowe, still kneeling, looked up. Yarmon raised a hand, fingers clawed, and aimed it at him. He felt his body freeze, and knew he could not move even if he wanted to. Some unseen magic pinned him in place. Pain, worse even than the knife wound, started as if from nowhere, and spread through his entire body all at once. It was Yarmon. Somehow, the man was inflicting pain on him without touching him.

"Your mother—" He whispered the word repulsively and Marlowe would have recoiled had he been able to move. "—never helped us either. Said she had done her part—" A humourless cackle erupted from between Yarmon's cracked lips. "—and refused to tell my messenger anything when I sent him to find her. Got them both killed. We could have saved her, you know, if only she'd told us where she hid the key."

Marlowe felt invisible hands on his throat, around his heart, crushing the air from his chest as though he was pressed between the palms of an unseen giant. He tried to struggle but found he could not move.

He could see Atrimus, his mouth open, his eyes wide. He looked frozen too, but whether with fear or because some unseen force was being inflicted on him also, Marlowe couldn't tell.

Yarmon stepped back, but Marlowe found himself still unable to move, aching with a deep fiery pain that seemed to come from his own bones.

"Where is she? Where is your sister?" Yarmon asked.

Marlowe shook his head. "I don't know."

"I don't like liars." Yarmon flicked his fingers, a signal for the bird at his feet to move. It came with flurried flaps of its wings, battering at Marlowe; the wings, the claws, all of the bird was at him.

He couldn't move, couldn't fight. He could do nothing. Talons tore down his face, warm blood began to run.

Something shot from behind him, faster than the bird, faster than Yarmon.

An arrow. It found its mark, lodging in Yarmon's eyeball. Marlowe knew it, knew the implication of it, knew that he might live, all in the moment before the strange force pressing in on him ceased to exist and he collapsed to the ground.

Kyla.

She was there, behind him, having risen from the bushes like a Goddess, another arrow nocked into her bow. Before he could speak she let fly at close range, again, her arrow lodging in Atrimus' heartspace this time.

Kyla, Kyla, *Kyla*.

15

KYLA

THE SLAVERS' CAMP

Kyla raised one arm to protect herself from the Nilari bird that was squawking frantically, now its master was dead. The air was a storm of bird and wing and feather and beak.

She knew this bird, recognised its golden beak, its wild eyes. It had attacked her before. This time she didn't hesitate. She nocked another arrow and let loose. The bird fell, flapping on the ground a few times before all movement ceased.

Nearby, blood was bubbling at Atrimus' mouth. He was sprawled where he had fallen, trying to tug on the arrow in his chest, but to no avail. He gave one last sigh, red spattering from his mouth to the ground as he died.

Kyla grabbed Marlowe, hauling him up by one arm. "Quick, hurry. Get up. Can you stand?"

She let go and he stumbled, falling to his knees. He gripped her arm with a desperation that shot fear into her heart. She tried to assess the damage. His face was deeply scratched from his forehead to his jaw. Three stripes of bright red blood, running down his cheek.

There was a knife embedded in his shoulder. At least it wasn't his leg, but it didn't look good. She reached to pull it out and then decided against it. If he started to bleed, he would be too weak to walk, to run, and if they got caught not even Valora would be able to save him.

She knelt down so she was on Marlowe's level and looked him in the eye. His eyelids were flickering strangely; he was either in shock or he had been somehow poisoned. What was the magic that had held him in place? What power had Yarmon had?

"The bird, it was—"

"I know," Kyla said "It was the same one, from the attack at the plains."

"That man—"

"Followed us. I know."

"You killed them..." A wideness, a wondering, washed over Marlowe's features, mixing with the pain. "You killed them... to save me."

She snorted a dismissal and tried to haul him to his feet again. "Don't read into it." He gave a small groan as he struggled to stand, and she yanked him up one final time and said, "You can thank me later."

She pushed him towards Valora, whom she had left further off under cover of the bushes, and he managed to stay upright.

"The camp's in chaos. Worse than before." She cocked her head, listening. Men squealed and hollered, their shouts echoing towards where Marlowe and Kyla stood. Shadows darted between trees and in front of fires. "Go. Move off, further into the forest. I'll find you. Take Valora out of harm's way. Go straight. Look for Max." She flicked her arm back and forth, pointing further into the trees, but Marlowe didn't move.

"I'm not leaving you."

She ran her gaze over him, taking in his wounds, the blood, the pain written so clearly in his eyes. "You're no good to me."

A flash of insult sparked across his face, but immediately faded and turned to urgency. He looked over his shoulder, where the traders and slaves were still fighting, where the men were yelling and searching for Valora. It wouldn't be long before they were found. "We need to go. Come with me."

"I'm not walking away from a key that has the power to open the Isle of Ashes."

Marlowe gasped. "You heard that?"

Kyla nodded. "Where is it? Where did he put it? I don't see—"

There was a sound, like someone moving nearby. She looked back at where Yarmon's body lay, the arrow still impaled in his eyeball. Her heart gave a frightened lurch. He was moving!

He wasn't dead as she had thought, but was dragging himself towards the dead bird, his fingers running through the creature's feathers. A howl came from Yarmon's mouth, more awful than the screech the bird had made as it died. It was grief, as pure as Kyla had ever heard it.

He looked up, his one-eyed gaze falling on Kyla. Then he noticed Atrimus' fallen body and began to claw himself across the ground, reaching for something concealed in the the palm of Atrimus' hand.

The key!

In seconds he would have it. Kyla pushed Marlowe aside, yelling, "Go. Go now! Get Valora, and run!" She waited only a moment, to be sure Marlowe was heading in the right direction, before she lunged in the opposite one, grasping for the little key. Atrimus' hand was still warm, his fingers soft and pliable. It wouldn't take much to steal the metal from him. She began to peel his fingers back, but before she could grab hold of the key itself, a bloody hand crunched around her own.

She nearly screamed. The horror of it was unbearable. Yarmon. The arrow was deep in his skull and yet here he was, gripping her hand, lurching towards her, blood running down his face.

He spoke in a growl. "That doesn't belong to you."

Kyla tried to pull away but something prevented her from loosening her hand from his grip. He was exerting some intangible force, crushing her, holding her in place, making it impossible to breathe. This, she was sure, was what Marlowe had been experiencing when he had stood, unmoving, as the bird attacked him.

She couldn't speak. She couldn't call for help.

She tried to turn, to look for Marlowe or even Valora, but she couldn't move. There was no noise that might suggest the proximity of someone other than Yarmon himself. She was alone. Helpless. Her heart began to beat so fast it would surely break free of her frozen ribcage.

"The key is ours! You Moriyans think you can lay claim to anything you want? You cannot!" Yarmon wrenched the shaft free of his own eyeball, the arrowhead sucking and popping as he drew it out. He gave no indication he felt any pain, and Kyla wondered for a moment if he was even human.

He forced her hand from Atrimus' and grabbed the key himself. A croak of laughter popped from his lips, and blood that had trickled from his eyes down to his mouth, sprayed out. "When the key is brought to our King, he shall rise again and we shall have vengeance! We shall destroy Moriya, and tear down the temple where the Sages dared to hang his wings. No longer shall they dangle as a trophy to Moriyan wickedness!"

Kyla thought of the great wings that hung over the healing circle in the Moriyan Temple. She wanted to shout, to scream, to tell him that the Nilari King would never return, that all the Nilari were dead, that he, *stupid, stupid man*, was labouring under a cruel delusion. But her lips would not move, they could form no words.

Straining against the invisible bonds, Kyla felt a sudden twitch in her face, as if some of her outrage had broken through whatever spell he had cast over her. Yarmon had seen it too, for one eyebrow rose over his bloody-blind eye.

"You think I lie? You think my words are nothing more than the ravings of a lunatic?" He began to laugh that crazed, awful laugh again, bloody spit-globules spurting from his mouth.

After a few moments his laughter shrank back to a throaty chuckle as he prised himself from the ground. When he stood at his full height he flipped the key in the air, and it threw out black sparks that glowed in the darkness. "What do you have to say?"

Something snapped, her body released and Kyla suddenly found herself able to speak, although no other part of her could move. She spat the words with as much vehemence as she could muster. "The Nilari King will never rise again! The Nilari are dead, they're gone! They will never return!"

Yarmon wiped the bloody trail that ran from his eye down his cheek with the sleeve of his jacket. "Ah, but that is where you are wrong."

Kyla blinked, still unable to move. What was he talking about?

He must have noticed whatever fragment of confusion she had managed to express, for he chuckled cruelly. "The King is not dead. He is but trapped, in the Isle of Ashes. Raging, tormented... his desire for vengeance merely festering, increasing... I feel his vitriol burning in my own blood." He held up the key again for her to see. "And now, I am one step closer to releasing them. All I need is your little cripple to unlock the gate, and then—"

Kyla didn't even stop to wonder what role Valora might play in all this. All she knew was that she could never let it happen. "You'll never get her. Never."

Yarmon rocked backwards, his lips wide, his teeth sharp and white inside his gaping mouth, and laughed, one quick blast of laughter before he spoke again. "You think you have the power to change fate? That small crippled girl who wields the ancient Nilari healing power is our saviour. She is the only true saviour."

Kyla felt her fear curdle into anger. How could he claim that Valora's magic had anything to do with the Nilari? She was marked as the next acolyte of the God-Sage. Her power belonged to him, there was no contesting it. Kyla swore to herself that Valora would never belong to this crazed man, not whilst she herself was still living and breathing. Had Kyla not been held rigid by some magical means, she would have thrown herself at Yarmon and dug out his other eyeball with her own fingers.

She opened her mouth to speak again, but Yarmon reached out a clawed hand, snapped his fingers, and once more Kyla felt her body freeze, pain shooting through her veins. A scream rose up her throat, but there was no outlet for the sound.

Yarmon, seeing the distress on her almost-frozen features, smiled a cunning, delighted smile and brought his mauled face so close to hers that she could smell the leather of his jacket and the sourness of his breath, rancid with feather dust. He trailed one long finger, the nail sharpened to a point like a talon, across her neck. She wanted to pull back, to recoil, but could do neither.

He lifted his fingernail from her skin and said, "It would be fitting, really, for you to be the first to pay for all the evil your people performed on mine." A small gasp escaped between Kyla's lips, but Yarmon only smiled. "I could torture you right here, right now... slit your throat, tear you limb from limb, and burn your body until the sky is full of putrid smoke! Then, perhaps, you will have taken some small steps towards atonement."

Yarmon had barely finished speaking when a blade slashed before Kyla's eyes. His neck sliced from ear to ear. Skin peeled open. Blood gushed from the wound like water rushing over a waterfall, and yet a taunting smile was still visible on his face.

The force holding Kyla disappeared. She collapsed. Yarmon fell.

Marlowe.

He stood beside her, the knife that had been in his own shoulder now dripping with Yarmon's blood.

He dropped the knife and pressed his hand to the wound in his shoulder. He looked at her, not with pride or any satisfaction for what he had done, but with glaring agony apparent in every part of his being. His shoulder was bleeding profusely.

Marlowe grimaced and then the ghost of a smile twitched at the edge of his mouth. "You can thank me later."

Kyla, dazed, stumbled to her feet. "Let's go," she said.

"One last thing." Marlowe let go of his shoulder, his hand covered in blood, and knelt to pick up the little piece of metal, which had fallen from Yarmon's hand. He flipped it up and caught it again, but no dark sparks flew from it, no light, no fire. Whatever power had held her frozen, it was Yarmon's and not the key's. It was clear that Marlowe had no ability to make the key function or perform its magic.

He clutched the piece of metal, grimaced at some internal pain and said, "Now we can go."

Kyla stared at him, at the piece of metal in his hand, glinting with its strange, dark light, and all of a sudden every fibre in her body seemed to ignite. She couldn't let him have it, not if it really did possess the power Yarmon had claimed it did.

She snatched it from him, ripping it out of his fingers. She barely had it in her hand, catching only the briefest glimpse of Marlowe's shocked expression, before everything around her disappeared.

Marlowe was gone. She blinked, but the forest, the trees, the cool breeze rustling the leaves, the dirt beneath her boots, all of it had vanished.

All sound vanished too. She could no longer hear the shouts of the men in the camp.

The only constant was the little piece of metal, which she still held in her hand.

A strange energy shot through her body, vibrations rippling through her flesh. A buzzing or humming sounded in her mind, although she felt it too in her body, as if she was moving in resonance with the skin of a nearby drum.

Around her, a room began to take shape until she was somewhere else entirely. It was a room she recognised, a room she knew well.

She was home.

She stood utterly still, afraid to move. It was her father's bedroom. The polished wooden floorboards, the wide bed, the carved headboard, the thick velvet drapes at the window were all the same, but the room felt more vibrant, more lived in than Kyla had ever known it. The curtains were not faded, not thick with dust and in need of beating; even the tear in the velvet that she had made with a knife when she was a child, and for which her father had cruelly beaten her, was absent.

Two women stood at the end of the bed. Kyla could see neither of their faces. One was dressed in servants' attire, a long black dress, tied at her waist and sleeves rolled to the elbows. The other wore a white nightdress, her feet bare and her hair loose and thick, like the pelt of a dark-skinned beast hanging down her back.

Both of the women were peering at what seemed to be a bundle of fabric, lying on the bed. A soft mewling sound came from the bundle and Kyla realised that it was in fact a tiny swaddled baby, only hours old.

One of the women began to talk. "I didn't know, I didn't. I swear. I only did what I thought was best. Never, never did I think this would happen." The voice was unmistakeable with its Varoan twang. Kyla knew it well, and when the woman turned so Kyla could see her profile, the sharp nose and large, heavily lashed dark eyes, she knew for certain. It was Aida, her cousin's royal nursemaid.

Tears ran down Aida's face.

The other woman lifted the baby and turned to Aida. Holding the baby close to her chest, looking down at it, she kissed its forehead. A lock of her own hair fell across her face, and it was only when she hooked her hair behind her ear with one finger that Kyla was able to see her face, and it was one she knew.

The Queen. The Mad Queen of Moriya, in a nightdress, her hair wild and free, her cheeks flushed.

The realisation was swift and sharp. Kyla gasped, and then worried that the two women would notice her, but they paid her no heed. She did not exist to them. They were playing out a scene from the past, and Kyla was merely a silent observer. She came closer, so close now that she could have touched them.

What was the Queen doing dressed this way, in Kyla's own home?

Kyla reached out a hand to touch a strand of the Queen's dark hair, to know if it was real, but the woman suddenly turned as though she knew someone else was present, and Kyla let her hand fall. The Queen's eyes were alert, listening, and then, after a moment, hearing no confirmation of her suspicions, she turned back.

"Oh, what will we do? When they find out what I have done, peace between Varo and Moriya will be destroyed. They will kill us all, as surely as I stand before you now." Aida clutched at the dark-haired woman's arm. "What will we do, Virien?"

The name sent a full shiver rolling over every inch of Kyla's body. Virien.

The woman was not the Queen at all, but Kyla's own mother. The Queen and Virien were sisters, and so similar that they were almost interchangeable, only for the fact that Kyla's mother had been dead for all of Kyla's sixteen years. She had died in childbirth, at least that was what Kyla had always been told. *Your mother lost her life bringing you into the world.* Yet here she was, alive, holding a baby and yet in full health herself. How was it possible?

"How did it happen?" asked Virien.

Aida's hands fluttered from her mouth and back to her dress, which she flattened with both palms. "It was the key, the Dream Key. She said it could bring our deepest desires, our most precious dreams, forth into the world. That even barren women might bear children. She said a child could be born that would save the peace between our countries. A child to bring peace to all of Tolinaye. She lied. She tricked me. This child is no child of dreams, it is a child of nightmares! It will surely bring no peace. This child will start a war!"

"Aida, slow down. I can't understand you. Who said such things?"

Aida covered her face with her hands and spoke through her fingers, shaking her head all the while. "I don't know, I don't know. She had such a kind voice, but she must have been a witch, a demon, some deadly creature to have played me so! I never saw her face. She kept it covered with a hood, and where there would have been a face I saw only shadows. I don't know who she was. I swear it, Virien. She seemed so sweet and gentle. I thought she meant well. I only did what I thought would help..." Aida paced back and forth across the room, running her hands through her tangled hair. "I never would have done it had I known... Great God-Sage, the Sacred Core will hang us from the gallows until we are nothing but food for the birds. They'll kill us all. The Sages, the priests, they will come for us." Aida gasped, one hand clapped to her mouth. "Your husband, Lander. He'll kill you. He will kill me." She gave a muffled squeal. "He will kill the child!"

Virien's features hardened, even as she held the baby in her arms. "Lander will not find out. No one will ever find out. I will deal with this."

Kyla felt fear unleash from the base of her spine, knowing without doubt that the child was the secret the two women discussed. How did they mean to keep a living, breathing child secret?

Aida ceased her nervous movement and stepped up to Virien, putting one hand on her arm. Despite her stillness her voice quavered when she spoke. "What do you mean? What will you do? I beg you to do nothing that will compromise your own soul. *Murder must be paid in blood*, Virien."

Virien shook her head. "Do not concern yourself with what I might do. Go to the palace. Make sure no one sees you."

Aida stood rooted to the spot. "You must assure me of the child's safety or I will not leave."

A rumble sounded in the back of Virien's throat. "That's why you came, isn't it? So that I might clean up the mess you made?"

The two women stood still, staring at one another, and the baby let out a cry. Virien laid the child on the bed.

Again Aida pulled her palms down her cheeks, a small sob escaping from between her lips. "I... I—"

"Go, Aida. For the sake of the God-Sage, leave before I lose my nerve. Get out."

Aida, throwing one last glance at the baby on the bed, rushed from the room, and when the sounds of Aida's footsteps had died, Kyla's mother stepped up to the bed.

She bent over and began to unwrap the swaddle from the child, and then, as the cloth fell away, something fell to the ground.

A piece of metal.

It rolled to the floor. Rolled... like a wheel.

It was the very object that Kyla held in her hand. The little crooked wheel. There were two different versions of it, one in Kyla's present time and one in the time of this scene she was watching.

Her mother bent to pick it up, but she did not inspect it. She slid it into her pocket at once, as if its appearance held no surprise for her whatsoever. As if she already knew to expect it, and it was in fact exactly what she had been looking for when she unwrapped the child.

There was a moment of silence as her mother looked down on the baby. She bowed her head and pressed her fingertips together, offering up some silent prayer. "I claim this child as my daughter, and name her for the God-Sage. Kyla Tarthwen, Morden's heir, saviour of the Moriyan people. I pray that one day, I might be forgiven for what I am about to do."

Suddenly there was a knife in her mother's hand. Kyla wasn't sure where it had come from, but that it was there now was undeniable. Her mother raised the knife over the tiny child, who had begun the most pitiful ululating cry.

With a shock that ran through her whole body, Kyla realised she meant to kill the child lying on the bed. She screamed and flung herself towards her mother, grappling for the knife she held over her head.

Just as Kyla's fingers were about to clench around her mother's arm, she found there was nothing there to hold. Her hand passed right through, like a ghost, only not like that at all, because her mother was gone, the baby was gone, and there was only...

Marlowe.

16

—— ◆ ——

MARLOWE

THE SLAVERS' CAMP

Marlowe hadn't expected Kyla to move the way she did. One moment she had been snatching the wheel from him, the next her eyes had glazed over, taking on a far-off look as if she had gone elsewhere, and then all of a sudden she toppled forward, completely off-balance, one hand flailing through the air towards him. And yet it didn't seem as though she could actually see him. Her eyes were still unfocused, like she was daydreaming.

As soon as her hand made contact with his, her eyes flicked alert, awake, and he knew she could see him again.

She collapsed against him, thumping against the wound on his shoulder. He swore, louder than he should have. She pushed against him, righting herself, but pressing on his wound, her hand coming away covered in blood.

Kyla cursed, confused, staring at her hand a moment before wiping it on her trousers.

Marlowe clamped his own hand against his shoulder, stemming the flow of blood. "What... what was that? What just happened? You took the wheel and then—"

Kyla wasn't listening to him. She was staring at the little piece of metal in her hand, her expression one Marlowe couldn't fathom. Was it amazement or fear? "By the God-Sage," she whispered. "What is this thing?"

There was no time for him to answer. The shouts from the guards in the camp became louder.

Kyla's head jerked up, her eyes darting as she listened to the noise. "We have to go. Where's Valora?"

Marlowe nodded his head back to the bushes behind him where he had left his sister with strict instructions to begin to make her way back to Max. "She's not far."

A shout burst over the noise, louder than everything else. "There, there they are."

The men began to turn, mouths briefly limp with shock as they saw Marlowe and Kyla standing by the tent, the bodies at their feet. One of the men began to yell, crashing towards them, shaking a violent finger. "Atrimus! They've killed Atrimus!"

Kyla moved so quickly that Marlowe couldn't keep up. She grabbed him, pulling him behind her. She was trying to run, but he was slowing her down. He struggled along, allowing her to pull him through the trees.

But where would she lead him? If they ran for where Max and Valora were hiding they would give them away. What would be the point in revealing their hiding place after all this? Of going to all this trouble, only to reveal the others and all end up trapped? No. They couldn't do that.

Marlowe cast a quick glance backwards. One of the men was still charging at them, shouting at the top of his voice, the words booming over the noise of the fighting. "Her. She did it, she killed them."

Kyla stopped so suddenly that Marlowe felt himself totter off-balance, only just managing not to fall. She was pulling an arrow from the quiver and nocking it into her bow at such speed Marlowe could barely believe she could move so fast. But even so the men were getting closer with each passing second.

"What are you doing? There isn't time! We have to run!"

Marlowe was about to grab her when she flicked her gaze in his direction, searing him in place. He didn't dare move again.

She let the arrow fly. It sank into the shoulder of the man who was coming towards her, knocking him backwards. He gave a roar, stopped in his tracks, looked at the arrow where it stood out. He clenched a fist about the shaft and, in a great show of bravado, began to pull it from his flesh. When the second arrow hit he barely saw it coming, so preoccupied was he with the first.

It went right through his neck. He was dead before he had time to realise what had hit him.

His body collapsed amidst the dirt, the rocks, the embers of a campfire, throwing sparks into the air.

Kyla glanced at the body and then at Marlowe.

"Now we run," she said.

Together they dashed through the bushes, leaping over bodies, plunging through the trees, not caring that the thorns and branches scratched them.

There was something exhilarating about running this way, with Kyla at his side, as if, somehow, they were allies. More than that, perhaps. Friends.

She led him through the woods, back towards Max and the horses, moving with a deal more alacrity and deftness than he did. She was stealthy; he was lumbering, crashing across the forest floor.

When they had covered a fair distance, they had almost left the noise of the camp behind. Kyla grew still and Marlowe did the same, relieved to be able to slow down. Now that the sound of the leaves and branches crunching under their feet ceased, he was aware that this shoulder was throbbing worse than before. He could hear Kyla's breathing, as fast as his own, and then, far-off, the sound of the men, still fighting the slaves.

Where was Max? Where was Valora? Just as Marlowe was worried they had lost them entirely there was a flash in the bushes ahead: the red of Max's uniform.

Kyla must have seen it too, for she headed that way instantly, and moments later Max was striding towards them.

"Thank the God-Sage, you're alive—"

"Where's Valora?" Kyla spoke to Max, but gave a subtle nod in Marlowe's direction and lowered her voice. "He's wounded."

Max glanced quickly at Marlowe, shot an alarmed look at Kyla and rushed to help her support him. It was a relief to be able to lean against Max's strength.

"Over here." Max led them a little further into the trees, where Valora was crouched near the horses, huddled, fearful, waiting, peeking intermittently from behind a tree.

But the sight of Marlowe was enough to draw her out. She hurried towards him. "What happened?"

He could barely see her, so much blood was running down his face. And one of his eyes was almost swollen shut. He knelt down, keeping one hand pressed to the wound on his shoulder.

Max and Kyla stepped back as Valora's hands fluttered around the blood.

"Don't touch him," Kyla said. "If you do anything that creates a big blast of light, they'll know we're here. They'll come running. And I've run out of arrows." She flung the bow and empty quiver to the ground.

Valora dropped her hands to her sides and Kyla nudged her out of the way, coming to stand before Marlowe herself.

"Let me see," she said.

Marlowe met her gaze and gave a brief nod before he lifted his hand from the wound. Blood surged to the surface, bringing a rusty, salty tang to the air. He could tell from the subtle widening of Kyla's eyes, the lift of her eyebrows, that it was more than she had anticipated.

She gave a slight, concerned shake of the head and pressed her hand to the wound. Marlowe could feel it pulsing against her palm and knew he couldn't go any further like this. The scratches on his face were one thing, his swollen tender hand another, but they could wait. This shoulder wound... It needed attention *now*.

Kyla looked at Valora. "Do it. Heal him, when I lift my hand."

"What about the light?" Max asked.

"It's not that bad," Marlowe said, trying to wave them all away with his good hand. "I don't need healing."

"Don't be an ass. You need it," Kyla said.

Valora stepped closer, her eyes steely. "My whole life I had to listen to Mother and Father telling me what I could and couldn't do, and when they weren't there I had to listen to you." Marlowe blinked, unable to deny it. "I know you're trying to protect me, but this time you need me. This time, I'm making the decision."

Before anyone could stop her, Valora's hand was against the wound. Only this time there was no light, at least not like the last time, not like when she had healed Max. There was a slight glow at the edges, around her fingers, as Marlowe was familiar with from previous healings.

He closed his eyes, feeling the heat run from her skin into his, spreading like blood dropped into a bowl of water.

When the light vanished Valora slumped forward. Marlowe's eyes sprang open and he grabbed her. His movement was free, limber. There was no pain in his shoulder or his hand. Even his face felt better. Valora's magic had done its work. The flow of blood had ceased entirely. He held her weight, slight though she was, with no discomfort.

"What's wrong with her?" Kyla asked.

"She gets tired, after a healing."

"She didn't before. When she healed Max."

Marlowe hesitated, wondering how much he could share. She was staring, waiting for his explanation. "That was different. I suspected it then, and now I know for sure. Max's healing was no ordinary healing."

Ignoring Kyla's questioning eyes and gaping mouth, Marlowe helped Valora sit down. She looked dizzy, her eyelids fluttered closed and she leant into him, unable to keep herself upright.

She clutched at his shirt, murmuring the words into his chest. "Did you get it? Do you have it?"

Kyla took the piece of metal from her pocket, letting it lie flat in the middle of her palm. "We have it." But she made no move to hand the object over, instead curling her fingers around it again.

Valora was too weak to object, and just as Marlowe was about to tell Kyla to hand it over, a noise from the direction of the camp drew his attention.

Kyla too turned to look. Men were coming, crashing through the trees.

"We need to go," she said. "Get the horses."

There was little time to speak as they raced through the forest and out onto the plains in the direction of Moriya to the south east. Valora was still too tired to manage a horse alone so she was riding with Kyla and Max alternately. Marlowe wished she could ride with him, but Kyla wouldn't let them ride together... probably because she still suspected that they might try to escape if they were allowed to travel together.

Was she wrong? Escape was looking like a reasonable option.

Valora was the acolyte. She was branded as such, and they were heading for Moriya so she could dedicate her life to the God-Sage. But the small piece of metal their mother had hidden in a box and given to Valora to keep wasn't just a trinket. It wasn't simply a little piece of jewellery or a memento. A keepsake.

It was a key. A key to open the Isle of Ashes, where the tormented souls of the Nilari had been trapped for five hundred years.

And now Kyla knew it too. He shot a glance in her direction. What was she thinking? She hadn't said much at all since they had fled from the camp, but she must have questions. She must have as many as he had, if not more. She was lined up to become a member of the Sacred Core. She could hardly bring a girl who was the *saviour of the Nilari* into the temple to be initiated as an acolyte, could she?

Suddenly another memory surfaced, and he saw Yarmon in his mind's eye, as vivid as if he stood before him again. He heard the words Yarmon had spoken about his mother. That she had refused to share the whereabouts of the key, because she had already *done her part.*

What part was it that Yarmon had spoke of? Was it possible that she had colluded with the Nilari rebels in some way?

Had Valora's hopeful speculation that their parents were innocent been nothing but wishful thinking?

A leaden weight settled in the pit of his stomach, as he realised this was a secret he would have to bear alone, until he knew what it really meant.

If Kyla found reason enough to refuse to take Valora to Moriya as an acolyte, what else might she do? What was to stop her killing the two of them out here in the middle of nowhere? Marlowe stiffened at the thought, feeling tension run up his thighs and down his spine. He shifted in the saddle, glimpsing Kyla out of the corner of his eye.

Could he take her on? He knew she was better trained than he was, but he was sure he was stronger. He watched the sword sway gently from her hip as she rode. He knew it was sharp, and then there were the knives in her boots.

The knives. Maybe if he could steal that black knife again... But how? Kyla had both the knife and the wheel, and didn't look like she was about to give up either. At least she had ditched the bow and arrow. He could imagine stealing off with Valora on the back of a horse only to be shot down from behind by one of Kyla's arrows. The picture in his mind was so vivid he could almost feel the impact of the arrow in his back.

He shook his head. He couldn't risk it with Valora. The best way forward, surely, was to play the whole thing down. Pretend that his mother had nothing to do with any of it, and that it couldn't possibly be the case that the little piece of metal did anything as powerful, as spectacular, and as ultimately threatening as opening the Isle of Ashes.

Yet again Marlowe had to admit that Valora would be safer in Moriya, as an acolyte, than anywhere else. If he could make that happen, if he could convince Kyla to take his sister there, then maybe, just maybe, they would survive.

17

KYLA

THE DREAM KEY

"You killed the priest?" Max was all agog, staring at Marlowe through the heat haze above the campfire they had built.

They had ridden as far as they could, and had set up camp as night fell. If Kyla's estimation was right, they were only a few days' ride from the city, although what she would do when she got there, she wasn't sure.

"I finished him off." Marlowe looked up at Kyla as he spoke. There were scars running down his face. Valora's healing had sealed the skin, but hadn't returned it to its original, perfect, state. His face was marred forever. Either he hadn't realised or he didn't mind, for as he looked at her his lips formed the slightest, almost conspiratorial, smile. Kyla didn't return it and Marlowe, briefly unsettled by her rejection, turned back to Max. "Kyla shot an arrow through his eye. You could say his death was a joint effort."

Max, mouth hanging open, looked at Kyla, who stared down at the toes of her boots and rubbed them into the dirt. Her thoughts were a mess. How could she begin to untangle everything she had learnt back at the camp? Everything she had done?

Yarmon's words echoed in her head, the image of him, blood pouring down his face replayed in her mind. The men she had killed... She could remember the look on each of their faces...

"Kyla, you shot him?" Max asked.

She resurfaced from her contemplation and nodded, slowly. "He was going to kill us. He was going to..." Her heart gave an awkward thump and she waved her hand in Marlowe's direction.

He was going to kill Marlowe.

Max frowned, and Kyla knew he understood her awkwardness, but there was so much too that he didn't, no, *couldn't*, understand, and the idea that he might attribute her anguish solely to her feelings for Marlowe was another irritation she couldn't stomach.

Marlowe hadn't noticed her hesitation, or if he had he'd ignored it, for he was continuing to regale them with the story. "I ripped the knife out of my own shoulder and used it to slit his throat."

Valora, recovered from the healing, was sitting cross-legged at Marlowe's feet, gazing up at him, hanging off his every word. She adored him; there was no question about that, even if she didn't always approve of his choices. When Kyla had first met her, she had seemed meek, but in her own way she had backbone; a great irony given the shape of her spine.

But who was she *really*? Who were her parents that they had possessed such an item as the one Kyla still had in her pocket? Marlowe hadn't yet asked for it back, although she had seen him casting glances towards her pocket, as though he could see it through the fabric of her trousers. In fact, she was sure Marlowe was much more uneasy than he was letting on. His bravado felt hollow, and even the smiles he kept throwing at her had a nervous edge to them, the usual mischievous glint missing from his eyes.

"And what about the wheel?" Valora asked.

Kyla felt her breath hitch in her throat and she laid a hand over her pocket. Marlowe cast a glance in her direction and began to speak, faster even than before.

"I snatched it, right out of the priest's dead hand." Marlowe scrunched his fingers in a fist. "Just like that."

Valora blinked up at him. "Where is it now then?"

Marlowe's gaze settled, hard, on Kyla.

She stiffened. Whatever she felt for Marlowe, she still wasn't sure she could trust him. How could she explain what had happened when she had held the wheel? Even now she was sure she felt a strange tingling in her fingertips, a memory of the sensation that had filled her body back by the tent.

Marlowe looked at her, his head cocked to one side, seeming to ask *What's wrong*? But there was a shrewd look in his eye that told her he had known all along that she was keeping something back.

Until this very moment she had assumed that he had not realised anything was amiss, and that the duration of her vision, the time spent in that alternate reality, had been but a meaningless fraction of a second for him. But now, feeling his gaze, as intense as if it was his hands that touched her, she knew that she had underestimated him.

She pulled the piece of metal from her pocket. "What else do you know about it?"

The question had been too direct, too clearly in need of an answer, and she wished she could retract it and start again. But it was too late. Valora tilted her head, meeting Kyla's gaze with a look that was more innocent inquiry than suspicion. Yet there was an edge, a sharpness, to the way the girl's eyes narrowed when she spoke her next words, like the question wasn't entirely a surprise. "What do you mean?"

Kyla stood up and began to pace by the fire. She could feel their eyes on her, watching every movement.

She waved towards Marlowe, trying to keep her voice calm. "You heard what Yarmon said. This isn't just a piece of metal. It's not some trinket that looks like a wheel. It's a key. A key that opens the Isle of Ashes."

Max, who had missed everything they had overheard back at the camp, spluttered to indicate his incomprehension, but Kyla silenced him with a quick sideways look. Valora too stared, eyes as wide as her gaping mouth. Clearly Marlowe had not shared what had happened with her either.

"What else do you know?" Kyla asked again.

Marlowe shook his head. "Nothing."

Kyla, in an impulse that was more anger than thought, took her sword from its sheath and pointed it at him. "I know you're keeping something from me."

Marlowe held his hands up and pulled his head back. "And you from me."

My mother. My own mother held this key. "I am not obliged to share anything with you," she spat back.

Marlowe's face hardened. "I know nothing more than you do. I swear by the God-Sage."

She took one step closer to him. "Don't swear by the God-Sage. Swear by something you actually care about. Swear by Valora's life."

Marlowe hesitated.

Kyla waved the sword. "I knew it. You do know something. What is it?"

Marlowe shook his head, slowly. "Very little. It belonged to our mother. She kept it, hidden, in a box. That's all I know. I swear it. I swear it on..."

His voice faded. He couldn't do it! He couldn't swear on his sister's life. He *was* lying. Kyla cursed, louder and worse than she ever had, the vile words flying from her mouth in an impenetrable stream of vitriol. The colour drained from Marlowe's face. When she had said everything that ran from her angered mind to her rapid tongue she took a deep breath.

They were all staring at her like she had lost her mind. Even Max. Marlowe had a protective arm around Valora.

Kyla closed her eyes, breathed deep. Then she looked up, meeting Valora's gaze, and spoke in a tone as level as she was able.

"I'm taking you to Moriya, to be the next acolyte, a handmaiden to the God-Sage himself, and you've been carrying around something that—"

"Something that what?" Max asked.

"Something..." The next word stuck in her throat and Kyla forced it to form on her tongue, her lips. "...magic. Something so deeply imbued with Nilari magic that a Nilari rebel was chasing it across the country." She met Max's concerned gaze. "You were right. The birds that attacked us on the Great Plains, they were *his* birds. Yarmon's birds. They were following us, because he wanted this." She held up the wheel, shaking it in the air. "He was going to buy it. For a lot of money. A lot of gold." Kyla slashed an arm through the air, anger shooting through her as she turned to Valora. "He was going to buy you! He called you the *true saviour* of the Nilari people. Those exact words." Kyla could feel herself beginning to shake, but she could not stop. "And this—" Again she shook the piece of metal. "—opens the Isle of Ashes and releases the souls of the Nilari back into the world!"

Valora had turned very pale. She reached for Marlowe's hand, and gripped it so tight her knuckles blanched more than her cheeks.

Max stood up. "What? Kyla, that's insane."

"Is it? Is it?"

Marlowe too stood up, his hands held out towards Kyla. "Please, put your sword away."

Kyla did no such thing, keeping the blade leveled at Marlowe. "Don't move. Don't you dare move or I'll kill you both."

Marlowe tipped his head to the side, his eyes narrowing. He fixed his gaze on her, his dark eyes full of trepidation, and for a moment she didn't want to be standing opposite him, threatening him, causing that look upon his face. She wanted to be beside him.

He must have sensed her thoughts, for the corners of his lips lifted, tugged upwards by the hint of a smile. A confused one, but a smile nonetheless. She stepped toward him, her sword pointed at his chest.

He stepped backwards, both hands raised. "All right, all right." He paused and then Kyla heard the click of his tongue as he prepared to speak again. "I do think, though, that killing us now would be a waste of all your hard work."

The smile was real now, and his eyes gleamed with amusement. He was trying to close the rift between them, and she was sure his smile had closed many such rifts in the past, but it would not work on her. She spun on her heel, turning her back on him, and put one hand on Max's arm, pinching it harder than she needed to.

"Come with me," she said, shooting a violent glance back at Marlowe as she and Max moved away together.

She heard Marlowe curse, low, under his breath, staring at her from beneath lowered brows. What must he think of her?

She didn't care. She dragged Max with her, out of earshot, until they were behind a cluster of nearby trees. She could still see Marlowe and Valora if she peered round. They looked too shocked, too confused, to move. They were standing, staring in her direction, Marlowe's arm around Valora again.

Max was whispering rapidly. "This is huge, Kyla. Huge. If all of this is true, it changes everything."

"Do you think I don't know that?" She could feel her body begin to tremble, but whether through rage or fear she wasn't sure. Max glanced at her hand, still holding the sword, now shaking at the hilt.

Max was waiting, but what was she going to say to him? What was safe to share?

"What's wrong?" he asked. "Tell me. I knew something wasn't right, ever since you got back from rescuing Valora. Tell me what it is."

She slid back behind the tree so that Marlowe and Valora could not see her. She could feel the unwelcome prickle of tears behind her eyes.

"Aside from the whole 'this piece of metal has the power to raise the dead and unleash our enemy'?"

Max grimaced, looking at Kyla from beneath lowered brows. Was he afraid she was going to scream and swear again? "Aside from that," he said.

She held the wheel in her hand, unfurling her fingers so he could see it. Max flicked his gaze from the metal to her face and back again.

"When I first held it, I saw something. A vision." She took a deep breath. "No, it was more than a vision. It was real. I was transported to the past. I was walking around, in another time."

Max shook his head, but said nothing, and Kyla tried her best to explain what had happened, what she had seen, but the words were jumbled and the story was confusing, even to her.

When she had finished Max said, "Are you sure it was your mother?"

"Yes. Aida called her by her name."

"And the baby?"

Kyla felt a thick swelling in her throat and her next words were a struggle. "Me. It was me. She was going to kill me. I tried to stop her, but before I could touch her I was back here, with Marlowe. It was over."

Max was silent for a moment. He raised a hand as though he meant to touch her, but decided against it and let his hand fall to his side. "You're alive. She didn't kill you. It never happened. Maybe it wasn't real."

"It was real." Kyla clenched her teeth to hold back the sobbing that so desperately wanted to rise. It didn't matter that her mother hadn't killed her, what mattered was that she had *wanted* to.

"What else?" asked Max tentatively.

Kyla shook her head. None of it made any sense.

"Tell me," Max said gently.

"This fell out of the swaddling." Kyla indicated the little wheel. "It fell out when she unwrapped the baby, and she wasn't even surprised. The key to the Isle of Ashes. She picked it up and put it in her pocket like it was nothing."

"Oh Kyla..." He frowned. "Maybe she didn't know what it was. Maybe..."

Kyla shot him a hard glare and he immediately stopped talking. He began to rub the thumb of one hand into the palm of the other, watching his own fingers. Then, a few moments later, he looked up and said, "What do you think it means?"

Kyla closed her hand tight around the little wheel. "I've no idea."

Max stared at her, and she knew he was urging her to piece the puzzle together. Her vision, the key, Yarmon's words. But it was all too much. She couldn't do it. Instead, she said, "We need to take it back to Moriya. We need to find Aida. We have to ask her what she knows. She was there, Max! If anyone can explain this to me, it's Aida."

Max looked at her. "We don't know that. We don't know what we're doing. We don't know—"

She shook the piece of metal in his face. "My mother had this when I was born, and their mother—" She waved her hand back towards Marlowe and Valora. "—kept it. I don't know what any of that means, but I know it means I'm tied to them. Connected to them, in some way I don't understand."

Max rested a hand on her arm and she felt herself calm at his touch. "What do you want to do?" he asked.

She wanted to weep, but there was no space for that now. She took a breath, shook his hand from her arm, and said, "If this key does open the Isle of Ashes it needs to be locked away, or destroyed. And even if it doesn't open the Isle of Ashes, we know it's powerful. We've seen it, on the banks of the river at Edmund's funeral. Yarmon Sacfron won't be the only rebel looking for it. And once word reaches across the northern mountains that we've killed him..."

Her voice faltered. What repercussions might Yarmon's death have? Who else knew? Who else was there to find out?

Until the day of Edmund's funeral, she had believed that all Nilari priests had been killed long ago.

"Who would send word across the mountains?" Max asked.

"The birds! They're his messengers, they must be. Who knows how they communicate, but we know they do because the birds from the plains must have told Yarmon where we were heading. And the bird he kept with him... You should have seen the way he treated it, talking to it like it was... like it was his child. And when..." Her words tripped over the memory of Yarmon's grief as he had stroked the bloodied feathers of the dead bird.

"You killed the bird too, though?"

Kyla nodded. "But it won't be the only one."

Max looked back at his hands and then, struck by some thought, he snapped back to look at her, but his voice, his words, were slow. "The key... Would you let me hold it? Perhaps... perhaps I can find out something."

He held her gaze and held out his hand for the key.

"You mean..."

"To connect with the dead. The history of it. Will you let me try?"

Kyla held it tighter, questioning for a moment whether she should let him touch it, and then, before she had a chance to change her mind, she dropped it into his palm.

Max cupped it in both hands and closed his eyes. His eyelids trembled and his breathing grew shallow. Kyla waited.

His eyes popped open. He took a deep breath, rapidly sucking in air. "It's too much. I can't. It's so... noisy. It's not like the rings at all. Those were... pure. This is... There's too many... too much." He tried to pass it back to her, but she wouldn't take it.

"There has to be something. Please Max, try again."

He nodded. His eyelids flickered, exposing the whites of his eyes between the lashes.

He began to sway on the spot, and Kyla was sure he was about to give up again when his eyes opened, but it was clear he couldn't really see her. He was elsewhere, almost as she had been when she had seen her vision. But Max wasn't merely watching as she had been. He was speaking the exact words that were being spoken wherever he had gone. The voice that came from his mouth was not his own. It was Atrimus'.

"I'd say there is no price you can put on this small piece of Varoan craftsmanship! There is magic woven into the metal itself. Have you Nilari worshippers not been seeking it for hundreds of years? The key that will unleash the souls of your dead, setting them free after centuries of torment?"

Max paused to give a mock shiver, eerily like the man Kyla had watched on the stage at the auction, the man she herself had killed.

"Imagine it," he continued. "The skies flooded with dead Nilari, soaring through the sky, ripping out the hearts of the Moriyans, making them pay for the slaughter they executed all those hundreds of years ago... Terrifying. Quite terrifying. So," he rubbed his hands together, "why should I sell you such an item? It would destroy the world as I know it. You would have to pay me handsomely to let go of such a thing. And guarantee my safety, when the great unlocking takes place."

He took a noisy inhalation, a great whoosh of breath, and then collapsed. Kyla grabbed him, only just managing to stop him falling.

"Max... Are you all right?"

His hands were tight around her arms, his eyes darting here and there. When he was able to steady himself, he said, "There's more, Kyla. There's another voice. A more powerful one. I'm afraid of it, Kyla. Afraid if I let it in..."

Kyla's heart thrummed in her chest. "What? What do you think will happen?"

"It will never leave me."

"You mustn't do it then. You mustn't Max. Don't—"

But he was already closing his eyes. The pupils rolled back, the whites exposed between trembling lashes. It happened so fast that Kyla wasn't even sure he had had any choice in the matter.

His eyes flicked open, and he began to speak. But it wasn't Max's voice. It was clear, familiar, and sent a rippling chill right through her.

Yarmon Sacfron.

"I knew you would come," he said. "I knew you would need more, Kyla Tarthwen." She gave an involuntary shiver. He must have remembered her name from the auction. "Let me tell you what you fear to know."

Kyla felt herself unable to move, barely able to breathe, as the voice exerted its power over her.

"You saw the death eels that day at the river, and back at Traitors' Lake too. The eels that killed your friend. Did you wonder where they came from? Why they were there? What evil could have brought such monsters into being?

"You wish to blame us, to call it Nilari poison, a plague, a disease, when it is no such thing. It was you, your people! How many Nilari lives were lost during the Sage Rebellion? Thousands! The untimely separation of so many souls from their bodies is not a crime that is easily forgotten!

"Do you know what happens when you wreak such evil on the world? That evil doesn't just disappear, it transforms. Mutates. It coagulates, like blood, and seeps into the earth. And when it rises again, it opens up dark chasms in the surface of the world, through which spill wild creatures, untold horrors, things of nightmares. Traitors' Lake is one such place. A crevice of death and torture, created by your ancestors!"

Max turned the whites of his eyes on her, but between his fluttering lashes she saw no sign of her friend. There was only malice and hatred. "You think yourself a soldier, a saviour, but you are just like them. You are nothing but a butcher, spreading poison with your sword!"

Kyla couldn't believe what she was hearing. That Traitors' Lake and its vile infestation should be attributed to the Moriyans, to *her*, was unfathomable.

She could stand and listen no longer. "No, no! The Nilari deserved it! They tormented us. Wounded and healed us over and over, ripping our organs out and letting them grow again and again until we were so ruined that no magic could heal us. Not even the healing circle itself. It is *you* that deserves to die, for continuing to worship such a bestial race of beings."

Max, or Yarmon, did not notice her distress. Rage boiled in her chest, but she could do nothing as the voice continued.

"The Nilari will have their revenge! Too long have they been locked up, sealed into the Isle of Ashes. The key will bring us all to freedom! The Dream Key! It holds the power to bring your dreams into reality. It is my dream, our great Nilari dream, that every one of you will die a death as painful and brutal as you inflicted on the Nilari people." Max began to laugh, that same crazed laugh she had heard come from Yarmon's mouth. The effect of it, the mismatch between the face and the voice, was nightmarish. She had to make it stop. She grabbed Max, began to shake him, trying to wake him from his vision, his... possession. But Yarmon kept laughing. Louder, and louder.

Kyla shouted, shaking Max, forgetting that the body she shook was that of her friend and not her enemy. "I'll kill you, I'll kill you before you can touch—"

"Why, Kyla," the voice continued, quieter now. "I am already dead."

That Yarmon was not here with them in any real sense suddenly struck Kyla with full force. She let go of Max, whose head rocked back, and a cackle cracked from his lips, the most hideous laughter yet. "We will come for you, Kyla Tarthwen! We will come for you and your cripple!"

The words echoed over and over, the voice magnified by some magical power, only fading when Max's voice began to break. As he closed his mouth, a wisp of smoke and the scent of feather dust escaped his lips.

He fell to the ground, an empty body that had served its purpose, and lay pale and limp in the dirt. Kyla slammed down beside him, her knees smacking onto the hard earth, but she barely noticed the pain. Her hands hovered over his face. "Max, oh Max!"

"What happened?" Marlowe was standing over her, Valora not far behind. "That voice... It was Yarmon—"

"I told you not to move," Kyla snapped.

Marlowe's eyes flitted between Max and Kyla, and she knew he was wondering how she could still be angry with him after what had just happened.

He spoke slowly. "I don't take orders from you. You don't get to threaten my life, my sister's life, and then leave us, waiting for you to declare our fate. I'm done with you Moriyan soldiers, taking control of everything. We're here to help you, to help Max. If that's what you want."

Kyla said nothing for a moment, and then, before she could change her mind, she nodded. She had been so engrossed in Max and his possession that she hadn't noticed their approach, but they must have heard everything, and there seemed no reason to hide anything from them now. She turned her attention back to Max.

He was beginning to come to and Marlowe knelt beside her, helping her assist Max into a sitting position. They propped him up, so his back was supported against the tree.

Max put a hand to his temple, rubbed it lightly and looked from Marlowe to Kyla and back again.

"Are you all right?" Kyla asked.

Max stared up at her. "I did it, didn't I? I accessed the spirits of the dead?"

Kyla nodded. "You did. Are you sure you're all right?"

"Yes, yes." Still he rubbed at his temple with his other hand, as he struggled to sit up.

All of a sudden Max sat bolt upright, no longer leaning against the tree. His dazed expression transformed to one that was sharp, alert.

"The key. He said it had the power to bring dreams into reality."

At these words a rigidity spread from Marlowe to Valora, so slight a change in the way they held their bodies that Kyla might not have noticed it, had Marlowe not spoken so fast. "Whose dreams?"

Kyla narrowed her eyes, observing the wariness that hung about Marlowe's shoulders. She was sure he was thinking of his mother. It had been her key. It was only natural that any information about the key would lead his thoughts that way.

And now she had seen her own mother holding that very item too. What did it mean? Kyla felt a bubble expand in her chest, move up her throat and nudge the lump that was already there. She was so close to having everything she wanted, so close to becoming a member of the Sacred Core, and yet still it felt so far away. Did she really want to ask more questions? Every question opened yet another chasm, a void, and it was only by virtue of her faith that she hadn't fallen into one yet. She felt herself teetering on the edge.

Max shrugged, seemingly oblivious to the tension that had risen around him. "If it really could release the souls of the Nilari, then—" He glanced at the metal he still held in his hand. "—it's dangerous, for us and for you." He nodded at Marlowe and Valora.

Marlowe eyed Max, his eyes dark beneath lowered brows. "Dangerous...how?"

Max's words were rushed, his voice breathy. "If this was in your possession, and your intention was to open the Isle of Ashes, to unleash our enemy, the Sacred Core would have no choice but to execute both of you."

Valora seemed to shrink, pressing herself closer to Marlowe. He, however, gave no sign that he had noticed her movement, and when he spoke, his voice was hard as flint. "And how would we prove it wasn't our intention?"

"Kyla would have to swear it. She's a Tarthwen. Her word is gold in Moriya." Max shot a tentative look at Kyla, checking that he wasn't out of line to speak about her as though she wasn't there. Kyla gave a small nod to allow him to continue. "It's the only way. It's the safest option you..." Max took a breath, correcting himself. "...*we* have. All of us. We bring the key back to Moriya, and claim its power for the God-Sage."

As Max's words faded, Kyla heard Atrimus' voice, as Max had spoken it, echo once more in her mind. *It would destroy the world as I know it.* He had said those words in reference to the key. How much did she have to fear from this little piece of metal?

A sudden fear tore at her heart. It wasn't enough. She had to know the truth, or at least some part of the truth. She directed a hard yet desperate look at Marlowe. "Your mother kept it. You said so yourself. Why?"

As she held his gaze, and he hers, Kyla was flooded with the knowledge that his answer was more important to her than she could ever admit.

If Marlowe was a traitor, a true traitor to the God-Sage, she would have to kill him.

From the Author

Thank you for reading The Dream Key. It gives me so much joy to think that my book has made its way into your hands (and that you've read to the last page). It's the second book in the Chronicles of the God-Sage, so it means even more because you've already made my way through the first book to get here!

If you enjoyed The Dream Key, it would mean the world to me if you would leave a review. Honest reviews are still one of the most important tools for authors. They can boost sales and attract new readers, both of which enable me to continue writing.

If you want a bit more from Kyla and the world of the God-Sage, head to my website at www.rachaelwatson.com and sign up for my mailing list to receive a FREE prequel story. You'll also gain exclusive access to all updates, bonus content and any other news about my publishing journey.

— • —

ACKNOWLEDGMENTS

Writing my second book was a much faster process than writing my first one, which was both a relief and a surprise. Firstly I have to thank Emily, the coach and editor who has held my hand and taught me such a lot in a very short space of time.

A huge thanks has to go to all those readers who have discovered my bizarre attempts to market my own work on social media, and taken a chance on an otherwise unknown author. Thank you so much. I have delighted in every encouraging and positive message, and I appreciate you so much.

Thanks also to my beta readers. Your thoughtful comments and insightful feedback helped this book become what it is now. I appreciate the time and energy you put into helping me become a better writer. And to all the ARC readers as well, without whom this book would have to linger on the internet for its first few days of life without any reviews to shield it from the world.

The most heartfelt thanks has to go to Tom, my husband, without whose constant love and support I would probably have given up on the dream of writing my own books a long time ago. Thank you so much, for being wonderful every day. I mean this sincerely even though it sounds trite and, had I written it in the body of my novel, you would certainly have scored it out on the first read through.